CW00432949

AN ALLOTMENT OF TIME

RIPLEY HAYES

Copyright © 2022 by Ripley Hayes

All rights reserved.

No part of this book may be reproduced in any form or by any electronic or mechanical means, including information storage and retrieval systems, without written permission from the author, except for the use of brief quotations in a book review.

❀ Created with Vellum

WELSH…

There are a few Welsh words and one Welsh sentence in this book. To non-Welsh speakers a translation may be helpful.

Cariad means _dear, darling, sweetheart, my love._ A term of endearment.

Croeso means _welcome, you're welcome_

Diolch means _thank you_

The sentence Mal uses in Chapter 1 ("_Oeddech chi'n golygu byddwch yn flin, syr?_") translates as "_I think you mean you'll be sorry, sir._"

1

A WALK AND A WORRY

Daniel Owen had been a policeman for fifteen years, and he didn't know how to be anything else.

THIS FEBRUARY WAS COLD. The sky was a silvery grey, lowering the horizon, pressing down on anyone foolish enough to be outside. It drained colour from the scene. In sunshine, the little north Wales town and all its surroundings would be picture-postcard pretty. Today it was dull. That the weather should start improving in a few weeks didn't stop everywhere feeling dreary, or the chill getting under his clothes, even in the house.

The desire to stop being a policeman had been overwhelming, he thought, and not for the first time. Leaving the police had lifted so much weight from his shoulders he felt he could fly. But if he wasn't a policeman, what was he? He came back to it most days around this time, drinking his second cup of coffee, sitting on the battered sofa, gazing out over the valley beyond the French windows. Flora, the little black and white dog he and Mal had adopted, snuffled in her sleep at his feet, curling herself into an ever-tighter ball, nose tucked under her tail. One ear was always left half pricked, *just in case.* Daniel wrapped himself for warmth in the bright crocheted blanket that his sister had given him. He made himself breathe slowly, feeling chilly air on his nostrils on the in-breath, allowing his shoulders to drop as he breathed out. He counted the breaths, and the space between them, hoping for clarity.

It had been growing, his misery, case by case until he could no longer force it to the back of his mind and keep going. He'd helped some friends who worked in private security and used his detective's skills and experience. That had felt OK, but they worked in the city, and the one thing he was certain about was that he didn't want to spend his time looking for light and greenery among the high rises and fighting his way through crowded streets. No, he wanted to stay here, where he could see the hills beyond the town. He needed to get his hands in the soil, to listen to birdsong, to smell new cut logs, and watch the seasons pass. He could grow food, bake bread, cook and clean for Mal and he knew that slowly, bit-by-bit, his time could be filled with activity.

And I will be bored silly within a year.

He needed to *be* something, to have a profession, a title. He wanted to be able to say "I am a —" when people asked what he did. The problem was, he didn't know how to fill in the blank.

So, he had resolved to fill this day with a long walk, and to hell with the weather. If it rained, he would get wet, if it was cold, he would freeze, but he would not spend the day moping round the house waiting for Mal to come home. He and Flora would have an adventure. He would talk to people who weren't police officers or his counsellor. He would find somewhere, or something new in the town where he'd lived for most of his life. And he'd keep doing it until he found his purpose.

***

In the glass box that was Melin Tywyll police station, Mal

Kent was trying to resist the urge to bang his head on the desk. He was tired, frustrated and irritated beyond reason. But he wasn't going to show his annoyance if it killed him. He knew that his black hair was perfectly combed and that his face was as closely shaved as it could be, and that he smelled expensive. His black suit was cut to fit tightly, emphasising his broad shoulders and solid muscles. He wore a rainbow striped tie. The big office was spotless, his desk empty but for a closed MacBook. Shaded windows looked out over the town. A civilian secretary was there to stop them being interrupted. Mal's expression said that if the man opposite didn't like what he saw, then he could suck it up.

Because I'm in charge, and you are going to have to live with it, you homophobic piece of shit. How did I finish up with you as a replacement for my lovely Daniel? Who is beautiful and lithe and graceful, and who can think?

DI Carey looked, as he always did, as if the world was letting him down. In Carey's mind, nothing was ever his fault. Mal imagined every deposed dictator and defeated politician had the same feeling.

"There are too many of these complaints, DI Carey," Mal said.

Carey shrugged and Mal wanted to hit him, to smash his fist into Carey's horrible, ugly, self-satisfied face until the blood ran down onto his perfectly ironed white shirt. Carey's face was fleshy, his nose red and pockmarked from spending too long in the pub after work. Hs hair was receding and looked greasy with poorly chosen product. He smelled of cigarette smoke, and cheap aftershave. His clothes were well cared for, but a size or two larger than he needed, in an attempt to cover his beer belly. Mal shuddered inwardly at the thought of a pair of skinny legs below that stomach. Carey wasn't the only overweight cop in the station, but he was easily the least healthy. He was also a malign influence, attracting those officers who resented having a gay man as a boss, or a woman, or anyone who wasn't white, straight and male. The attitude spilled out into their dealings with the public. White men were believed. Their reports were taken seriously and followed up. Black complainants were assumed to be lying, women to be exaggerating. Children weren't listened to at all.

The report on Mal's computer was from DS Bethan Davies, but he wasn't going to betray his colleague by sharing the information about the author with Carey. It was better if Carey thought he, Mal, had spies everywhere. Which, to be fair, he did.

"CID has been following the Khan family for months," Mal said. "I sanctioned an investigation based on your initial report, but there is no evidence at all that any member of the family has any connection to drugs. None. They are two doctors with teenage children who also want to become doctors. They are the kind of people this town needs, and they are being made to feel unwelcome."

Carey opened his mouth. Then closed it again at the expression on Mal's face.

Mal leaned forward. "If I have one more report that any police officer from this station is harassing any member of the Khan family, I will be holding you, Adam Carey, personally responsible. Do you understand me?"

This time Carey did speak. "You'll be sorry. We don't want their type here, and we'll prove it. Or we could, if you'd stop poking your nose in."

Only he said it in Welsh, assuming that Mal wouldn't understand.

"*Oeddech chi'n golygu byddwch yn flin, syr?*" Mal said, enjoying the sight of Carey turning bright red. Mal had been waiting for this moment for a while, savouring the thought of Carey's realisation that just because Mal chose not to speak Welsh, it didn't mean that he couldn't understand it. It hadn't always been the case, but he'd dragged his schoolboy Welsh out of the mental box where he'd left it years before. A mixture of lessons and speaking Welsh at home with Daniel had almost got him up to speed. Enough to catch Carey out at least. It was a nice moment, but it wouldn't last. Dealing with Carey was a Sisyphean task.

Carey's body language as he left spoke volumes of defiance. But Mal wasn't the youngest Detective Chief Superintendent in the county because he was stupid. He rang the front desk. "Kate? DI Carey is on his way down for a smoke any minute now. I'd like to know who joins him please. CCTV would be great."

"I can leave my phone out there on record, sir."

"Thank you, Kate, that would be helpful."

She sent him the recording later. It was as useless as ever. Just Carey and his mate PC Kelley moaning about how awful their bosses were, and making remarks about women that Mal hoped Karen hadn't listened to.

***

Flora pulled on her lead, dragging Daniel towards a gap in the high yew hedge lining one side of the road. The un-marked gateway led to the town's allotments: small patches of ground divided by grassy pathways, now turned to mud. Sheds, cold frames, stakes for fruit bushes, dark black kale, and the last of the Brussels sprouts were stark and dark against the wet soil. Neglect seemed rife, but Daniel knew that tools were being cleaned and sharpened in the tatty sheds, seeds were being grown in heated propagators and greenhouses and the black plastic and cardboard held down by stones was allowing the soil to warm. He knew all this, because he had left the same apparent mess back on the smallholding he and Mal called home. The smell of rotting compost and damp earth filled his nose, and he wiped spots of drizzle from his face. The little black and white dog led the way eagerly on to the site, tail wagging, and Daniel followed.

A Mazda Bongo campervan decorated with stickers of flowers was parked outside a large grey-painted tin shed covered in notices. The notices proclaimed the building to be the headquarters and shop for the Melin Tywyll Allotment Society. The shop would open every weekend, for the sale of fertiliser, weedkiller and other horticultural supplies. A rota was attached. The metal door was padlocked shut.

Daniel smelled smoke, and looking up saw wisps rising slowly in the far corner of the site. Flora pulled him towards it, and after a moment he realised that her nose had picked up another, more enticing scent — bacon. A muddy path led in that direction, and Flora was insistent on taking it. He knew the little dog would charm most people, and hoped that she would charm whoever had the fire. It would be a conversation, a human connection with someone new. He needed it, and maybe they did too. If bacon-person was the owner of the camper van, he was disposed to like them already. He arrived at the plot to find a woman sitting on an upturned bucket in front of a cast iron fire basket in which a few logs burned. She had long brown hair, streaked with grey and plaited with ribbons, topped with a hand-knitted beanie, and a kind face. Her skin was tanned, or rather, like his own, weatherbeaten from being outside every day. There were smuts of smoke and blobs of mud on her hands and clothes — a brightly patterned wool skirt, red leggings with the tops of hand-knitted socks poking out of her wellies. Her coat was an old anorak, torn in places that showed the padded lining, also well covered in mud.

Behind the woman was a shed painted what would have been a bright blue in any other light. The overcast skies made it look grey. The door was open, and Daniel could see well-cared-for tools hanging on hooks, plant pots neatly stacked, and a potting bench in front of the window. The shed itself was elderly, patched here and there with bits of timber showing evidence of former existences as packing cases or floorboards. The cold frames next to the shed were made from old windows, and the raised beds were — Daniel looked closely — bookcases laid flat on the ground and filled with soil. He liked what he saw, because this woman had made her plot into a smaller version of his own.

"Hi," she said, reaching out to pet Flora, stroking her head, and scratching behind the little dog's ears.

"Hi," Daniel said. "This is Flora. Her manners are not the best when she smells food."

The woman smiled. "Sorry, lovely, I've just finished my sandwich," she said to Flora. Then she looked up at Daniel. "But I've still got tea if you want to pull up a bucket." She gestured to another upturned bucket beside the fire, and picked up a flask.

"That would be great, thanks." He sat down. "I'm Daniel Owen, and I love what you've done to your plot."

The woman's cheeks flushed pink. "Thanks. Not many people round here would agree with you, but I like it. It's a community allotment. Pandy Melton." She held out her hand. "Sorry, I'm a bit grubby. Tea's hot though." She opened the flask, filled two small cups and handed one to Daniel. The tea steamed in the cold air. It was the bright orange milky brew that Mal loved, smelling of tannin, but the hot cup warmed his hands, for all that he would have preferred something herbal. He blew on the liquid and took a drink, hoping for the sweet spot between burning his mouth, and being able to taste the tea. If there was one thing worse than hot orange tea, it was cold orange tea.

"Cheers," he said, raising his cup in salute. "So, tell me, what's a community allotment?"

2

COMMUNITY ALLOTMENT

"**A** Community Allotment is a space for local people to learn about growing, especially children and families, and to have some fun doing it. I'm trying to attract people without gardens of their own, or who thing veg-growing is for old men in flat caps. Growing is for everyone. It's therapeutic."

"How's it going?"

Pandy gestured at the empty space around them. "About as well as it looks. A few people come, but most don't stay. The rest of the allotment holders aren't welcoming, don't want people with mental health problems, don't want children here making noise and running about."

"You mean enjoying themselves?" Daniel thought about his nephew and niece, and his friend Sasha's daughter Arwen, and the way they loved to get muddy, 'helping' around the small-holding. "I did notice that most plots are the vegetables-in-rows kind."

Pandy nodded. "Double digging, fertiliser, weed killer, slug pellets, peat-based compost."

Daniel grinned. "Runner beans, forced rhubarb, courgettes by the metric tonne, sprouts that no one wants, tomatoes with thick skins, Dahlias."

They smiled at each other.

"I have a smallholding," Daniel said. "I've let most of it re-wild. My neighbours hate me with a passion. They farm sheep, and claim subsidies. I keep us in fruit, vegetables and eggs—to be fair, the hens keep us in eggs—and use only a tiny bit of land to do it. The disapproval flows towards me in waves."

"I'd love to see it. It sounds like paradise."

"It is. You'd be very welcome to visit, but I'd like to see more of what you're doing here too."

Pandy looked at Daniel, as if seeing him for the first time. They'd been speaking in Welsh without thinking.

"Do you have a brother who's a policeman? You look familiar. Were you at my school? Though you'd have been a first year when I was doing my A'levels."

Daniel pulled at his hair, that was curling over his neck in a way that was becoming familiar, and ran his hand over the two-day stubble. "I used to be a policeman. I left. And if you went to school here, we went to the same school. But sorry, I don't remember you."

"I wasn't very memorable. Mostly, anyway." Pandy gestured with her cup. "More tea?"

Daniel shook his head. "This was fine, but builder's tea is more my partner's drink than mine. I'm trying to make him appreciate Earl Grey, but it's a battle. Not that I'm not grateful for the warmth."

Pandy didn't bat an eyelid at his revelation. "Is that why you left the police? Because you're gay? Or is that too much of a personal question for someone I only met twenty minutes ago?"

Daniel re-arranged his bum on the cold bucket, trying to

move it closer to the fire without sinking in the mud. He poked the fire with a long stick making the logs settle and begin to produce a few yellow flames. They didn't make a lot of actual heat—his face and hands were warm, but the rest of him was well aware that it was February and about 10 degrees. The smell of the burning logs added to the impression of warmth, but the thing that was keeping his feet from freezing was Flora, curled up on them as usual.

"It's not easy to be gay in the police, or female or a person of colour. The default setting is male, white, cis, straight. But that's not why I left. My partner is still a policeman." Daniel paused, trying to get his thoughts in order. He knew why he'd left, but it was hard to explain in a few words. There was something about this idea of a Community Allotment, and Pandy's friendliness that made him want to attempt an answer.

Sometimes policemen have to be violent. They see violence. I didn't like the violent man I was becoming. I made some misjudgements. People died. I met a man and fell in love and police work screwed us both. We've sorted that out. It's helping. But I don't know who I am any more.

He held up his hand, the one with two missing fingers. "I got injured. It doesn't look like much, but I got sepsis. Spent weeks in hospital. When I came out, I realised I didn't want to go back. I don't have any idea what I'm going to do instead. Which is probably TMI."

"No, it's interesting." Pandy got up and went into the shed, returning with an armful of logs and two brightly coloured blankets. She threw the logs on the fire and handed him one of the blankets.

"I would say that getting your hands in the soil is the best therapy, but you already know that. But a community allotment is also a place to talk without pressure. Or to sit and stare into the fire and say nothing."

Daniel had a lot of things to say, and perhaps Pandy was the first person he'd met who he might be able to say them to. Probably because she was a stranger. He had always talked to his twin sister, until she moved to Spain with her family. They still talked, but it wasn't the same, not being able to drop in when he felt like it. And he missed his nephew and niece. But he wasn't ready to talk yet. So he looked into the fire, and let his breathing slow, counting the breaths in and out. It was peaceful. After a while, Pandy asked, "Can you fix things? Like cold frames? And shed floors?"

It took Daniel a moment to focus on what she was saying.

"What's up with the shed floor?"

Pandy stood up, folding her blanket, and Daniel followed suit. She led him to the shed. It looked funky and quirky from the outside, with its painted flowers and butterflies, and it was neatly organised inside. But the floor was sagging, rotten in places, with a large hole in one corner. Daniel stepped in gingerly, feeling it sink under his weight, and squatted down to look at the hole, poking the crumbling wood with his fingers. Cold air blew through the space, and the rest of the floor was damp and disintegrating.

"Do you want my diagnosis?" he asked.

Pandy grinned. "I know exactly what's wrong with it. It's buggered. I don't have the right tools to fix it, and I don't know what I'm doing anyway." She let her voice trail away.

"What time tomorrow? I'll bring everything I need. And my own tea. Shed floor repairs are one of my superpowers." They chatted for a bit longer and when Daniel set off to walk home, he felt lighter. The sun came out, and the world seemed a more cheerful place. "I think we may have made a friend," he told Flora.

***

Mal was no stranger to being disliked by his fellow officers. He was ambitious and a perfectionist, and no one loves a perfectionist as a boss. He'd been grudgingly accepted when he'd moved to Melin Tywyll because of Daniel. Daniel, who knew everyone and everything in Melin Tywyll. Daniel, who could talk to anyone, and would make friends on the moon. Daniel, who Mal loved to distraction. And now Daniel was no longer a policeman but was trying to make a different life. Mal looked at his office. A big fake wood desk smelling of aerosol polish, a leather chair for him (he suspected his predecessor had paid for it) and two blue fabric chairs facing the desk. A round table with more fabric chairs for meetings. A couch and a low table. Bookshelves. Bethan Davies brought pot plants, and his secretary watered them, and he suspected, polished their leaves. Daniel had given him a rainbow mug, and a box of strong Welsh tea bags. He made himself what Daniel called 'orange tea' all day. The only personal things he kept in the office were spare clothes. The pictures of Daniel and their friends were on his phone, rather than in frames on his desk. He looked at them often, especially after dealing with Carey. The contrast between Daniel's open-minded determination, and Carey's lazy thinking, and mistrust of anything outside his immediate experience was maddening. Mal got his phone out to look at the picture of Daniel leaning against a tree, with a glass of champagne in his hand at Mal's brother Huw's wedding. It reminded him of the warm sun on their skin, Daniel high on champagne and their friends' happiness, the two of them kissing on a rug on the soft grass. The memories made him itch to get home, to wrap Daniel in his arms and make love in front of the fire. He sighed and put the phone away.

Instead, he opened his laptop and started going through his emails. A report on the number of women killed by violent partners after the police had failed to respond made him angry. *We should do better than this.*

Robert Cowlishaw, the Police and Crime Commissioner, was making domestic abuse this month's priority. There were targets to achieve, and new training on offer for all officers. He sent the report to DI Sophie Harrington—though she probably had it already—and asked for an update on the number of active cases on their books. Then he gathered his things up, washed his mug and left. There was plenty of work he could be doing, and if he was going to leave early, he should hit the gym or get the Audi a much-needed wash, but all he wanted was to be at home with Daniel.

Daniel's muddy Land Rover was parked outside the house, and as Mal slammed his car door, Flora's frenzied barking told everyone in the neighbourhood that Mal was home.

"Be quiet, you silly dog," he said, picking up the wriggling fur ball and cuddling her, regardless of the effect on his clothes. The stove was bright with yellow flames behind the glass, and the living room was warm, the red velvet curtains they had bought from a charity shop closed against the darkness outside. Low-level lighting added to the cosiness, as did the smell of rich tomato sauce and newly baked bread coming from the kitchen. He changed his shoes for the thick woolly socks they both wore around the house and walked quietly into the kitchen.

Daniel was stirring something in a pan on the stovetop; from the smell, the tomato sauce. He was wearing a pair of his most ancient jeans, washed to velvety softness, and an equally ancient and velvety sweatshirt, all wrapped round in an apron. Mal liked the way Daniel's blond hair had begun to curl as it grew out of its police-approved short back and sides. Mal slid his arms around Daniel's waist.

"Hey," he whispered in Daniel's ear, making sure to blow gently. Daniel quivered and leaned back against him.

"Hey, yourself." Daniel tried to turn round, but Mal held him still, breathing softly into Daniel's ear and kissing his neck where it met his shoulder. "I missed you today."

"Missed you too. That's why I'm making you a delicious

dinner." Daniel tried to wriggle free, but Mal held him with one arm and took the wooden spoon from Daniel's hand. Then he moved the pan off the heat and switched the hob off.

Daniel wriggled again. "Not hungry, then?"

Mal didn't answer. He ran his hands over Daniel's body, loving the soft cotton against his hands, knowing that underneath he would be able to feel Daniel's ribs, and the wiry muscle that was slowly returning after Daniel's illness.

"Come into the living room. We can eat later," he said. This time he let Daniel turn round and kiss him.

"If we're going to make out, at least take your jacket off, Maldwyn."

Mal slipped the jacket onto the back of one of the dining chairs then pulled Daniel into the living room and onto the sofa. "Come and lie down with me," he said, knowing that there was plenty of room for both of them. "But maybe lose the apron?"

Mal held Daniel, feeling the warmth between them grow into heat, and something more urgent than a cuddle at the end of a long day.

"I love these soft clothes," Mal said. "But I'd love your naked body even more. I'll make it worth your while."

"Back atcha," Daniel said, and their clothes were soon in a pile on the floor.

Mal wrapped his arms around Daniel, loving the contrast between the dark hair on his own skin, and Daniel's winter paleness. They lay chest to chest, their dicks against each other, with the slightest movement sending delicious electric pulses through Mal's body. It felt to Mal as if they were merging, despite their physical differences, as if he hardly knew where he ended and Daniel began. Then Daniel pushed him onto his back and moved to kneel between Mal's legs, looking up with an ear to ear grin.

"Close your eyes, Maldwyn." Mal did as he was told, and

felt Daniel's hands, lips and tongue on his cock, sucking for a moment, then drawing back and licking up and down his length, fingers massaging his balls, until Mal groaned with pleasure.

"You're playing with fire," Mal gasped, trying to hold onto the sensations for as long as he could without coming. Which was when he felt Daniel's lips close round his cock and take it deep into his throat. He thrust, trying to hold back, once, twice and then his orgasm overtook him, and nothing else mattered.

He felt Daniel move so that they were lying next to one another again, and he opened his eyes to see Daniel's blue eyes inches from his own. "I owe you," Mal said. "And I like to pay my debts quickly."

Daniel sighed a sigh of contentment, and rolled onto his back. "I like the sound of that."

Afterwards, when the post orgasmic haze had faded, Daniel put his sweatshirt back on, and got up to put another log on the fire. Mal laughed at the sight of his half-naked boyfriend heading to the kitchen to reheat the sauce and turn on some pasta.

"I love you, Daniel Owen."

"Of course you do. You just got laid, and your dinner is on its way. All you need is your slippers warmed and you have the perfect life."

Mal looked down at his feet. "I'm still wearing my slippers, and so are you. When did we get so old that we have sex in our socks?"

"If your colleagues could see you now... DI Carey would have all his prejudices confirmed. Gay men really do have lots of sex."

Mal shuddered theatrically. "Don't. I had to talk to him today. I truly hate that man."

"By contrast, I met a very nice woman, and I'm seeing her

again tomorrow. She's hot for a guy with a toolbelt. I think maybe a shower and some clean clothes before we eat?"

Mal could easily have melted into the sofa, dressed only in his socks and a crumpled shirt, but Daniel was right.

"Only if you tell me about this woman. Because, gotta say, I'm not into sharing the hot guy with the toolbelt."

3

DOMESTIC ABUSE

D aniel took Flora, his tools, a pile of reclaimed timber, sandwiches and a flask of coffee to the allotment the next morning. There were more people around, as the busiest part of the horticulturalist's year began. Daniel told himself not to panic, as he did every year at this time. *Nature always catches up. Let the soil warm and the days get longer.*

Pandy was waiting for him, and a look of relief crossed her face when he appeared. "So many people say they will come back, and I never see them again." She seemed anxious, springing up off the upturned bucket, and wiping her hands on her clothes.

Daniel didn't know her well enough to comment on the anxiety, so he grinned. "I always turn up — I'm never going to miss an opportunity to show off."

Some of the tension left Pandy's shoulders, and she smiled back.

The day was brighter, still mostly overcast and grey, but with the occasional patch of bright blue showing between the clouds. Daniel had dressed for the cold in jeans, thick socks, and a rainbow-coloured sweater his sister Megan had made him many years ago. It was showing its age and had been reduced to gardening-only status. Flora was wearing one of the many dog coats that Mal was never able to resist buying. This one was bright pink, with a fur-lined hood. Pandy was equally well bundled-up, in a thick skirt and more red leggings, with a shawl wrapped around her fleece jacket. Both had well-worn work boots and hand-knitted woolly hats. Daniel had never considered not keeping his promise to fix the floor, but seeing Pandy's relief at his presence made him happy. She'd created the kind of space he liked; nature and horticulture working in harmony, muddy and untidy though it might look on first glance. He resolved to make the shed solid and free of damp and draughts. He put his flask next to the fire pit and turned to the open shed door.

"We need to get everything off this floor," Daniel said. Pandy nodded and they moved piles of pots, seed trays and plastic bags outside.

"OK, now the floor has to come up." Daniel set about the rotten boards with his crowbar, and Pandy stacked the pieces outside.

As they worked, they chatted about how to attract people, especially children, to the allotment.

"I have a daughter, Cerys, she's seven, but I don't think she counts."

"What about her schoolfriends?"

"I might persuade her to bring her friend Arwen ..."

"Arwen whose mother is called Sasha? Who lives with my mate Hector Lord?"

"That Arwen. Wales is small and Melin Tywyll is smaller," Pandy replied with a smile.

Daniel thought that if Arwen was anything like her mother, she would round up half her classmates to come and enjoy a day at the allotment.

"We can get them to turn the compost, and let them make s'mores on the fire," he said, "and I'll organise a treasure hunt."

"Lots of creepy crawlies and a high yuck-factor. S'mores will be a good bribe. They might be an American import but they always go down well with kids." Pandy started to break the wood into fire-sized pieces, putting them into old compost bags to stay dry.

"Did I hear someone say s'mores?" The voice came from behind Daniel. He turned round to see two women with Pandy. They could have been sisters, but he thought they were most likely a couple, who liked the same clothes and the same haircuts. Both wore purple corduroy dungarees, thick red sweaters and flower-patterned Dr Marten boots. Both had short spiky purple hair, and faces rosy from exertion. Pandy looked pleased to see them. "Hey, guys, I've got a volunteer!"

Daniel dragged another piece of shed floor outside, dropping it next to the fire pit.

"Daniel, these are my friends Lizzie and Beth, yes, really."

Daniel brushed the bits of wood off his hands and smiled. "Hi. Daniel Owen." His eyes flickered between the two women. One was taller and thinner than the other, and her dungarees were muddier. The smaller women reminded him of his sister with her ability to stay clean and tidy regardless of the activity. "I'm helping sort the shed out."

The taller woman introduced herself as Lizzie, and the other as Beth.

"What's with the twinsies look?" asked Pandy. "Not that it's not great. I love the dungarees."

Lizzie answered. "We both wanted the same colour. But seriously, people here kept asking us if we were sisters, and then going very quiet when we said no, we're a couple." She looked at Daniel, as if waiting for the same response, before properly taking in his rainbow sweater.

"The sweater does not lie, ladies," he said. "There are

homophobes everywhere, but I am not one of them. Have you come to help?"

This time it was Beth who spoke. "You wish. No, we needed a break from one of the blokes near us. He keeps giving us death stares, and mumbling about us planting weeds."

"We're planting willow whips and comfrey. Weeds."

"They do willow weaving classes," said Pandy.

"Just wreaths and Christmas decorations so far, because we have to buy most of the willow. But if we can grow our own, we can do baskets, and maybe bigger stuff. But a few of the old fellas complain about new-agers and hippies."

Daniel wasn't surprised. He had the same responses from his farming neighbours. "Osier beds are an ancient form of sustainable growing. Nothing new about it at all. Or about comfrey for that matter."

"Preaching to the choir," Lizzie said. "Anyway, we've had enough for today. Nice to meet you Daniel, see you Pandy."

The two women walked towards the car park hand-in-hand.

Pandy was relaxing to work with, thought Daniel. He and Mal had built a hide for bird and badger-watching, and Mal was always willing to help on the smallholding, but none of it was instinctive. Mal's practical talents tended towards the care of clothes, hair-cutting and car washing. He could cook, but regarded all tools, especially power tools, as dangerous and to be avoided. Pandy was used to working with her hands and getting dirty. She got the fire pit going, feeding the old floor into the flames. They soon had the floor out, leaving a lattice of timbers resting on a concrete slab.

She moved the two upturned buckets next to the fire. "I declare a tea-break before the sun goes in."

Daniel poured himself a coffee. "Some of the supporting timbers need replacing, but I should have what we need in the car."

A male voice interrupted them. "It all needs replacing. It's falling down. Makes the place look a mess."

Daniel looked up. On the other side of the fire, a man stood looking disdainfully at the shed. He was probably in his seventies, thought Daniel, dressed much less colourfully than he and Pandy, but still in work clothes and a woolly hat. His face was creased and weathered, with blue eyes set below deep frown lines.

"Hi, Hayden," Pandy said, and Daniel heard the forced cheerfulness in her voice. "Hayden, this is Daniel, who's kindly helping sort out the shed. Daniel, Hayden Bennion."

Daniel stood up and held out his hand. He was probably a foot taller than the older man, but they shared the same wiry build. Hayden shook hands, trying not to pull away when he saw that Daniel was two fingers short.

"I know who you are. Copper. Haven't we got enough crime to keep you busy?"

"I'm not a policeman any more. I'm leaving crime to other people. Do you have an allotment here?"

Hayden jerked his head towards where the cars were parked by the tin shed. "Chair of the Allotment society. I've got my plot over by the entrance. A proper plot. Not like this."

Daniel took a drink of his coffee. This was an argument he had often, and he'd learned that he could never win. He took a couple of calming breaths, and looked around him. "There's plenty growing here—salad, chard, kale, garlic and the onions are in. Some of these piles of brush are probably hiding hedgehogs. There's more than one way to grow food."

"Aye, and some of them piles of rubbish will be hiding rats."

"If they were, I'm sure Flora would have found them." Daniel kept his voice quiet and calm, but his words rolled off Hayden like rain off wax. "I need to get some wood from my car." He finished the coffee and put the cup down. He gestured towards the car park, as if to push Hayden in front of him, giving him little choice but to leave the Community Allotment. Daniel felt Pandy's relief as a tangible thing.

***

Mal opened Sophie Harrington's door, to find his friend and colleague talking on the phone, searching the papers on her desk and responding to pings on her computer. A whiteboard covered in notes showed what her officers were working on, and another, who was on duty and when. As he watched, she rubbed out one of the numbers and marked it as *sick leave*. "Dammit. I know the guy is ill, but I just don't have anyone left to cover." She put the phone down, and collapsed into her chair, pulling her hair out of its ponytail and tying it back up, using the computer screen as a mirror. She looked good in her uniform, and comfortable in her body. Sophie exuded competence. "There are some days when I hate this job. I want to go and stand outside 10 Downing Street with a placard." She found a half-drunk cup of coffee behind a pile of papers and took a sip. "Ugh, it's cold."

"Meditation's not working then?" Mal asked, moving a folder from the spare chair and sitting down.

"You know me too well. I'll get back to it, once I've restored some kind of order here. Anyway, I did your report, so there wasn't time for meditation. It's that folder you were about to sit on."

"Did you read my email about paperless offices?"

"It's here somewhere." Sophie gestured at the piles of paper.

They smiled at each other. Sophie frequently told Mal he would lose the ability to write with a pen, and he told her that her body would be found one day under an avalanche of printing.

"Anyway, we have too many cases of domestic abuse, and we're nowhere near getting on top of them," Sophie said.

"How seriously are we taking it? Honestly?"

"Honestly? We have a regular conference call with social

services, Women's Aid and support workers, and we update
each of the individual cases every week. We should *know* who's
in danger. But you know as well as I do that the victims have to
call us, and we have to respond." She pulled her hair out of its
ponytail and re-tied it again. "It was bad enough when we had
enough officers... And not everyone takes it as seriously as we
do. How am I supposed to choose between a fight kicking off in
the town centre and a broken-off call from one of our regulars?"

"How do the dispatchers prioritise?"

"Depends on the dispatcher. And how many bodies we've
got to dispatch."

Mal stood up, with the report in his hand. "I'll see what I
can do." Domestic abuse wasn't usually detective work, unless it
was very serious. The victim and the perpetrator were already
known. But sometimes CID were needed, and Mal wondered
whether he could take some of the pressure off the uniforms.
Not that he had any spare resources himself.

Back in his spartan office, he read the dispiriting stories of
violence, coercion and threats. Men who the courts had told to
keep away from their former partners turning up and banging
on the door or breaking windows. Men putting their wives in
hospital after a night at the pub. A name sprang out at him.

Ms Pandora (Pandy) Melton, neé Nicolson. The woman Daniel
had been working with at the allotments. Divorced with a ten-
year-old daughter, Cerys. Ex-husband James had beaten her
badly enough to serve time in prison, and there was a power of
arrest attached to the injunction keeping him out of Melin
Tywyll and its surroundings. The most recent addition to the
case was a report that James Melton had discovered his ex-
wife's phone number and begun ringing with threats.

What is wrong with these people?

***

Daniel was struggling to keep his voice calm and his body
relaxed as Hayden Bennion lectured him about the correct way

to grow vegetables, pointing out the *decent* allotments as they made their way towards the grey tin shed.

"This community allotment business. It's nonsense. The council is paying that woman to show people how to grow potatoes in old tyres. No one wants to know. They just want somewhere to leave their kids, if you ask me."

Daniel had no intention of asking Hayden anything. Not that it shut him up.

"Says we mustn't use slug pellets, or pesticides. She goes on and on about bees and peat-free compost as if we just stepped off a Christmas tree. I've been growing veg since before she was *born!*"

Spittle flew out of Hayden's mouth as he said the final words.

Daniel took a deep breath. "I like the idea of encouraging children to learn about growing food. My nephew and niece love getting muddy and digging for veg in the ground. They would love to come and help, and all my friends' kids too."

Hayden looked him up and down, taking in the rainbow sweater and the hair curling coyly from underneath Daniel's cheerful hat.

"No children of your own. Your sort don't." His meaning was clear, and Daniel was done with being pleasant.

"I'm gay, Mr Bennion. It's got nothing to do with whether I have children, and nothing to do with how I garden. In fact, it's got nothing to do with you at all. But I can see why people are wary of coming here if this is the way they get spoken to." He turned away, and went to the Land Rover to collect the wood he needed. He felt Bennion behind him, trying to come up with a rejoinder.

"Melin Tywyll doesn't need *gay gardeners*."

Daniel burst out laughing. "I think it's too late. We're already here. Now please move and let me get this wood shifted."

He giggled all the way back to the community plot, muttering *gay gardeners* under his breath. *I should have a T-shirt printed.*

Pandy didn't find it as funny. "They're nasty, and they run the place. I went to one of the meetings with some friends. It was horrible."

Daniel thought about the plots he'd seen. "Not every plot holder here is a weedkiller junkie. You aren't the only one growing organically."

"No, I'm not. The AGM of the allotment society was a few weeks ago. Some of us wanted the shop to stop stocking Roundup-type products and peat-based compost, so we went." A shadow passed over Pandy's face, and Daniel thought that she might be about to cry. "Most people didn't care much, just wanted to be able to buy what they always buy. But a few of the committee got personal. I think they're going to try to get the community allotment stopped..."

"Hayden says the council pays you to run it?"

"What? I get a grant to pay for seeds and tools. That's all. *I'm* not getting a penny." Now she did cry, sinking on to one of the up-turned buckets and putting her face in her hands. "I'm not doing *anything* to those men and they hate me."

"The best revenge is success," said Daniel, moving his bucket next to hers. "I'll do everything I can to help defeat the forces of darkness and environmental catastrophe."

4

FROM TINY SEEDS

Daniel was first up the next morning. "The days get longer, and breakfast gets better." Daniel put three fresh eggs in a bowl on the kitchen worktop. "Fried or boiled, love?" he called out in a high-pitched and utterly fake cockney accent. "Don't come any fresher than this, darlin', straight out of the hen's arse this morning."

Mal put his coffee down on the table and pulled Daniel onto his lap, running his hands under Daniel's tatty sweatshirt, pinching a nipple. He loved the sight of Daniel in his pyjama pants and the washed-out sweatshirt, feet in woolly socks and his 'outside crocs'. And he loved the feeling of Daniel's slender body in his arms, Daniel snuggling close, his curls brushing against Mal's newly shaved face. Things hadn't always been this easy between them, but over the last few months Mal had begun to feel their happiness would last.

"Maldwyn, I must stink of hens and you're dressed for work." But he didn't move.

Mal ran his tongue up Daniel's neck sniffing noisily at his skin. "You smell delicious. And taste nice too."

"Don't start anything you aren't prepared to finish." Daniel wriggled in his lap, and Mal had a sudden and intoxicating image of where this could lead.

"Do that again."

But Daniel stood up. "There isn't time, dammit. Scrambled eggs on toast and then you can go and keep the peace and I will go and fill the children of Melin with sugar, before returning them to their parents."

The eggs were bright yellow, and though Mal knew it was the chicken feed giving them the rich colour, they seemed to taste of the grass the chickens played in. He'd helped Daniel build the safest possible run for the bronze Warrens, rescued, as Daniel said, 'from the pie factory'. He'd never expected to like chickens, but he had come to love their insatiable curiosity, and the way they stood on his feet with their blunt claws, and consented to feathery cuddles. And they didn't smell.

"So," Mal said between bites, "what are you doing with a Tesco bag full of chocolate, marshmallows and digestive biscuits? I thought the kids were supposed to learn about growing stuff. I'm assuming this is why you have been ringing all our friends with promises of fresh veg if they will only come along?"

"I'm going to teach them that growing stuff brings rewards. In this case, s'mores by the fire. I persuade them to get filthy, planting seeds and turning the compost, and then they get to stuff their faces. We're hoping to get half a dozen, and that they will tell their friends and so on. But it's not till this afternoon."

"And what are their parents supposed to be doing while you bribe the kids?"

"Looking respectable. I have persuaded Hector to bring Arwen, with the promise of many drinks. I want him to go and talk to as many of the old farts as he can about what a *marvellous* job Pandy is doing."

Mal poured some more coffee into his mug. "You really like her, don't you?"

"Yes, I do. What she's trying to do is worth supporting. Most of the other plot holders might not grow veg in the same way she does, but they don't object to someone doing things differently. But there's a few bullies, and they won't be happy until they drive her out."

Mal thought about the entry in the domestic abuse file. He wondered whether any of the bullies were James Melton's friends. A few months ago, he would have shared his information with Daniel. Now he couldn't. He stood up, and put his breakfast things in the dishwasher. Then he put his arms round Daniel and kissed him, wishing that he'd sacrificed breakfast for a return to bed. He took the imprint of Daniel's body with him to the police station.

***

Hector Lord arrived at the allotments in his oldest jeans, green wellies, and a Barbour jacket that had seen better days. He had his partner Sasha's daughter, Arwen with him. Over the last year, Hector had changed from being Arwen's 'Uncle Hector' to 'Daddy Hector', and once he and Sasha married, he was hoping to become simply 'Daddy'. Arwen was her mother's daughter — strong-minded and ready to claim what she thought should be hers. He hoped she'd claim him. He knew that today she would be claiming leadership of the other kids on the community allotment. Cerys he already knew from sleepovers and school events. Her mother Pandy stood up from 'supervising' the planting of dozens of seeds. "Hi, Hector, thanks for coming. Hi, Arwen."

"Sasha needed homework time, and it's not actually raining, so here we are. What would you like me to do?" Hector's cut glass accent always surprised Pandy. He looked so *normal.*

Daniel appeared from behind the shed, bringing the odour of rotting vegetation with him. He had a spade in one hand and a pitchfork in the other. "Circulate, Hector, charm the other plot holders. Make us look respectable. Make friends." He waved Hector away, and leaned towards the children still poking seeds into pots of soil. "Who likes worms?"

Hector sighed. Talking to random strangers was an improvement on playing with worms. Probably. He told Arwen to be good, and set off to 'circulate'.

He estimated that about a quarter of the allotments had people working on them, though it wasn't always easy to see where one plot ended and another began. The muddy paths were lined with edging boards in some places, and in others the grass had been trimmed to keep it from spreading onto the growing space. He was surprised by how much produce was growing — lots of kale, some Brussels sprouts or cabbagey things, and what looked like small onions, half buried in the ground. All the plots showed signs of recent industry. He made his way towards the car park and the big grey tin shed with the notices on its door. When he got there, a man was dumping half a dozen plastic garden chairs which had once been white, but were now green with slime and mould. Hector thought of the upturned buckets and old tyres which were the only seating on the community allotment.

"Are you getting rid of those?" he asked.

"I'm hoping someone will find a use for them." The speaker was a small, wiry man with greying hair and glasses. He was very neatly dressed for a man manoeuvring filthy garden chairs. Even his wellies looked clean. "I don't like to see things go to waste."

"Oh, absolutely agree," Hector said. "Are you sure no one else will want them?" He noticed that the man didn't have the out-in-all-weathers look shared by Pandy and Daniel. He looked tired, and rather grey, with watery, pale blue eyes behind his glasses, and thin lips. He'd missed a bit of his chin while shaving. There was a water butt next to the grey tin shed, and next to that, a tap with a long hose pipe. Hector pointed.

"Would it be OK for me to use the hose, do you think? To wash the chairs?"

The man shrugged. "Water's cheap."

The man didn't seem keen to get back to his plot, but Hector was finding him hard going. He arranged the dirty chairs in a row, and turned on the tap. "Have you had your plot here for long? I must say, it's all very impressive. I grow a few tomatoes in my garden, but that's about it. My friend Daniel gives me a hand. He's over at the community allotment now, showing some children how to sow seeds." He realised that he was gabbling, but carried on. The man appeared to be listening. "My daughter — well my fiancée's daughter — will be bossing them all about by now. She's that kind of girl. But it's a lot of fun having her around." Hector thought he saw a look of pain cross the man's face, but it was gone as soon as it arrived. The chairs were beginning to look a bit better, although Hector was glad they were on the gravel car park rather than the soil, as gallons of water soaked into the ground. He turned the hose off for a moment. "I'm going to get a cloth, or a brush or something."

The man nodded. "Get the stubborn bits off, and they'll be good."

"I think the adults will be glad of somewhere to sit after their efforts this afternoon. Let the kids sit on the overturned buckets." Hector tried a smile.

"Community allotment. Free childcare. That's what people want. Can't wait to get rid of them."

"Oh no. No kids without a parent. Definitely." He wiped his hand on his jeans and held it out. "I'm Hector Lord, pleased to meet you."

The man jerked into life, and shook hands, rather feebly, Hector thought.

"David Jones," he said. "I don't approve of all these hippies coming here, but you can still have the chairs." Then he turned away and left. Hector followed him with his eyes up to a plot on the road side of the allotment field. It had a new looking shed. David Jones opened the door and went inside, closing the door behind him. Hector shrugged. *Well, I deserve full points for trying.*

***

At the Community Allotment, the parents and children sat around the fire pit toasting marshmallows on sticks to make s'mores with chocolate and biscuits. Sparks danced from the fire as the afternoon drew to a close. The children gave small screams as the sparks came too close, or their marshmallow burned. It was cold, but they'd been working, so faces were flushed from effort and smudged with dirt and smoke. Hector had brought his newly cleaned chairs, referring to them as the 'executive seating'. Pandy had supervised the planting of dozens of seeds, and promised that if the children came back next week, there would be green leaves to see. Childish voices had talked of digging a pond, and building a greenhouse from plastic bottles. By five, they had all drifted away. Hector and a couple of others were on a promise to return the next week, and the children talked excitedly about bringing friends. Pandy's daughter Cerys went with Hector and Arwen for a sleepover.

When they'd gone, Daniel sat in one of the executive chairs and put some more of the wood from the old floor on to the fire. His knees were hot in their jeans, where they were close to the flames, but the rest of his body was cold, though not cold enough to make himself move. He fished one of the last marshmallows out of the bag and toasted it, waving it around until it was cool enough to eat.

"I know you wanted people without gardens or growing space of their own, but if the kids can persuade some of their mates, and the word goes round ..." He offered the bag of marshmallows to Pandy who shook her head. He tossed his toasting stick into the fire. "You're right, they are pretty disgusting. But the kids love them."

"It was good, today. You were great with the kids. I can teach them how to plant seeds, but I wouldn't have thought of s'mores."

"I had fun. I like kids."

"You don't have any plans for your own?"

Daniel liked the way that Pandy asked about children so casually, as if it wasn't a whole pile of hideous decision-making and complications.

"I was a detective. I worked insane hours, and my partner Mal still does. We could barely look after the dog when we first got her. Now? Maybe, but we haven't talked about it."

This time Pandy threw some wood on to the fire, sending more sparks shooting into the growing darkness. The smoke drifted towards them, and then away again, and Daniel could smell it on his clothes. He let his thoughts drift towards the possibility of children. Mal wasn't keen, but he wasn't completely set against the idea either. Mal had his own nephew, baby Emyr, and Daniel saw the look in Mal's eyes as he let the little boy clutch at his fingers. Perhaps a baby would be too much for them. His friend Veronica wanted them to apply to become foster carers, and they'd talked about it on and off. His mind drifted away, as it seemed to do easily in front of the fire, with Pandy's undemanding company.

"Have a blanket," Pandy said. He hadn't noticed her leave and had no real sense of how long she'd been gone. He wrapped the blanket around his shoulders, shivering slightly, as the cold fabric touched his body. But it would warm up.

It was intimate, sitting here in the twilight, listening to the last few plot-holders putting their tools away and getting into their cars. Quiet voices drifted towards them, saying goodbyes and sharing hopes for another decent day tomorrow. Headlights briefly lit up the tin shed by the entrance, then disappeared through the hedge onto the road.

Daniel said what had been on his mind all day. "I'd like to keep coming here, if I can. I've got my own planting to do, and it's a busy time of the year, but I've enjoyed it. I, um, have a friend who is a social worker, and I could ask her if there are any people she knows who might enjoy it. Maybe people with kids but no gardens... If you think that's a good idea?"

Pandy reached out from under her blanket and took his hand, squeezing it briefly. She smiled, teeth and eyes bright. "Daniel, *please* keep coming. You know how to talk to people. All I know is how to get grants from the council."

"I don't know what I'm doing though. In the police when we *worked with the community* it was about getting information about illegal activity."

"It doesn't matter. You know how to grow vegetables, and how to mend sheds." There was a pause and Pandy started to giggle. "The thing is, if you are going to volunteer regularly, I'll need to get you police-checked to make sure you haven't got a criminal record I should know about..."

"*That* tells me I'm not a policeman any more. It's a strange thought. It's like I've swapped sides."

"Is that how it feels?"

Daniel considered it, his body starting to chill even with the blanket as the fire began to die. He put a small piece of wood on, for five more minutes thinking time.

"I've been a policeman longer than I've been anything else. I knew I wanted to stop, but I don't know what to do instead, so I'm drifting around as an ex-copper. I thought the smallholding would fill the gap, but I've learned that I need to be with other people, as well as with trees and chickens. The long and short of it is that I don't know. But this has helped. I think I've been lonely." He was embarrassed. Those were things he could barely say to Mal, let alone a virtual stranger. he stood up, evicting Flora from his lap and folding the blanket. "We should lock up and get home. You need your evening of peace in front of the telly."

Pandy rosę to her feet, a little stiff after sitting in the cold for too long. "I don't know what you'll finish up doing, Daniel, but trust me, you can come here as often as you like."

They stacked the executive seating, made sure the fire was safely out and locked the shed. Solar lamps poked into the ground provided a feeble light around their plot, but once on the path back to the cars, they needed their torches. The Land Rover and Pandy's van loomed out of the darkness, a streetlight catching a sliver of the tin shed, and the shine of the Land Rover's windscreen. Pandy went round to the driver's door of her van and Daniel heard a gasp.

"What?" he called.

"There's something here." Pandy sounded panicky.

Daniel ran around the vehicle, and when he saw, he took Pandy's arm and eased her gently away. "Ring for an ambulance," he said, and bent over the figure slumped on the ground, feeling at the cold skin on the neck for a pulse. There was none. But the skin was warm. And, he noted, wet. He turned the figure onto its side, opening the mouth to look for obstructions. He found nothing. He heard Pandy talking to the dispatcher. "I'm going to try CPR," he said, loud enough for the dispatcher to hear. "But I think it's too late. Send for the police."

Pandy came round to his side of her van, holding her phone, with the dispatcher still talking. "Who is it? Daniel? Tell me!"

Daniel blocked her view of the body with his own, counting as he breathed into the man's mouth, and compressed the chest.

"Hayden Bennion."

5

LOCUST TIME

The ambulance arrived first. It didn't take long for the paramedics to confirm what Daniel already knew: Hayden Bennion was dead. Daniel had seen enough dead bodies to be largely immune, but Pandy was shocked and distressed. She was soon wrapped in a silver foil blanket, still shaking. Daniel made her get into his Land Rover and turned the engine on to warm them both up. The air was still, cold and damp, and the exhaust fumes from his engine hung in clouds. Its acrid smell filled their noses, even with the doors and windows closed. The ambulance had turned its siren off, but the blue light pulsed, turning the faces of Pandy and the paramedics a ghostly colour as it flashed and dimmed, flashed and dimmed. It was joined by another blue light as the first police car arrived: PC Morgan, squeezed behind the wheel of a marked four-wheel drive.

Thank God it's him, Daniel thought, as the big man rolled towards them, light-footed, despite his bulk.

Daniel got out of the Land Rover, closing the door behind him to preserve the heat inside for Pandy.

"Sir," PC Morgan said, as if Daniel was still in charge. "What have we got?"

Daniel led him to the end of Pandy's van, and pointed: "The body is a bloke called Hayden Bennion. I've met him. He was the chair of the allotment society, but that's all I know. I tried CPR because he was still warm, but he was already dead. Paramedics confirmed death. His body and clothes are wet."

"Did you find him, sir?"

Daniel indicated Pandy's figure in the silver blanket, lighting up with blue flashes. "That woman is Pandy Melton, and this is her van. She was about to get in it when she saw him." Daniel looked round. "Not my job to tell you what to do, Morgan, but if it was, I'd ask you to tape off the whole area, probably including my car. The area round the body is screwed up, but as far as I know, nothing else has been disturbed. I'd do that before I did anything else, to keep the gawkers out, and stay on the right side of the CSIs."

Morgan, nodded so firmly that it was almost a salute. "Perhaps you and Ms Melton would like to go and sit in the back of my car for a few minutes? I expect someone from CID will be along soon."

Daniel switched his engine off, then helped Pandy into the police car. PC Morgan had left the engine running, so it was warm. They sat close together on the back seat.

"What happened to him, Daniel?"

"I don't know. His clothes were wet, and his hair and skin." Daniel's own sleeves were wet and chilly where he'd moved the body, and his coat, where he'd leaned over to breathe into the man's mouth. "But you know my friend Hector, who was here today, is a pathologist. He'll be here soon, and he'll find out. And I'm going to call my partner, because I think we need to get you out of here, and into the warm."

"How can he be dead? I thought he'd gone home." Pandy

started crying, deep sobs and hiccoughs. She wiped her eyes with her hands. "I didn't like him, but how can he be dead?"

Daniel wrapped his arms round Pandy, feeling the rough wool of her clothes against his hands, and her long braid of hair on his neck. She smelled of woodsmoke, and a little of chocolate.

This is why I left the police, Pandy love, this shit, day in, day out. Because if he had felt the broken skin on the back of Hayden Bennion's head, Hector wasn't going to miss it. Nothing about this situation felt like an accident. Everything felt like murder. He moved her slightly to get his phone out of his pocket.

"Maldwyn? Can you come to the allotments? You, yourself." Mal would know about the body, but his job wasn't to look at the scene. There was a time when Mal would have argued, but that time had passed.

Daniel heard the sound of a laptop being closed and chair legs moving on a carpet.

"I'm on my way. But DI Carey will be there first."

PC MORGAN WAS MIDWAY through taping off the scene when Carey arrived, demanding to know what PC Morgan thought he was doing. Morgan could look like a stone man when he needed to, and his face held all the expression of a tree stump as he answered. "Taping off the scene, sir, but I can stop if you don't want it done."

"Of course I want it taped off. Get on with it."

Next for the Carey treatment were the paramedics, who didn't have to call him 'sir', and would leave as soon as they had their next call. So Carey's anger was in full flow when he reached the car with Daniel and Pandy. Daniel got out, hoping that Mal would arrive before Carey had a chance to shout at Pandy.

If Carey was intimidated by Daniel being at least a foot

taller than him, he didn't show it. Carey might not have come directly from the pub, but he smelled of beer and cigarettes.

"Fancy seeing you here, Danny boy. Just can't keep away from dead bodies. How long until Kent arrives to get you out of trouble?"

Daniel resisted the urge to knock the obnoxious man onto his back, counting his breaths as he'd learned to do since his illness. He did his best to look at Carey from underneath his eyelashes, a la Princess Diana. "Oh, am I in trouble, DI Carey? Do tell me what I've done."

In the corner of his eye, Daniel saw PC Morgan cover his face and fake a cough to cover a snort of laughter. He looked away before Carey noticed. Daniel leaned one hip against the police car, and took his hat off, the better to run his hand through his new curls. It annoyed Carey just as Daniel knew it would.

"If I were still a detective, DI Carey, I'd be asking questions of the man who tried to save the victim's life, but I'm sure you have your own methods."

Carey's breath came in rasps, his always-red face turning purple in the strobe lights. A glossy black Audi drew up next to them, carefully not blocking the ambulance. Mal got out, as immaculate as his car.

"Daniel, Adam. What do we have?"

Daniel was sure that he could hear Carey's teeth grinding. "Sir," he said. "I've only just arrived myself. I was just going to ask Mr Owen about what he found."

Mal held his hand out, palm upwards. "Go ahead, don't mind me."

Daniel was careful not to look at Mal, and to keep his face serious. After all, a man is dead, he told himself.

"My friend Pandy Melton found the body," he said. "Less than a minute before we called you. He was lying on the ground, curled on his side, not breathing, no pulse. But he was warm, so I tried CPR. He was wet. Most of his clothes and his hair. His name is Hayden Bennion, and all I know about him is that he's the chair of the allotment society. We had a small event here today, and I think he was here, but I didn't talk to him, though I have talked to him in the past. Dr Hector Lord was also here today, so you should talk to him, too." Now Daniel was positive Carey was grinding his teeth.

More police cars arrived, like the descent of a swarm of locusts, bringing DS Bethan Davies and DC Charlie Rees, as well as more uniformed officers. All except Bethan called Daniel 'sir', and each time, Daniel saw Carey's face harden. He could almost hear his replacement grinding his teeth. Carey snapped at Bethan to "Get this scene bloody organised, for God's sake." The CSIs arrived in a van: Paul Jarvis and a woman Daniel hadn't met. Dressed in white coveralls, masks and shoe covers, they erected a tent around Hayden Bennion's body and Pandy's van. The rest of the parking area was taped off, and plastic 'footsteps' put on the ground to provide a single route for the investigators.

Finally, Hector arrived in a taxi.

"Daniel, Mal, sorry it's taken me so long. Had a drink with dinner and had to wait for a cab." He sniffed, pointedly, in Carey's direction. "One glass of wine, and I didn't finish that. But I guess I'm not the only one who was enjoying their Saturday night."

Mal lifted one eyebrow, in a way that Daniel had tried hard to imitate for years. Carey blushed again, the red of his neck visible in the headlights. "I'm on duty, not drunk, thank you very much," he said, in Welsh, knowing that Hector wouldn't understand. Daniel obligingly translated.

"My mistake," Hector said airily. "Let's have a look at this body then." He looked between Mal and Carey as if to ask who he should report to.

"This is DI Carey's case," Mal said. "Pretend I'm not here."

DI Carey and Hector suited up and ducked into the tent.

Mal moved close to Daniel. "So you told Carey everything?"

Daniel nodded. "Except that I felt a bump on the guy's head as if he'd been bashed, but Hector will tell him that. The other thing I didn't say was that Bennion was one of the bullies I was talking about before. Shouted at Pandy and patronised me."

A low whine from inside the police car reminded Daniel that Pandy and Flora were still waiting patiently. "I think Pandy needs to go home. She's cold and she's had a shock. Her statement can wait. That's why I asked you to come. Carey would make her stay here."

"I thought you wanted my manly protection?"

"That's just a bonus."

"Take my car, get her home and I'll send Bethan or Charlie over to get her statement later." Mal handed Daniel the keys to the Audi.

"You mean DI Carey will send someone," Daniel said, grinning.

"Of course I do. Now clear off before he realises you've gone."

***

Mal waited patiently for Hector and DI Carey to finish inside the tent. Bethan had the scene organised, with uniformed officers searching the car park with torches, and DC Charlie Rees trying to find information about possible key-holders for the big grey tin shed. PC Morgan was dispatched to keep the entrance clear of gawkers, both those curious plot holders, and those pretending to have business on the site. Mal thought that the team was working well despite Carey, rather than because of him. Carey had been drinking, no question. Time to find out more. He rang Sophie Harrington at the station, suspecting rightly that she'd still be there.

"Have you got anyone trustworthy in the building?"

"Me. Friday evening? When someone's been finding suspicious bodies? How many coppers do you think we have here?"

"Point. Carey has turned up here stinking of booze, and he's supposed to be on duty. I wondered if someone might like to have a nosy around his office while it's quiet. There's a spare key in the top right-hand drawer of my desk if you need one."

There was a giggle down the line. "How fortunate that I fancied stretching my legs. I'll get back to you."

6

THAT WAS THEN

Daniel drove Pandy back to her house in a quiet street Daniel had passed, but never entered. It was a kind of mews, he supposed; converted stables, red brick, a single storey high, with a half-storey above which must have been for storing hay. Old-fashioned square lamps lit the grassy cobbles. The houses were on one side of the road only. The other side was a high red brick wall, dividing a walled garden from the mews. Parked cars and wheelie bins brought a jarring note of the twenty-first century.

Inside Pandy's house, there was a single room, maybe twenty feet long and twelve wide, with open wooden stairs rising in the middle. The living area was at the front, and a kitchen to the rear. A partially open door in the kitchen suggested a utility room. The feeling of a converted stable was enhanced by the stone flagged floors and white painted raw brick walls. Without Pandy's trademark style, it would have been bleak. But she had covered her furniture with rainbow throws, painted her kitchen units in the same blue as the shed at the allotment, and covered the walls with hangings and photographs. The draining rack beside the kitchen sink held the morning's washing up; not a single matching item, but every plate and cup patterned and brightly coloured. The only source of heat seemed to be the log-burner, so Daniel started making a fire.

"Can I make you a hot drink?" he asked, when the logs had caught. "Hot chocolate? Builders' bright orange tea with lots of sugar? And something to eat. Tell me what you've got."

"God, Daniel, I'll never eat again. But I'd love some tea. Without sugar."

He put the kettle on, found the teapot, mugs, milk and a tray. With a quick search through the cupboards, he located a packet of biscuits, probably meant for Cerys's school lunches, and added them.

"You need to eat something sweet. You're in shock. Believe me, sugar works."

Pandy kept shivering. "I'm so cold." She held her hands out to the fire.

"That's shock, and trust me, sugar helps."

She gave a feeble smile, and unwrapped one of the biscuits, looking at it without interest. But she took a bite, and then another. She picked up her mug, warming her hands, and a moment later, taking a tentative sip. "Too hot." She put the mug down again and finished the biscuit. Daniel unwrapped another, handing it to her with a smile.

"It was Hayden? And he was dead? Thank God Cerys wasn't there."

"Eat your biscuit and I'll tell you."

The room was starting to warm up. Daniel fed more logs into the fire, feeling his damp clothes begin to steam gently in the heat. Pandy noticed. "You're all wet. How did you get wet?"

Daniel checked to make sure Pandy had started drinking her tea. "Hayden's body and clothes were wet, soaking. When I tried to revive him, I got wet too. Before you ask, I don't know how he got wet."

Although I have a theory, and I bet I'm right.

A tear ran down Pandy's cheek, and she drank some more tea to hold the sobs at bay. "Why am I crying? I didn't like him."

"He was a bully, Pandy. But it's natural to cry. Have you seen a dead person before?" She shook her head. "It's shock. We'd had a good day. Hayden didn't spoil it, despite his best efforts, and we were headed home thinking about having a nice evening. Then — this."

Daniel filled Pandy's cup from the tea pot. He saw her remember that he didn't like orange milky tea. "If you don't like builder's tea, there's some herbal stuff in the cupboard. You must be cold too."

Daniel was starting to feel unpleasantly warm and sweaty, but he did want a drink, so he made himself some mint tea and came back. Pandy had relaxed enough to sit back in her chair. Suddenly she jerked upright. "You've left your dog in the car! She'll freeze. Go and bring her in."

Daniel knew that Flora would be curled into a tiny ball on her blanket, and not at all cold, but she'd be much happier in front of the fire. Having Pandy stroke her ears would be nice for Flora, and calming for Pandy. "Some people don't want dogs inside, but I'll get her if you don't mind."

When they were settled again, Pandy said, "That policeman, the dumpy one with the red face, is he in charge of finding out what happened to Hayden? Because I didn't like the look of him. And who was the other one, whose car we borrowed? Is that your boyfriend?" A pause. "What does it mean that all those police were there?" Pandy's voice started to rise, with a note of panic.

Daniel took Pandy's hand. "We don't know what happened to Hayden. He was fine earlier and we don't know why he died. It's the police's job to investigate suspicious deaths. The policeman you didn't like is called DI Carey, and he's vile. The other one is my partner, Maldwyn Kent. He's in charge. He came because I wanted to make sure you got home, and Mal would make sure no one stopped you."

Pandy gave the merest hint of a smile, as she began to relax. "He's very good looking."

"And a very good detective."

Pandy smiled, properly this time. "Which did you choose him for, looks or brains?"

***

At the allotments, Mal was beginning to wish he'd taken Pandy home himself, rather than let Daniel drive away in his nice comfortable car. Hector and Carey were taking a long time to look at Hayden Bennion's body and Paul Jarvis had set up blindingly bright floodlights so that he could fingerprint every smooth surface. The other CSI was examining the ground minutely, picking up items with tweezers, replacing them with a little numbered sign and taking multiple photographs. The implication of this activity was that Carey had told the CSI's that the death was more than a simple heart attack. Only no one official had told *him*. He added it to his mental list of charges against Carey.

After an age, Hector and Carey appeared, pulling down their hoods and masks. Carey spoke first. "He was murdered, sir, according to the doc."

Mal knew that would grate on Hector, who never drew conclusions, merely reported his findings, and abhorred being called 'doc'.

"Really?" said Mal.

Hector moved towards Mal, took his arm and tugged, gently. "Excuse us for a moment, DI Carey," he said. Hector led Mal away from the taped off area, and into the darkness. "Where did you get that idiot? Central casting? I'd heard about him, but it's nothing to the reality. And he smells."

"I'm working on it. I keep hoping there's a good detective in there somewhere, but no signs of one yet. So, was the guy murdered?"

"For your ears only, almost certainly bashed on the head, then pushed face down into the water butt until he drowned. It's not a proper water butt, just an old barrel."

"Which is why he was wet."

They were disturbed by the sound of the mortuary van joining the crowd of vehicles in the car park. Hector took hold of Mal's sleeve again. "I have to go. But DI Dickhead knows that Daniel was here all day, and he thinks it's 'significant' that Daniel found the body, and that you dashed down here. He's out to make trouble. Watch your back."

***

Daniel didn't want to leave Pandy on her own, so he made toast and unfroze some soup from her freezer. She seemed more relaxed. Tea, biscuits and stroking Flora's ears were all working their magic, but hot food was another antidote to shock. His clothes had begun to feel drier, and the house was warm enough that he could strip off the top layer.

"Thank God Cerys went home with Hector and Arwen," Pandy said. "She doesn't need to know about this. Do you think the police will want to talk to me? Because I don't want her here then. She's had enough policemen in her life. Me too, come to that."

Daniel put that aside for later. "They will definitely want to talk to you. We can probably fix it so they come before Cerys gets back."

"Will you find out what happened?"

Daniel thought that he already had a pretty good idea of the *what*, but no idea about the *who*. "I can't find out anything officially."

"Unofficially?"

Daniel felt the squeeze as the rock and the hard place

moved closer together. "I can't get involved. I'm not a policeman any more."

"The thing is that Hayden wasn't always nasty. I was at school with Rhys Bennion, even went out with him for a bit, and Hayden was always OK when I went round there."

"Rhys Bennion being...?"

"Hayden's son. Married and living in Australia. There's a daughter too, Eluned. She lives in Shetland with her girlfriend. We're Facebook friends."

Now Daniel was on safe ground. "Eluned Bennion? That's Hayden's daughter? I remember Eluned Bennion. Shaved all her hair off for a bet when we were at school. She said it was for charity, but everyone knew better." He smiled at the memory, even though he couldn't remember who had challenged Eluned. Somehow he wasn't surprised to hear that Eluned was living with another woman.

Pandy smiled too. "She was just a kid when I was seeing Rhys, but we're friendly now. She was kind when I got divorced. Invited me and Cerys to visit them. I'd love to go, but we've got no money." The smile faded.

They both started as someone banged at the front door, then rattled the letterbox. Pandy spilled her tea as she moved to put it down on the table, managing to catch Daniel's just dried sleeve with the liquid. The clammy feeling on his arm came back. He opened the door to DI Carey and a uniformed constable waiting on the mat. Carey made to push past, but Daniel could hold his place like a dog reluctant to leave a particularly good smell.

"Is Mrs Melton here?" Carey snapped. His white coveralls had been replaced with a new-looking dark green wool coat with a black collar, the kind Daniel mentally called a *spiv coat*. Its newness couldn't disguise the smell of sweat, cigarettes and breath mints. It was speckled with tiny rain drops sparkling in the light from the open door.

"It's her house," Daniel said flatly, stepping aside to let them in, pointing at the row of shoes next to the doormat and his own stockinged feet. Carey took off his shoes — muddy black oxfords — but the uniform seemed reluctant to remove his. *Hole in the socks* Daniel thought, remembering that the thin-faced constable was called Kelley, and that he was the nearest thing DI Carey had to a friend in the Melin Tywyll force.

"Stay there," Carey told PC Kelley. "We won't be here long." He turned to Pandy. "Mrs Melton, we'd like to ask you some questions down at the police station."

"Do I have to go?" The question was directed at Daniel.

He shook his head. "Not unless they arrest you, and I don't think they want to do that."

But Carey's face was hard. "It's just questions at the moment, Mrs Melton. It's easier for everyone at the station. We could call your husband to look after your little girl if you like."

Daniel saw the impact of the words hitting Pandy like a sledgehammer. Her body slammed back into the back of her chair, and the blood rushed from her face, leaving her lips and eyes stark against ghostly white skin.

"Or perhaps not," Carey said. "Perhaps you'd like to come and answer my questions and then you'd be back here to put your daughter to bed, and no need to bother your husband at all."

Pandy was struggling for breath. "He's not... not... he's not allowed near us. You can't tell him where we are."

"Oh, my mistake." Carey didn't sound the least repentant. In fact, he seemed pleased with the response he'd achieved. Daniel's heart pounded in his chest, and his hands curled into fists. What a truly evil man. Carey turned to Daniel. "I want to take her to the station, because I need some fucking questions answered. You can call your precious boyfriend if you like, to make sure I don't beat her up. That way, this address doesn't feature in my report."

Daniel recognised blackmail when he heard it. So did Pandy. Trembling, and still white as a sheet, she stood up.

"Pandy, you don't have to go. I'll call Mal. This is totally unacceptable, and I'll be making a complaint."

Carey openly sneered. "You're in this up to your eyeballs, Danny boy. Go ahead. Complain. Drag Kent into your muddy business. You're all compromised." Daniel felt the anger in the back of his throat, closing it until he could barely breathe. Only his refusal to allow Carey to see his desire for violence kept him calm. He forced his hands to uncurl from the fists they had formed, and walked stiffly over to Pandy to put his arm around her shoulders. Her entire body had frozen. "I will bring Ms Melton to the police station and I will arrange for her to have a solicitor with her when she answers your questions. Now get out of her house."

7

IT'S ONLY GARDENING

D aniel waited for Pandy's solicitor to arrive once they got to the police station. The battered blue carpet in the reception area was drearily familiar, and he imagined how it must seem someone like Pandy, who hadn't been there before: the scratched acrylic screen between the civilian receptionist and the public, the uncomfortable chairs around the small space, the endless coming and going of dirty feet across the floor. The automatic doors hissed open and closed, letting cold air in every time, so that the receptionist had to keep a heater under her desk. Carey was waiting by the metal door next to the reception desk. He beckoned Pandy, but Daniel said "We'll wait here for the solicitor, thank you."

On the other side, Daniel knew the police station proper began, with interview rooms and the corridor to the cells, and the medical suite for blood samples and breath tests. This was where the custody officer sat, behind another screen. The area would smell of disinfectant, covering the odour of drunks who arrived with depressing regularity. But all this was barred to Daniel now. He waited in one of the horrible chairs, keeping his gaze fixed to a piece of chewing gum ground into the carpet, rather than the two lads in tracksuits waiting to answer their bail, and the elderly homeless man having a warm, while pretending to fill out a form of some kind. He texted Mal to say that he was there, but wasn't surprised not to get an answer.

Marcus Scott, the solicitor Daniel had called, arrived fifteen minutes later. Daniel dragged him and Pandy outside and explained as succinctly as he could and Carey was in full-on bully mode.

"Don't worry," Scott said. "I've come across DI Carey more than once. I'll deal with him."

Daniel sent another text to Mal, got another silence, and decided to head home. The house that had seemed so full of life and promise this morning seemed empty and cold when he got back. The chickens had put themselves to bed, their internal clocks reacting to the dusk by sending them to roost inside their house. He let himself through the outer fox proof barricade, and into their domain: scattered straw, a few surviving bits of grass, and hollowed out areas for dust bathing. As usual, corn and chicken feed were strewn untidily around the space, fair game for any wild birds who were small enough to get through the wire mesh fences. Daniel loved that some of it would sprout every year, producing all kinds of non-native grasses and corn plants. He probably should have uprooted it all, but he never did. He shone a light into the chicken house, counting the birds and ensuring that no predators had managed to find a way in. The chickens chuck-chucked sleepily. "Good night, ladies," he said, and closed the door, turning the wooden peg to secure it.

Flora was waiting impatiently in the kitchen. "Dinner?" he asked, and got a nudge on the leg as answer. Once Flora was fed, Daniel went through the motions of lighting the fire, showering, putting his dirty clothes in the wash, and pouring himself a beer. They felt like the things he ought to be doing, when what he wanted was for Mal to come back and talk to him about Hayden Bennion. He wanted the phone to ring and Pandy to say Carey had believed her story, and she was now home, with a glass of wine, having said goodnight to Cerys, happy at her sleepover. With neither of those things on offer, he kept adding more logs to the fire, until the room was almost unbearably hot. Then he looked for a book, any book, to catch his interest, on the shelves at the back of the room. He plumped cushions and folded the crocheted blanket on the back of the sofa. He cleaned the already clean kitchen. He spun the washing and hung it on the clothes horse. He made popcorn, and ate it with another beer. He tried a crossword, but it defeated him, and he resorted to computer games, until he felt his eyes begin to close and he went to bed, still having heard nothing from either Mal or Pandy. Flora was already asleep, curled into a tiny ball in her basket, paws twitching occasionally.

The bedroom was painted white, like the rest of the house, with lamps and more dark velvet curtains to make it cosy in winter. One wall was covered with cupboards for clothes; mostly Mal's clothes, Daniel always told everyone. Daniel had constructed the bed himself, because he'd wanted to try something more complicated than a shed, or a hen house. His sister had been so impressed that she had made him a huge rainbow blanket. It weighed the duvet down, so they could barely move, but in winter, they were glad of the extra warmth. Daniel wriggled under the duvet and switched the lamp off. Then he got up and opened the curtains, hoping for a moon and stars. Clouds covered the sky. He closed the curtains and went back to bed. He practiced his meditation exercises for what felt like a year. Then he switched the light back on, reached onto the floor for his fleece, found an old envelope and a pen in his bedside table, and did what he had wanted to do since finding Hayden Bennion's body. He wrote down everything he could remember from the last few days: the people he'd met, the things they'd said, the events of this afternoon and the days running up to it.

Pandy: some kind of history. Not just DV? How does Carey know about DV? Relevant? I can't give complete alibi — drifted off. But could she have gone further than shed? Interview all plot holders who were around today, also ask about history Question Eluned and Rhys. Other schoolfriends? Hector's findings?

Daniel fell asleep as the pen fell onto the floor and the envelope found its way under the pillow, gripped in his hand.

He woke to feel a warm body pressed against his own. A faint light was creeping round the heavy curtains, creating a dim haze. He could just see Mal's dark hair against the pillow. Mal had obviously been too exhausted to do more than drop his clothes on the floor and crawl into bed naked. Daniel felt Mal's chest rise and fall against his own body as he breathed, and he found himself breathing in the same rhythm. He slid his free hand round to caress the soft hair on Mal's stomach, and then upwards onto his pecs. His fingers found the nipple ring. Mal"s breathing never changed. He was asleep, but his body was beginning to stir, and so was Daniel's. Reason said *let him sleep.* His body disagreed. Daniel's fingers moved lower, finding Mal's cock hardening, and it hardened more as he played. He missed his absent fingers, but smiled inwardly as he told himself to do the best he could. Then Mal's breathing changed. A hand gripped his own. Held it in place. Daniel responded by wriggling further into Mal's warmth, his own erection pressing into Mal's arse.

"What are you doing?" Mal sounded hoarse, and still mostly asleep.

"What does it feel like?"

"Like the best sort of dream, but don't expect me to move."

"Let go of my hand then."

Daniel fucked Mal as if they were both dreaming. Sliding first one lubed finger inside his warmth, then two, which is all he had. Finally, after a long time of soft movements and gentle noises, he rolled an uncomplaining Mal onto his back and pulled a pillow down to lift him up. Pushing into Mal, feeling Mal pushing back, reaching for his neck and kissing him as they moved together still felt like a dream. Mal never opened his eyes, just breathed, and whispered *Fuck, I love you, Daniel*. His orgasm built quickly, and he didn't stop it, letting the sweet waves roll over him, then resting in the aftermath. He withdrew and moved down the bed, running his lips over Mal's body, teasing his hard nipples, swirling his tongue in Mal's navel, and finally taking Mal's cock into his mouth, licking and sucking until Mal came too. He ignored the mess of the bed, just threw the pillow onto the floor and dragged the covers over them both and snuggling into Mal's shoulders.

"I missed you," Daniel said, feeling a sting of tears in the corners of his eyes.

"Go to sleep", Mal answered, so he did.

DANIEL WOKE up to the sight and smell of a mug of coffee held by a dark hairy man dressed in a towel, and smelling of soap.

"What time is it?" he asked, as Mal put the mug on the bedside table.

"Nine. I have to go in. But we need to talk before I go, so drink your coffee. There will be toast." Mal disappeared out of the bedroom, and Daniel heard his bare feet going downstairs, and a few minutes later, coming back, this time with a plate, and another mug. Daniel lifted the covers and Mal dropped the towel and got back into bed.

Daniel took a piece of buttery toast from the plate. "Wassup?" he asked after the first bite had gone down.

Mal held up a crumpled paper. "This. Your notes about Hayden Bennion."

Daniel recognised the envelope he'd been scribbling on the night before. "Only a few thoughts."

"A few thoughts about an investigation that you can't be part of."

"I am part of it though. I was there. And I was there when Carey blackmailed Pandy by threatening to tell her ex where she lived. I don't know what went on, but Pandy was terrified. Carey was totally out of order."

"I know about Pandy's ex. I didn't know you couldn't give her an alibi."

"They are *notes*. We were sat by the fire talking and I started thinking about something. Then I kind of came to as Pandy gave me a blanket. I'm sure I'd have heard if she'd gone past me. I'm sure she just went to the shed for the blankets. I wasn't asleep, lost in thought is all."

"Daniel. This says you couldn't give her an alibi. She was at daggers drawn with Bennion. She argued with him at the Allotment Society AGM. Charlie talked to a couple of plot holders last night. They describe two camps at the allotments; Pandy and her mates, and Bennion and his."

"Bennion was a bully."

"Exactly. Witnesses say he was trying to drive Pandy and her mates away, and that would lose her the money she gets from the council for running the community allotment. And now I find out that she hasn't got an alibi for the time of the killing."

Daniel put the remains of his toast back on the plate and sat up properly. He looked at his partner, wondering where the astute detective he'd fallen for had disappeared to.

"In the immortal words of John McEnroe, *you cannot be serious!* Maldwyn this is *gardening*. No one gets murdered over a disagreement about peat-based compost or slug pellets. I can't believe you've fallen for the crap about Pandy making money from the community allotment. Do some police work and stop listening to gossip. Fucksake Mal."

"Are you sure you know everything about your shiny new friend, Dan?"

Daniel wanted to pick up the toast plate and throw it. Mal knew exactly how to push his buttons, but Daniel knew that Mal was hitting out because he wasn't sure of his ground.

"Read the note. It says *find out the history*."

Mal put his mug down and got up. He went over to the cupboards and started to get dressed, methodically picking out socks, underpants, a shirt, tie and one of his many tightly fitting black suits. He hung the jacket, still on its coat hanger over the wardrobe door and went to brush his teeth. When he came back, he said: "*I* will find out the history, Daniel, not you. You have to keep out of this, or we're both compromised. Your car is back at the station, you can collect it any time. Keys on the kitchen table. I already let the hens out."

"Love you, Mal. Have a great day."

Mal made what sounded suspiciously like a growl, and left.. He could almost feel sorry for the officers Mal was going to see today, especially the ones who'd taken the gossip about Pandy making money from the allotments at face value. On the other hand, if he thought Daniel was going to sit at home doing embroidery, he had another think coming. But first, another pot of coffee, and then he would call Pandy, and Hector.

8

MAN IN PUB

Mal's spies reported back to him regularly. He knew, for instance, that Adam Carey was attempting to recruit to the anti-gay-boss faction from amongst the smokers who hung out together at the back of the police station. He knew that Carey had a bottle of whisky in his filing cabinet drawer, behind a pile of out-of-date files. He knew the rate at which the level in the whisky bottle was going down. He also knew that Carey looked at misogynist websites on work time. Carey was a divisive presence in the station, but Mal knew that he was himself divisive. *Except I'm in charge.* He had long realised that being the boss meant not having any friends at work, and he was fine with that. But his spies were letting him down on the question of how Carey had found out about Pandy Melton's ex, and the rumour about her being paid by the council. He decided to take the battle into enemy territory; in this case, the main CID office. He walked up the stairs, looking through rain-streaked windows at the car parks between the police station and the hills beyond.

CID was chilly — the result of an architect whose love of

glass didn't take the British climate into account, any more than they had cared about how a glass box would fit into a historic town centre. The consequence was that for a few weeks in spring and autumn, the offices were filled with light, and providing it wasn't raining, the views of the hills were magnificent. The rest of the time, the glass either magnified the effect of sunlight, or lowered the temperature to the extent that people kept their coats on all day. The open plan CID space was too big to be heated or cooled effectively. It was just a bad design Mal thought, but he bet it had looked great in the architect's sketchbook.

There was no sign of Carey in CID. Bethan Davies was at her desk, as were Charlie Rees and Abby Price. All looked up as he came in. "I'm looking for DI Carey," Mal said. No one answered, and Mal felt a wave of tension between the three detectives. "Am I missing something?" he asked.

Charlie Rees spoke up. "He's gone out, sir."

The others nodded.

"When are you expecting him back?"

"We expect him when we see him," said Charlie, for whom the phrase *no filter* was a perfect description.

Bethan shot him a *shut up* look. "The DI has forgotten to put his whereabouts on the board," she said.

Abby looked embarrassed. Actually, Mal thought they all looked embarrassed.

"So, no idea where he is, or when he will be back?"

Charlie muttered something under his breath.

"Excuse me DC Rees? Something to share?" If anyone was going to dump Carey in the clart, it would be Charlie, and he did.

"Sir, I said try the Slaters Arms. I'm sorry, sir, but it's got to be said."

"Thank you, DC Rees. Shall we go and look for him?"

Charlie looked horrified, as did the other two. Knowing that

Carey had taken time out of the day to go to the pub was one thing. Having it as public knowledge was something else. Carey was unlikely to forgive and forget, and if he couldn't take it out on Mal, he would take it out on Charlie. But Mal thought the time had come to stop pretending that Carey was in any way a competent detective. Time to get the battle lines drawn and it all out into the open. They had a murder to investigate.

THE SLATER'S Arms was an easy walk from the police station. The building wore a blue plaque on its long, low stone facade, proclaiming it to be one of the oldest buildings in the town. Anyone over about five foot six tall had to stoop to enter the arched doorway, with its heavy studded oak door, weathered grey by time. Through the first door was a porch of remarkable inconvenience. The inner door was at right angles to the outer, and in such a small space, politely holding a door open for another was a recipe for confusion and entanglement.

Inside, the entanglement theme continued. The proprietors had long since given up any attempt to make a living from selling alcohol alone, and the space was taken up by a confusion of different shapes and sizes of dining tables. Mal assumed the pub had been given a collection of randomly sized tables and the owners were determined to fit them all in, even though there clearly wasn't room. The consequence was that getting to the bar, or to the toilet, meant edging your way around someone's chair as they tried to eat.

Lunchtime proper had not yet begun, so the bar was quiet, and still smelled of the morning clean: furniture polish, toilet cleaner and yesterday's beer. The fire had been lit, but without a crush of people, the temperature was still cool. Food service wouldn't start for half an hour, although the menu was already chalked onto the big blackboard next to the bar. The bar itself was made of the same warm brown stone as the outside of the

building, as was the inglenook fireplace and the bay window —
filled with a table naturally. A tiny nook, also filled with a too-
large table, had been left unpainted, but the rest of the walls
had been roughly rendered and lime washed. Four red leather
bar stools, with legs of polished brass and dark wood, stood in
front of the bar. Three of them were occupied, none of them by
anyone Mal recognised.

"He's not here," said Charlie, with obvious relief, turning to
leave. But Mal pointed to the half-drunk pint on the bar by the
fourth, empty, bar stool, and when the door to the Gents
opened, Mal was not surprised to see DI Carey emerge. Mal
almost wanted to give Carey credit for the look of challenge on
the man's face. Carey had no official reason to be drinking at
eleven thirty in the morning, in the middle of a murder case.
Mal jerked his head towards the door, and led the way into the
street.

"My office," he said, then "Thank you, DI Rees. Please talk
to me immediately if there is any come-back from this morning's events." He looked at Carey as he spoke. The three men
walked back to the police station in silence. For a miracle, the
lift was working, and Charlie jumped in. Carey tried to follow,
but Mal touched his arm. "I think we can manage one flight of
stairs, DI Carey." All the executive offices were on the first floor.

Mal didn't sit down behind his desk, and Carey had to stand
on the other side. Mal saw no fear, only defiance, on the
smaller man's face. Carey's lips had adopted their usual half
sneer, and he stood with his legs apart, and his fists clenched.
Nothing Mal could say would change Carey's opinions; all he
could do was try to contain him, as he continued to collect the
evidence he needed to get rid of the wart once and for all.

"Run me through where you're up to on the Hayden
Bennion case," he said. "In view of this morning's episode, we'll
be having daily briefings at eight and five. You will lead them
and I will attend. So, let's start by getting me up to speed."

"We've spoken to the next of kin, and I've interviewed Mrs Melton. I'll be interviewing her again later. She's the obvious suspect. The autopsy report should be here soon. CSI's have found Melton's fingerprints all over near where the body was found. Open and shut."

Mal raised an eyebrow.

"Sir," said Carey.

"What other evidence did the CSI's find near the body? Evidence of other people being there?"

Carey shrugged.

"You didn't send anyone to the autopsy?"

Another shrug.

"To sum up then, you have decided that as Ms Melton's fingerprints were found near the body, which is to say, *on her own vehicle*, she must be the guilty party?"

"She and the victim had more than one altercation, *sir,* and he was threatening her livelihood."

Mal sat down, opened a drawer in his desk and took out a notepad and a pen. He pulled his chair up to the desk and jotted down a few words in a list.

"What I don't understand, DI Carey, is how you can get information that you shouldn't have, but utterly fail to get information that a probationary constable could have obtained in five minutes." He looked up.

"Sir?"

"Ms Melton received no renumeration for working at the allotments. It was a rumour. Your job was to check it. You didn't." He made a mark on his pad. "But you were able to obtain information about Ms Melton's violent ex-husband, and use it to bully her. This suggests to me that you had already decided she was your best suspect, and you went deliberately looking for leverage to use against her — specifically the threat that you would tell her ex-husband where she was, and ensure that he had access to their daughter. If you knew that, you also knew that Melton faces prison if he comes within ten miles of either of them. Perhaps you could explain your thought processes, DI Carey?" Mal smiled, the smile of a cat who realises that the mouse is within pouncing distance, and has nowhere left to run. But the cat likes to play with its prey. Mal leaned back in his chair.

"On second thoughts, don't bother. I'll find out another way. And while I do, you can begin investigating who killed Hayden Bennion. A proper investigation. Start by finding out who else was at the crime scene. Get the autopsy report, make sure you understand it, get contact information for everyone who was at the allotments on the day of the murder, and set up interviews, and find out everything you can about Hayden Bennion. Bring it all to the briefing at five. And get rid of the bottle of scotch in your filing cabinet. I don't want to smell drink on you ever again. Take this as your first warning. Unless you have an explanation?" Mal waited for a few seconds. "Thought not. You can go."

Carey didn't move. "Your luck will run out one of these days, *sir.*" Then he left, leaving the door open behind him. Mal concentrated on breathing in and out until he heard a light knock at the door. Bethan Davies stood in the doorway. She looked at neat and tidy as ever, despite the cold, in a long-sleeved dress and a warm-looking cardigan that somehow managed to look like office wear, as opposed to something put on to keep the cold at bay.

"Bethan, come in. What can I do for you?"

She came in, and quietly closed the door behind her. Mal gestured her to a chair. "Sir, I think you made a mistake this morning. Taking Charlie to the pub."

"I needed a witness. And I made it clear to DI Carey that there was to be no victimisation."

Bethan took a step forward and accepted the offered seat. "The victimisation might not be from DI Carey, sir."

Mal sighed. Bethan was right, and he should have thought of it before he acted. "It's a small country, Bethan. Of course Carey knows someone. Who is it?"

"Robert Cowlishaw, sir, the Police and Crime Commissioner.

9

CAN I BORROW A HEN?

Sasha listened contentedly to the two little girls playing hide and seek. They were banned from going outside or coming into the kitchen, but the rest of the house was fair game. As neither her own daughter Arwen, nor Arwen's friend Cerys were capable of being quiet for more than 30 seconds, the game involved a lot of running about and yelling. The sound of stampeding buffalo across the prairie was as nothing compared to two ten-year-old girls clomping up and down the uncarpeted stairs of Sasha's home. *Well, Hector's home really*, she reflected, though it felt more like hers every day. She was supposed to be planning a wedding, but instead, she was trying to read about diseases of the heart. The smell of baking bread filled the kitchen. She glanced at the timer: five more minutes. Two of the set of faux 1960s orange and leopardskin glazed ceramic mugs waited for her to make coffee for Daniel when he arrived. She ran her fingers over their shiny surface, loving their garish colours and glassy finish, wondering if she could get matching plates, then deciding they would clash horribly with any food she served.

The battered wooden kitchen table was covered in her

university work. A laptop sat charging on the chair beside her, plugged in to one of the work-top sockets. Open textbooks were arranged around her notebook, and a bulbous blue mug with the phases of the moon badly painted on the sides held her pen collection. It had been a present from Arwen, and was impossible to drink from. She'd told her daughter that it was *perfect* as a pen holder, and this way, would be seen every day.

The rest of the kitchen was spotless. 1980s 'cottage style' wooden units that a previous owner of the house had stained a dark reddish-brown colour and varnished thickly dominated the space. Some of the eye level units had glass doors with fake leaded diamond shapes. Sasha had cleaned them all when she moved in. At that point, three quarters of them were empty. Her stuff had filled another quarter. She and Hector often wondered what could possibly have filled this exuberance of cupboards.

"Hens," Hector suggested.

"The materials for making prayer flags," Sasha countered.

"Sweets," Arwen said hopefully, no doubt imagining opening one of the doors to find boxes of lollipops and chocolate jammed in and ready to fall into her waiting hands.

"You should have looked when you came to view the house," Sasha had said. "Then we'd have known."

"It would have been something boring. I'd rather think it was hens in straw lined boxes. Clucking to get out, but safe from foxes."

Sasha had filled a cardboard box with packing straw, added a patterned ceramic egg and some chocolate and left it in one of the empty cupboards. So far, no one had found it. If she had to, she would borrow a hen from Daniel.

The timer for the bread went off as Daniel opened the back door and slid in, closing it quickly behind him.

"Jesus it's cold out there."

"Could I borrow a hen, do you think? Only for a couple of hours. And hello," Sasha said.

A loud crash came from above them, followed by a howl of outrage, or possibly pain. "You go, and I'll get the bread out," Sasha said.

Daniel dropped his coat onto a chair, took off his shoes and headed for the stairs.

***

Daniel had been friends with Hector since Hector's appointment as head pathologist at Wrexham hospital. Sasha he'd met on the first case he'd investigated alongside Mal, and technically he had introduced them. But it was their shared delight in the stories told by dead bodies that had brought his friends to the point of marriage. Sasha was studying biomedical science at university, and their dinner conversation could be alarming. Daniel had never been the kind of policeman who worried about watching an autopsy. He worried far more about what happened to someone when they were still alive. He didn't share Hector and Sasha's fascination with decaying tissue, brain damage, or stomach contents. He did love the way Hector's cottage was slowly turning into a family home: not by design, but by increment, though he dreaded finding *un-named things in jars* used as ornaments.

The stair rails now had fairy lights wrapped around them, and the magnolia paint which had been used to make the house ready for sale was decorated with stickers, scuff marks and pencil drawings. On the first floor landing, Arwen's PE kit was neatly packed into a bag hanging on a hook marked "PE Kit Tuesday and Thursday". A bookshelf held novels. The bedroom doors had the names of their occupants painted in a childish hand onto small pieces of wood. The study was simply marked "Work" and the bathroom had a picture of a shower head. Photographs of the three of them had been blown up onto canvas and fixed to the wall. They showed Arwen and

Sasha playing in the surf on Anglesey, Hector and Sasha dressed up at Sasha's sister's wedding, and finally a picture that Daniel had taken of the three of them in their garden, looking tanned and happy on a picnic blanket.

Giggling came from behind the bathroom door. Daniel lowered his voice. "Where are those naughty girls? Unless I find them soon, I will be sending for the police and they will have to go to jail."

The giggling got louder, interspersed with little shrieks. "It's Uncle Daniel. Go away, Uncle Daniel!"

"Have you made a mess? Do I need to call the police?"

"No!"

But his nose told him something different. The smell of coconut shampoo, and some kind of fruity body wash was strong. There was a panicky scrabbling of small feet and he heard the bath taps running. He tied to sound as fierce as he could, fighting his own urge to laugh. "I'm coming in."

More shrieks. He pushed at the door, feeling the weight of two little girls trying to keep it closed. He imitated the sound of a police radio: "Cccchhhh come in two seven... I need back up at the bathroom door, suspected shampoo spillage. Cccchhhh."

The door opened. Arwen, a smaller version of her mother's tall stringiness, grabbed his leg. "It just came out, Uncle Daniel, honestly it did."

Cerys looked a lot like her friend: tall for her age and thin. But she had her mother's dark hair. Both the girls had grey-blue eyes, and both looked as guilty as sin.

"I think I should call the police anyway," he said.

"You're not the police any more," Arwen said. "I'm sure this is only a minor offence, so Uncle Mal won't worry about it." Cerys watched them both with wide eyes. She knew who Daniel was, but she wasn't sure about all this talk of the police.

"It's a fair cop," he said. "I only came to see if you were all right. We heard a crash."

"It was nothing," Arwen said, trying for a grown-up innocence that had Daniel howling inside with hidden laughter.

"If you're sure?"

"We're sure. We're going to play with dolls in my room. Aren't we Cerys?" Cerys nodded solemnly, and the two girls headed for Arwen's room, carefully closing the bathroom door behind them.

"OK." Daniel went back downstairs.

"God only knows what they've done in the bathroom. I'd expect shampoo all over the floor, but they were very careful not to let me see," he told Sasha.

"Good. Guilt might keep them upstairs for long enough for us to have a coffee. There's a cake." The cake was on the table—dense yellow sponge with bright red cherries—along with black coffee in the over-the-top 1960s mugs. Sasha had made space by piling the open books and the papers on top of each other. Daniel pulled out one of the mismatched ladder back chairs and sat down.

"I like what you're doing to the place," he said, only half in jest.

Sasha laughed. "Some of us have more important things to do than pick out the perfect tap, or the ideal shade of white paint."

Daniel ran his hands through his hair, leaned back and crossed his legs at the ankle. "It's all about the *ambiance*, darling. Things have got to be *right*."

"In your universe, maybe."

"Seriously, it feels like a family home, and I'm envious." He realised that he was. The progress on his own house had been agonisingly slow, because he insisted that every detail had to be right. His car might be a mess, and he might attract mud every time he stepped outside, but he really had spent a ridiculous amount of time choosing the perfect tap for the kitchen sink. He took a drink of his coffee: hot and strong. Sasha pushed the cake plate towards him. The cake was delicious: the sponge melting as he ate it, contrasting with the firm, sweet cherries. He helped himself to another piece.

"I wanted to talk to Hector about the guy Pandy found dead at the allotments," he said. "Hayden Bennion. And to see you of course."

"Mal won't tell you then?"

"He can't. Ongoing case and I'm not a copper any more. But I was *there*, Sash. Pandy didn't kill the guy any more than I did, and there's nothing I can do. He says he's *compromised enough already* by trying to keep Carey from arresting Pandy and charging her with murder. Carey is a fuckwit of the first order."

"So you've come round here to try to get the information from Hector?"

Daniel nodded. "And to check on Cerys, who is obviously living the good life while her mother is answering the same questions over and over, and running up a solicitor's bill she probably can't afford to pay."

"Cerys can stay as long as she likes. Really."

Daniel thought how easily Hector had acquired a family. Neither he nor Sasha would see forty again, but they could conceivably have another baby if they tried. He had no idea if they wanted more children, but if they did, they would be able to get them so much more easily than he and Mal. Even if Mal wanted to try, which wasn't certain. He saw the big fridge by the back door, covered in childish drawings, and next to it a calendar covered in appointments for Arwen: piano lessons, ballet, horse riding, birthday parties, swimming, parents' evening. Sasha saw him look. "The glamour of childcare," she said. "A combination of constant tidying-up, being a taxi-service and listening to which friend is being mean to which other friend."

"But you love it."

"I love *Arwen*. It's not the same."

"I'm afraid I'll never know that."

"Jeez, Daniel, stop moping and talk to Mal. He'll do whatever you ask, and if you haven't realised that by now, I can't help you." She re-filled his coffee cup. "Look at you lounging about, doing your Sebastian Flyte impression. Get with the programme."

"Fuck you, Sasha," Daniel said, but there was no heat in it. He sat up straight. "The problem is that I don't know what the programme is. I could do a better job of finding out what happened to Hayden Bennion than Carey, even with Mal watching over his shoulder and Bethan holding his hand. But I made such a fuss about leaving the cops, and I've left Mal in the lurch. If he told me what he's already found out, I could sort it, but he's not going to — so I'd have to go behind his back."

"But if you *don't* investigate, your mate Pandy's going to get charged, and Mal's going to get his name dragged through the mud, because Pandy is your new BFF. It'll probably drag Hector in too, because he was there at the Community Allotment thing. All of which is why you are sitting in my kitchen, eating my cake, stopping me from doing my homework, and why my fiancé is going to tell you everything he knows, or no sex for a week."

Daniel looked at his friend. When he'd first met her, she'd had leggings, a teddy bear fleece, blue hair and a Valleys accent you could cut with a knife. She still did, except the hair was now blonde. But she fitted in here, with Hector, with his private school education, aristocratic connections and country cottage, and he thought that he was lucky in the women he knew. She was right. Carey would arrest Pandy, he would come after Mal, and though he wouldn't win, he would leave a swathe of damage behind that might take years to repair.

10

WATER END

I f Daniel was being honest, he would not have called his
friend good looking. In part that was because Daniel lived
with a man who looked like a movie star, but mostly it
was because Hector simply didn't care. He was clean, properly
shaved, and his clothes were good quality and fitted him well.
He had regular haircuts and smelled of soap and a good
cologne. He had dark brown hair, and light brown eyes. In the
summer he was tanned, in the winter, pale. Beyond that, he was
without vanity. Having met Hector's mother, Lady Belinda,
whose effortless style and looks left even Mal in the shade,
Daniel understood that Hector's role was to admire, never to be
an object of admiration himself. Despite that, Daniel was
drawn to Hector, as he was drawn to anyone with an intelligent
enquiring mind, and a sense of humour. He'd slept with Hector
once, and remembered the event as a moment of happy
comfort when they both needed it. He'd wondered whether
Hector had wanted more, especially after his next, disastrous,
boyfriend had been a Daniel lookalike. But then Hector had
met Sasha, and that was that. That Sasha, like Daniel, was tall,

thin and blonde (at the moment) wasn't something Daniel was going to lose any sleep over.

The man himself stood in the kitchen doorway with an expression of nervous anticipation. Daniel wondered whether he expected Daniel to hug him, or Sasha to tell him off before kissing him senseless. Then the reason for the expression came thundering through the door and threw herself into his arms.

"Daddy Hector! You're back! Mam said we could have ice cream when you got back, so can we have ice cream? Please?"

Hector put Arwen back onto the floor, along with his briefcase.

"If she really said that, it's up to your mother to get the ice cream out."

Sasha gave her daughter a stern look. "Arwen, I said you and Cerys could have your *tea* when Hector came back, and that there would be ice cream for pudding." Cerys stood in the doorway to the hall, looking from one to another of the adults, wondering how this was going to play out. "The pair of you, go and wash your hands, and you can take your food upstairs." She produced a plate of sandwiches, and a bowl of cut-up carrots and apples. "Hands, go. I'll bring your ice cream in a bit."

They went.

Hector pulled out a chair and sat down, his eyes falling on the cherry cake. He reached over and cut himself a slice. "I am going to become a fat man, surrounded by thin females." It didn't sound like something he was worried about. He looked at Daniel. "Autopsy, Hayden Bennion, right?"

Daniel nodded.

Without appearing to have moved, Sasha plonked a mug of tea in front of Hector, and sat down. "I want to know, too."

"Bashed and drowned," Hector said. He pushed his cake plate aside and put his briefcase on the table. From it he produced a series of photographs. "This is the back of his neck." The picture was not of anything recognisably human, just an A4 glossy close-up of black and dark red smears. Looking closer, Daniel could see hair mixed in to the mess.

"It looks like road rash," he said.

"My guess is that it was some kind of metal bar, and it dragged on the skin as well as knocking the guy insensible. That's what you're seeing. Some of those marks are rust, and if you look *here...*" Hector produced another photograph. "... you can see tiny spots of paint—green and blue. I've sent the rust and the paint off to the lab, but I think I know what was used." He held his hand up as Daniel opened his mouth to speak. "I'll get to it."

The next two pictures showed horizontal red marks across pale skin. The skin wasn't broken, and Daniel couldn't tell what part of the body he was looking at. Sasha did though. "He was pushed onto something sharp—across the top of his chest? Or was he hit with something sharp?"

"Right first time." Hector's finger traced the red line. "You see there's a very slight curve? This is the top of the water barrel. Someone pushed his head into the water, and the edge of the barrel pressed into his skin and left these marks. They must have put a lot of weight behind it, because he was fully dressed in thick winter clothes."

"And they held his head in the water until he drowned," Daniel said. "I hope he was unconscious, poor bugger."

Hector nodded. "I can't swear to it; I wasn't there, but that blow to the back of the head would probably have knocked him out. There's no sign that he struggled—these red marks wouldn't be so clear if he'd been trying to get away. Nope, I'm pretty sure that he was out of it when he drowned."

Hector got another file out of his briefcase.

"Mam! We've finished!" The cry came from upstairs.

"I swear that child has a loudhailer," Sasha said, and got to her feet.

While Sasha fulfilled her ice cream promise, Daniel looked through the pictures again. "This looks like it was done by someone stronger than Pandy," he said. "Could she have done it?"

Hector wiggled his hand in a *yes, no, maybe*, gesture. "But I think the initial bashing was done with *this*." He produced another photograph, of what appeared to be a length of rusty iron railing. "From the angle of the wound, whoever hit Bennion was smaller than him, but then, he was almost six feet tall. *You* couldn't have done it, but that still leaves a big field."

"I could have bent my knees."

"If you did, you could save everyone a lot of trouble and just confess."

"I take it this admirable weapon provided no useful clues?"

"The tiny spots of paint on the wound look—to me—as if they could come from this bit of old iron. But that's not my area of expertise *as you know*. More to the point, it was dropped into the water butt at some point, thus relieving it of much forensic evidence. You will have to find another snitch to tell you more."

Hector put the photographs away in his briefcase and twirled the combination lock. "Not things I want the kids to find," he said. And finished his tea and cake.

"Don't you think it's strange?" Daniel asked. "I'm trying to reconstruct it in my head. I come up behind you with my trusty fence post, bash you on the back of the neck and knock you out. You are going to fall over, right?"

Hector nodded.

"So why don't I just give you another bash? I've seen what the post can do; one more good bash and the job's done. Lifting an unresponsive body up just to push its face into a water butt makes no sense. It's also bloody hard. That's why environmental protesters go limp. Humans are heavy."

"That's why you're the detective and I'm a humble pathologist. I give you the facts; it's up to you to construct the story."

Daniel ran his hands through his hair, and rested his forehead on the table. "I'm not a detective though. Not any more."

"But if you don't find out what happened, who will?" And that, Daniel thought was the rub. It wasn't his job, but Carey had fixated on Pandy. She was physically strong, probably strong enough to move Hayden Bennion in order to drown him, but wouldn't he, Daniel, have noticed if she'd disappeared for long enough to murder someone? She'd also have been wet, and surely he'd have noticed that?

"You have to talk to Mal about it." Hector sounded firm.

"I have. He says we're both compromised already. No, I can find out what happened, but I can't involve Mal as I do it."

"Just present him with a neatly gift-wrapped solution?"

"If that's what it takes to get the truth, and Pandy out of Carey's clutches. She's being interviewed again today—which I guess is why you've still got Cerys."

Hector shrugged. "Sasha sorted it out. She's a nice kid. They're like sisters, her and Arwen. But she's worried about her mum. Wonders why she can't go home, even though she speaks to Pandy all the time on the phone. I think whatever happened with her dad has left some deep scars."

Daniel added it to his mental *find out* list. Whatever had happened had given Carey his opening, and it was always easier to fight back when you have the same information as your opponent. "I have to go," he said. "I have to find out what Bennion was like before he was killed. I met him once, and didn't like him at all, but there must have been more than his dislike of *gay gardeners*."

Hector snorted. "Pass me that cake, and I'll tell you what I know." Daniel passed the cake. There wasn't much left, but Daniel was becoming used to Sasha's ability to cram more activity into a day than most people achieved in a week. There would be another cake.

"Bennion was married, and his wife cried over his body. She

brought her own sister, as well as Bethan Davies. Bethan told me that her kids both live too far away to get here quickly. Bethan also told me that Mrs Bennion said that she *knew that allotment would be the death of him*, and the sister said, *yes, but not that he'd be murdered there, love.* She—Bethan—said they rattled on about Hayden spending all his time there, and how they could never go on holiday because he couldn't trust anyone else to look after his plot. So that's a start on your researches. You could ask Bethan yourself."

Daniel smiled and shook his head. Bethan had been loyal, and a terrific sergeant. She'd never really approved of him, preferring Mal's more by-the-book methods. But he was sure he knew where Charlie Rees would be once the opening time arrived, and he was quite happy to pump Charlie for information.

"Do you think Sasha would mind me staying for dinner?" he asked Hector.

"Not if you read those two brats their story," Sasha answered, having snuck in without either of them noticing. "Then you can bugger off out and I can get Hector to talk me through the problems of the heart. For my exam."

***

Charlie was not a regular in the Slaters Arms. Melin Tywyll had a wine bar; just one. It served wine, bottled beers with silly names, and food designed to mop up drink rather than please the palate. It had a limed oak laminate floor, and a projector played silent black and white moves over the walls and ceiling. The tables were mostly tall, for standing at with a drink, with only a few intimate booths along one wall. The only soft surfaces were the patrons, so noise bounced around the space like stones in a tin can. The overwhelming smell was of competing colognes. Even on a Sunday night, the place was busy. Not as busy as it would be on a Friday or Saturday, but there were still plenty of people with bottles of wine and bowls of bread and olives, or piles of nachos. Unfortunately for Daniel, none of them were Charlie Rees. He got himself a glass of wine and some completely unnecessary olives to pick at, and settled down in a booth to wait. He knew Mal thought he was spending the evening with Hector, and Mal himself would be late. He would give it an hour, and if Charlie didn't show, he'd go home and think of something else.

Charlie did show, alone, and after only fifteen minutes. Daniel waved and Charlie came over.

"Get you a drink, boss?"

"No thanks, got one," and Charlie disappeared back to the crowd in front of the bar. Five minutes later he appeared with a bottle of Chardonnay and several glasses. "I'm just getting them in. The others were all going to get changed and meet me here." Which meant Charlie's drinking companions were uniformed officers.

"So we don't have long." Daniel said. "Hayden Bennion."

"I was hoping you were going to ask me about that, boss, because no other bugger seems to care what the guy was like."

"Don't call me boss. Are you telling me that Mal doesn't care?"

"He's letting Carey have enough rope to hang himself, is what I think. I don't think Carey knows what he's doing, but *he* doesn't care, as long as he gets to stand at the front like the big man"

That was not a pleasant image. Nor was the idea that Mal wasn't directing the investigation from the front. But that wasn't a conversation he wanted to have with Charlie. Daniel didn't like himself for even talking to Charlie like this, using Charlie's past loyalty to undermine the official investigation for the sake of a woman he'd only just met. But he was going to do it anyway.

"Tell me about Hayden Bennion."

"Not much to tell, boss, um, yeah." Charlie had spent most

of his police career being cheeky, but calling Daniel by his given name *after* he'd left the service wasn't something he could do. "Bennion worked all his life at the timber yard—the one on the road to St Asaph. The rest of his time he spent at the allotment, at least according to his wife. Somehow managed to have two kids, but one's in Oz, and the other is some kind of bird warden in the Shetland Islands."

"So what about this feud on the allotments?"

"DI Carey is convinced that's why he was killed, but, gotta say, I don't see it. Like, The Committee—they talk about it as if it was the cabinet—don't want anything new, but that's all. We haven't done alibis yet, because to be completely honest, we haven't done much at all..."

Daniel was hoping for a list of the alibis that *had* been done, but it was too late. Charlie's mates were pushing their way through the crowd towards their table.

"Time for me to go." Daniel stood up as four uniformed officers, now in their civvies arrived.

Three of them nodded and smiled. One said "Evening, sir."

"Have fun, guys. Gotta go." As Daniel left, he overheard someone--Kelley, by the sound of it--say, "We don't have to call him *sir* any more. Fucking fairy," and Charlie's voice in reply.

"That fucking fairy could kick your arse into next week."

Daniel was less concerned about being called a fairy than he was that Carey would probably learn he'd been talking to Charlie. And that gave Carey ammunition to use against Mal. From here on, Daniel was on his own, and he needed to stay under the radar.

11

NOT A GOOD MORNING

Daniel was asleep on the sofa, head squashed uncomfortably onto a cushion and the crocheted blanket round his body, when Mal came home. He woke up enough to mumble, "Wha' time is it?" Then he woke up some more when Mal put the overhead light on and pulled the blanket off.

There was a discreet thud as Flora jumped off the sofa where she was not allowed to be. The fire must have gone out hours before and the room was cold. With the overhead light on, it *looked* cold too—the downside of painting a room white. Daniel sat up and blinked, and pushed his hair back. He pressed the button on his phone to see that it was two am. Mal's eyes were red with dark circles around them. He looked as if he had spent too long in the same clothes, and as if he had been running his hands through his hair for hours. His chin and cheeks were dark with stubble, though Daniel could see a few grey hairs amongst the black. He leaned forward to put his hand out to Mal. "Jeez, Maldwyn, what's up?"

Mal rubbed his eyes. "Charlie's what's up. He got jumped on his way home and I've just come back from the hospital."

Daniel opened his mouth to speak, but Mal held up his hand. "He's going to be OK. The worst is a broken rib, but he's covered in bruises and what the doctor called *contusions,* and I'd call a bloody mess. No concussion, thank God."

"Do we know what happened?"

Mal sank heavily onto the sofa, moving the blanket so that it formed a barrier between them. "You tell me."

"I didn't beat him up." *So much for doing things on the quiet.*

Mal frowned. "I'm not accusing you of beating him up. But you saw him. Tonight, I mean."

Daniel considered dissembling and decided against it. "I met him in the wine bar. Not by arrangement. For about fifteen minutes, then his mates arrived and I came home, and I've been here ever since. Which reminds me, there's a casserole."

Mal waved the idea of food away. "I know you met him because everyone and his dog has been queuing up to tell me all about it. The only person who *didn't* tell me was Charlie." Mal moved the blanket onto the back of the sofa. Daniel wondered whether he could move closer, have a lean against Mal's reassuring muscly shoulder, and decided that he could. Mal didn't push him away.

"Charlie told me you're giving Carey enough rope to hang himself," Daniel said. "I know it's nothing to do with me. I just wanted to know about Hayden Bennion, and Charlie seemed like the right person to ask. Then I saw that one of Charlie's drinking buddies was PC Kelley—Carey's friend. It was a mistake to talk to Charlie. I'm worried sick about Pandy."

"You should be. Carey has got her in the crosshairs."

"Shit. She's a good person, Maldwyn. She didn't do this."

Mal leaned back on the sofa, and allowed Flora to jump onto his lap. He stroked her ears, and they all pretended they hadn't noticed that the rules were being broken. *It's no wonder we can't keep her off the furniture,* Daniel thought.

"My hands are tied, Dan. I can tell Carey what to do, and

watch as he doesn't do it, but I can't run the investigation myself. I've got a fucking Everest of paperwork, I'm already doing twelve-hour days, and now I'm another body short."

"Then let me help."

"You can't. Carey already wants you in to give a statement about your own row with Bennion. Look how quickly Carey's lot found out that you'd been talking to Charlie. Small town, Dan, small town."

Yeah, but my small town, Daniel thought. *Was Charlie attacked because of me? Why is Carey so keen to fit Pandy up for this?*

But what he said was, "Bed."

***

They were both decidedly dopey the next morning, and stared at each other blearily over coffee and toast. Flora looked between them, hoping for dropped crumbs, or discussion of adventures of interest to dogs. Daniel propped his chin on his right hand, feeling the beginnings of a beard. He didn't think he had the energy to shave. Mal looked as perfectly groomed as ever, despite the bags under his eyes.

Daniel began, "I'm going to--"

"Don't tell me," Mal said. The message was clear. What Mal didn't know, he couldn't be held responsible for. Except they both knew it didn't work like that. They were a team, had been a team for years, and no one would believe they weren't acting as a team now.

"I am going to go to the briefing," said Mal. "Then I'm going to meetings and writing strategies all day, and then I'm going to another briefing, and then I'm bringing a pile of work home. Just so you know."

Daniel nodded. "I have no idea what I'll be doing. Probably go for a run. Into Melin and back." *So both of us will be seen not investigating Hayden Bennion's murder.*

As Daniel tidied the kitchen, he made a mental list of his

priorities. Visit Charlie. Contact Eluned Bennion. Think of an excuse to visit Bennion's widow. Talk to Pandy again. Find out who else was on the Allotment Society committee, and whether there was any truth in the "huge row at the AGM" story. Go to the allotments. All things he could easily have done with a warrant card, and his status as a police officer. Things that were going to be a lot more tricky now.

He started with a call to Charlie, in hospital.

"They're sending me home, boss. Bethan's giving me a lift, so maybe wait until she's gone before you come round?"

Daniel agreed, and then started trying to work out how he could get in touch with Eluned. They hadn't been friends at school, but they hadn't been enemies either. If they'd been sat next to each other in a class, or stood together in a queue, there would have been chat. It was enough. He went and got his laptop from the living room and started a social media hunt. Luckily "Eluned Bennion, Shetland," was an instant hit. He sent a message, worrying about what to say, in a way he'd never had to as a policeman. That felt odd, as did the thought that he had no way to compel her to answer. Flora started insisting that the time to go out had arrived, or was even overdue, but he looked up the Allotment Society and made a list of the committee members. Then he changed into his running clothes and went out with the intention of being seen *not investigating* by as many people as possible.

***

Mal didn't get the chance to attend the morning briefing into Hayden Bennion's murder. A "See me," message was waiting for him from the Assistant Chief Constable, Crime, Jack Bowen. He wearily went back downstairs, and got back into his car. The Audi was as comfortable as a car could be, and Mal could probably programme it to drive to the police HQ in Wrexham, while he caught up on some sleep. He and the car had been along this road at least twice a week for the last several years. The car needed cleaning, though. Mal loved it when it was sleek and shiny; he hated the trace of dust on the dashboard and the arches left on the windscreen by the wipers. He wasn't one for those scented beermats hung from the mirror, but he liked the car to smell clean, and it didn't. There was a faint odour of damp compost. If he opened the window, he would smell rain instead, but it was a desultory, half-hearted kind of rain, the sort of rain that made the road filthy, reduced visibility and made him long for sunshine and heat. He pressed the CD button, hoping for something cheering, and got lucky. He didn't remember putting the Buena Vista Social Club in the player, but it was perfect. The music brought the image of the elderly Cubans with their instruments on the stage in the Millennium Centre in Cardiff. He and Daniel had gone on a whim, and it had been fabulous. They, and the entire audience, had finished up singing *Somewhere Over The Rainbow* along with the band. Remembering made the hairs on his arms stand up, and brought a smile to his face. He was still smiling when he walked into the police station. It didn't last.

In Mal's opinion, the Assistant Chief Constable, Crime was the walking embodiment of promoting someone to the level of incompetence. On a bad day, Mal wondered whether he'd been promoted as the quickest way to get him out of whatever job he was in. Jack Bowen was only a few years from retirement, and it couldn't come quickly enough for Mal. *If he calls me Malcolm again, I swear I shall swing for him.*

"Malcolm, good to see you!"

"It's Maldwyn, sir," said Mal, as he did, every time, carefully unclenching his fists, and Bowen smiled and nodded, as *he* did, every time.

Bowen was a completely forgettable man. Middling height, neither fat nor thin, balding but not bald, greying but not grey. He must have been able to afford better suits than he wore, and glasses that were more stylish than the ones he chose. Mal thought that Bowen could get away with almost any crime, because no witness would be able to describe him. Except Mal didn't think Bowen was clever enough for even a simple crime. His office was a crime against taste: patterned brown carpet, fake antique desk, uncomfortable leather chairs, and walls papered with photographs of Bowen shaking hands with the good and the great. Mal was almost certain that on his first visit there had been a photo of Bowen with Jimmy Savile, but he wondered whether that was him projecting his dislike of the man onto something that never happened.

"This Hayden Bennion murder, Kent. You need to get that sorted out asap."

"Absolutely, sir. You may have heard that one of my detectives was attacked last night, so I'm even more short-staffed than usual."

Bowen looked concerned. Not concerned enough to do anything to help, rather a bland, indifferent kind of concern, the facial manifestation of the phrase, "I hear what you say".

"You got a new DI when that other chap left. Plenty of people would be glad of a new DI."

"About DI Carey, sir..."

Bowen interrupted, leaning forward slightly for emphasis. "Good man. Close to the Police and Crime Commissioner you know. Family values and all that."

He has no idea what he's talking about.

"DI Carey needs a lot of supervision, sir. I'm afraid he's chosen a suspect and has stopped looking for anyone else, and there is plenty of evidence that doesn't fit."

"That's what I wanted to talk to you about, Kent." Mal noticed a slight flush spread over Bowen's face. *It's relief. He's remembered what he's supposed to be telling me.*

"Micromanagement is never a good idea. Delegation is what executive officers need to be doing. Leave it to Carey, that's best."

"I have no desire to run the investigation myself. But I have even less desire to see a murderer get away because we've arrested the wrong person."

"Well, that goes without saying." Bowen stood up, the signal for Mal to leave. "I'm glad we've had this little chat."

Mal stood his ground. "Sir, DI Carey is focussing on an individual who has an alibi, a very flimsy motive, and who probably doesn't have the physical strength to have carried out the murder. This is not a proper investigation, and the CPS are not going to go for a charge on the evidence. In the meantime, we are letting time go by and not doing our jobs."

"Well, that's for you to sort out, I think. Carey's good for your image. Melin Tywyll was getting a bit of a *reputation* you know. Now, I'm sorry to hustle you out, but I have another meeting." Bowen held out his hand and Mal shook it, somehow resisting the temptation to crush the other man's fingers until the bones cracked.

12

THE COMMITTEE

C harlie opened his door, and led the way to his flat, visibly wincing from his bruises, so that Daniel felt guilty for making him get up. Charlie's home was everything Daniel expected. It was small, untidy and smelled of pizza, beer and socks, all of which were in evidence. Charlie had an armchair set up in front of a huge flatscreen TV. It was obviously where he spent his time; not watching TV, but playing games. The game-playing urge had never troubled Daniel. He looked around in vain for books, even magazines, but apart from a couple of glossies with reviews of, naturally, computer games, there was no reading material.

"I always wonder how people get to sleep without a book to read," Daniel observed.

Charlie looked at him oddly. "What do you mean?"

"Well, what do you do when you're lying in bed at night? Actually, don't answer that."

Charlie blushed.

Daniel went into the kitchen, which stood at one end of the room. It was surprisingly clean given the rest of the place. "Coffee?" he asked, and Charlie nodded. Daniel could see Charlie struggling with the notion of Daniel making coffee for him, but there was no way he was going to let Charlie move again when he obviously ached all over. Daniel knew the misery of being forced to try to sleep in hospital, and he'd been assaulted once or twice so he knew about that too. Looking at Charlie's face, drawn and ashen, he realised that Charlie had been frightened. There was always the terror of that first unexpected blow, the fear that the assailant would be armed or that no one would come.

Daniel gave Charlie his coffee, then went to the door for the box of cupcakes he'd brought as an offering to the wounded. He'd seen the way Charlie grabbed for the gooey sugariness when they were on offer, and when he opened the box, Charlie's face showed Daniel that he'd made the right choice.

"Did someone tell you how much I love these?" Charlie asked.

"I'm a detective, young grasshopper, or I was. Now eat your cake and tell me who assaulted you. Remember I'm a detective, so don't bother to say you don't know."

Charlie took a bite from the most chocolatey of the cakes, inadvertently depositing a lump of icing on the end of his nose. He chewed, swallowed, and licked the icing from his fingers. Daniel leaned over, and wiped the blob of icing from Charlie's nose. "Now you see why I don't eat those things. They should be eaten in the bath, like mangoes." He offered the icing to Charlie on the end of his finger. Charlie's face showed a moment of panic, then he slurped it up.

"Thing is, boss..."

"Don't call me boss. You just slurped icing from my fingers. The combination of that, and calling me boss is ... not good."

Charlie blushed even harder.

"The thing is, I don't know who assaulted me, except I think that one of them was PC Kelley. I'm not sure, I just thought I recognised his voice."

"How many?"

"Three," Charlie had to clear his throat. "It was very quick. Someone thumped me hard and I stumbled, then they kicked my legs from under me and I rolled up in a ball... there were a couple more kicks and then they ran off."

"Bastards. What did you hear the odious Kelley say? I mean, you'd been drinking with him all evening."

"That's just it. I hadn't. He buggered off not long after you. No one likes him much, so to be honest, we were glad to see him go. All I heard him say before he ran off was something like *Let's get out of here.* I wouldn't want to swear to it in court."

"So, you met me, Kelley saw us together, then he cleared off and was part of a posse who beat you up on your way home. But no one said anything about why? They didn't steal anything, or give you a message, just thumped you and ran off?"

Charlie nodded, winced and nodded again more gently. "I've been awake half the night thinking about it. I think someone must have been coming, or they thought someone was coming. Because it makes no sense otherwise."

"But no one came?"

"No. I rang in, and PC Morgan came and took me to A and E. Before you ask, he didn't see who attacked me, or anyone else come to that."

"Do you know what I think Charlie? I think you were bloody lucky."

Charlie nodded again. "Are you going to work this case, b-- Daniel? Because Carey is a complete fuckup."

Daniel shook his head. "It's not my job any more. If Kelley and his mates beat you up because you were talking to me, I need to keep well out of everyone's way, including out of yours."

"But..."

"But nothing." Daniel got up in one smooth movement, "Eat your cakes, Charlie, and when you come down from the sugar high, go and stay with your mam for a few days."

. . .

NEXT ON DANIEL'S list was a quick call on Pandy. The house was quiet when he got there, another box of baked goods in his hand. He called through the letterbox. "Pandy, it's me, Daniel. I've got cake." The neighbours were out, so no curtains twitched. He heard the sound of shuffling feet behind the door, then the sound of bolts being pulled and finally a key turn in the lock. The door opened. Pandy looked worse than Charlie. Her hair was falling out of its plaits, and her face was white and looked bruised from lack of sleep. She was wearing a pair of flannelette pyjama bottoms in a garish yellow check, and a blue hoody from an American university he didn't recognise. It was clear that she'd been crying.

He put his box down and put his arms round her, pulling her close. "You poor lamb. What have they been doing to you?"

Pandy pushed away. "Sorry. I don't like ..."

Daniel gave himself a mental shake. This was a victim of domestic violence, and he was a man, grabbing her, without warning when she was already upset. He stepped back, and put his arms down, turning his palms towards her so that she could see they were empty.

"No, I'm sorry. I didn't think. I did bring cake, and if you sit down, I'll make some tea to go with it."

Pandy almost fell into the sofa, pulling her feet up and tucking them under her. She pulled the hood of her hoodie close around her neck and under her chin. The room was as tidy as it had been when Daniel first visited, and when he went into the kitchen he saw why. The two mugs they'd left on Saturday, when Carey came round, were still there. If Pandy had eaten anything since, she'd left no trace of it. He found a plate for the cakes, and made builders' tea for Pandy and mint for himself.

"You need to eat some of this cake," he said, putting the

plate on the coffee table in front of her. "It's special magic cake, designed to make you feel better."

Pandy shook her head and snuggled further into her hoody, "I want to see Cerys, but I can't let her see me like this."

Daniel sat on the coffee table in front of Pandy, making sure that there was a distance between them. "Pandy, why don't you eat something and drink the tea? We could video call Cerys. I saw her yesterday and she's fine. Maybe tidy your hair a bit, so she doesn't see you looking upset? But we don't have to. Really, Cerys is fine." She looked at him, but the words didn't seem to register. Everything he'd just said to Charlie went out of the window, though if he was honest, he hadn't meant it. "Listen to me, I'm going to find out who killed Hayden, and then all this will be over."

Pandy turned her head away. He saw tears roll down her cheeks. The competent, funny, cheerful woman of two days before had been reduced to this by a policeman's threats, whether of a murder charge or letting her ex know where she was, he didn't know. The image of a young man sitting on the parapet of the bridge, his legs dangling over the river in full flood came to him. Daniel had been a new PC, walking round the town in the late evening after dark. His first instinct had been to grab the youth, to pull him to safety. He'd taken a step forwards and the boy shouted, "Get back! I'll do it," and shuffled towards the edge. He'd talked that boy down, though it had taken over an hour. He recognised that he was in the same situation now. Hugging wasn't going to work, and sugar would only be effective once Pandy was back in the present. He started talking, slowly, quietly, describing how Cerys and Arwen had been playing the day before. "She misses you though," he said, because of course she would, even with her best friend by her side. He added that Sasha had taken the girls to school and would take them home again.

Pandy gave a small nod. "Sasha texted me."

He told her what he'd learned about Hayden, and reiterated his determination to find out the truth. "Because I know that neither of us killed him, Pandy. It won't be as easy as when I was in the police, but I know what I'm doing."

Slowly, very slowly, Pandy's face grew less tight, and she emerged from her hoody, like a tortoise from its shell. Daniel offered cake again, and this time, Pandy helped herself to a Danish and took a tiny bite. Daniel picked up her cup of by-now cold tea and went to make some more. When he got back, the first Danish was gone and Pandy was halfway through a slice of Bakewell tart.

"Drink this, and we'll see about that phone call." Pandy nodded, and mumbled through a mouthful of cake.

"Sorry," she said.

"Don't be. You've had one hell of a shock. Someone you know has been killed and you've been browbeaten and bullied ever since. This is not your fault. None of it. Drink some tea."

The magic of tea and cake began to do its work, bits of colour starting to return to Pandy's cheeks, and her shoulders falling away from her ears.

"But what must you think? I'm supposed to be a mother, and I've just abandoned my daughter." She started to cry again, pulling a very shredded tissue from her pocket. Daniel fetched some kitchen roll.

"Hey, stop that. Cerys is fine. She's with her best friend, and you're going to talk to her in a minute."

It took another half an hour, and Daniel could see the struggle on Pandy's face between going back to bed and pulling the covers up, or facing the day. Facing the day won. "This has brought it all back," she said, looking down at her lap. "Getting away from my husband, getting Cerys away and safe. It took a long time. I thought we'd never escape."

"He went to jail?" Daniel asked.

"Contempt of court. Not because of anything he did to us,

but because he wouldn't shut up when the judge told him to."
For the first time since he'd arrived, Pandy gave a small smile. "I
came back here because it felt safe. I can speak my own
language, and I wanted that for Cerys. But nowhere's safe."

Daniel wanted to hold her hand, to express comfort with
his body as well as with his words. "I can't remove every threat,
but I can get Carey off your back. I promise. And I'll talk to Mal
about your ex."

Though what Mal would be able to do, he had no idea. At
least he could try. Something of the reassurance he wanted to
convey must have got through because when she spoke, Pandy
sounded more determined. "What can I do to help?"

"Can you tell me about the AGM? When you and Hayden
had the row?"

"It wasn't much of a row. And it wasn't just me and Hayden.
Lizzie and Beth—you remember them?"

Daniel nodded.

"And a few others too. We wanted to persuade the
committee to stop stocking poisons in the shop. That big tin
shed is a shop, opens for a couple of hours every weekend. But
the others, mostly the committee, but not only them, wanted to
keep buying the same things they always bought. I said that
they could get those things from other places, and that we
ought to be setting an example. David Jones was there, and he
got a bit personal, but then he's hated me for years, so I didn't
read much into that. Hayden did his *I'm the chairman* thing and
made everyone talk in turn, and then insisted on having a vote.
Which we would have won, except someone dug up this
obscure rule that you had to have been a plot holder for a year
or something, before you could vote, and some of my friends
hadn't been."

"But all the old guard..." Daniel said.

"Since they came out of the ark. Possibly earlier."

"So there were no threats, or violence?"

Pandy smiled weakly. "No way. That's what I kept telling that policeman, that DI Carey. I feel really strongly that we shouldn't be using insecticides that kill bees, that we are risking all our futures. I'm pretty passionate about not digging up peat. I want to save the planet for all our children and grandchildren. There are people I might kill if I thought it might stop global warming, but Hayden Bennion isn't one of them." She paused. "That's what the Community Allotment is supposed to be about. Spreading the word. That's how I do things. It's pathetic, but it's the only way I can do it. Maybe killing people would be better, especially if I'm going to be prosecuted for murder anyway. It's not the first time I've been blamed for something I didn't do."

She sounded so bitter, and unlike her usual positive self, at least when she was talking about the allotment. Daniel wanted to know whether her ex-husband was the only person to have blamed Pandy for something she hadn't done. Seeing her so defeated was heart-breaking.

13

OLD FRIENDS

Daniel was still encouraging Pandy to eat and drink when his phone rang with an unknown number. "Daniel Owen."

"The Daniel Owen I was at school with? This is Eluned Bennion. You wanted to talk to me?"

"Yep, I'm that Daniel Owen. Thanks for calling. I'm sorry for your loss. Are you in Melin?"

"Got here yesterday. Why?"

"Could I come and talk to you? About your dad?"

There was a deep intake of breath at the other end of the phone. "Sure. Is it true that you joined the police?"

That wasn't a discussion Daniel wanted to get into over the phone, especially while he was still concerned about Pandy. "Yes, and no," he said. "Do you have half an hour this evening, and I can explain?"

"God yes. Am I old enough to drink in the Slater's yet?" Daniel thought about how easy, or not, it would be to find a private spot in the Slater's Arms.

"The Red Lion might be better." It was the town's least popular pub, where he was unlikely to run into another policeman.

"Seven in the Red Lion. Are you still the skinny, pretty boy?" Daniel looked at his phone in bemusement. Is that how people had seen him at school?

"I played rugby," he said, and Eluned laughed.

"I remember. Weren't you good at running?"

Daniel thought that he was still good at running, but the realisation that he'd been picked for the rugby team because he could run, and not because he was tough, was as shocking as a sudden splash of cold water. He knew with horrible clarity that it was true. He had been the skinny, pretty boy, and he probably still was. But fuck it, he had a job to do, even if it wasn't his job. This wasn't about him.

He said goodbye to Eluned, and turned back to Pandy. "How about you get changed and I'll run you over to Hector's, and you can see Cerys is OK? Bring her back home?"

Pandy looked down at her feet. "I think I have to go and talk to the police again tomorrow. I don't want Cerys to know. We had all that with my ex. She's better off away from me."

"But you want to see her?"

Pandy nodded. Daniel put all the encouragement he could muster into his voice. "Get showered and changed, and we'll go." Thankfully it worked. Pandy walked, rather than shuffled, towards the stairs. He looked round the tidy room with its bookshelves, and neat cupboards. There was a fold-down desk with a glass jar of pens on top, and a pile of post-it notes. He helped himself, and started writing a list. It wasn't that he couldn't have used his phone, but there was something about writing a physical list that helped clear his mind.

Committee Members—AGM—Pandy right? Ask Lizzie and Beth, other friends?

Jones? David?

Eluned and Rhys. Mrs Bennion?

Where was Kelley last night? Who are his mates?

Charlie—get out of town.

Mal.

He started with the last one, getting out his phone. "Can you talk?" he asked, when Mal answered his phone. He heard the sound of a door closing, and Mal saying goodbye to someone.

"Yes."

"I'm going to take Pandy over to see Cerys at Hector's, then I'm meeting Hayden's daughter. I was at school with her. Pandy is in bits. Carey's been bullying her, and there's some stuff with the ex-husband, and maybe something else. I'm concerned."

"You should be extremely concerned." Daniel wanted to scream *just tell me*, but there was no way Mal would tell him anything confidential, at least not while he was in his office.

"Can you find out where PC Kelley was last night? Because he wasn't in the wine bar for very long..."

"Stop there. You need to know that DI Carey had a tip off about the allotments and they carried out another search. One of the polytunnels was apparently being used to grow cannabis. Some people are being questioned. The other thing you need to know is that DI Carey would like to interview you under caution. Apparently you were seen talking to the alleged cannabis growers. There is talk of a warrant to look for cannabis on your land. I am not minded to ask for such a warrant at this time."

"You're not joking, are you?" Daniel didn't know why he was asking. Mal wouldn't joke about this.

"This is not going to get any better, anytime soon."

"Those people Carey is questioning for growing dope. Are they two women?"

"Yes. I have to go." Daniel heard the door open again, and Mal speak to someone before the phone went dead.

A door slammed at the top of the stairs, and a waft of warm, damp, shampoo-smelling air drifted towards him.

Am I going to be able to help her? Will Mal be able to help me?

He looked at his right hand, the one with only two fingers. It seemed a small loss, compared to the many other officers who had been killed or badly injured while doing their jobs. And there was guilt too. Maybe if he'd been better focussed on his job, and less on the misery in his life, the injury could have been prevented. But he heard his counsellor's voice: *This isn't your fault. You did the best you could. You are not to blame.* He took the breaths that she'd taught him, concentrated on them going in and out, centring himself in the moment, letting the sounds of the house fill his consciousness: the fridge buzzing in the background, a car on the road outside, the slam of a car door and a child's high voice. The moment broke with the sound of Pandy coming down the stairs. He and Mal had faced trouble in the past, and they would face this, and beat it.

"Let's get you over to see Cerys," he said. Pandy's smile was hesitant, but she was in clean clothes, her hair was washed and plaited again, and she held out her hand.

"Thank you," she said. "The last two days... let's just say they haven't been great. Some bad memories, and the idea that maybe Cerys would be better off without me." There was a pause, and then Pandy spoke with determination in her voice. "I think you know what I'm saying. But I'm OK now, honestly, and I want to see my baby."

***

Bethan was looking at Mal with dismay. Her expression was pained. He'd seen her look at Daniel like that when he'd had one of his wild leaps of intuition, but he'd never seen that gaze turned on him. She was as tidy as ever despite the coldness and discomfort of the office: hair in a French plait, cardigan buttoned, scarf tied around her neck.

"Daniel. Is. Not. Growing. Dope." he said. "You worked with him for years. You *know* him. You were there when he was attacked by a cannabis farmer. Jesus, Mary and Joseph, Bethan, what's got into you?" He saw her face begin to relax.

"I thought, maybe with him being ill. It's supposed to help with pain..."

"So does paracetamol."

"My boys smoke it. Weed. They talk about it like everyone does it. And he was hanging round with those hippies on the allotments. I'm sorry, sir."

This is how conspiracy theories get traction. Drip, drip, drip.

"Do tell me, sergeant Davies, is it now the view of CID as a whole that ex-DI Owen is a criminal and I am helping to conceal his crimes?"

Bethan blushed a dark red from the roots of her hair, down her neck and who knew how much further. She loosened the scarf and used it to fan herself.

"I'm so sorry," she said. "Of course it's nonsense, and I'll go back upstairs and say so."

"Thank you."

Bethan closed the door carefully behind her.

We're on our own. Mal looked out of the window into the darkening car park. The hills were being swallowed by grey clouds. There would be no stars tonight. He had complete faith in Daniel, but his own hands were tied. If the rumour about Daniel growing dope reached the ACC, or anyone in the executive corridors, then he, Mal, would be suspended and investigated. He pulled the desk phone towards him.

"Sophie? I need to borrow two of your constables right now. If one of them could be PC Kelley, that would be great. PC Morgan or PC Jones would be good too, if either of them are available. Get them to meet me outside in twenty minutes."

Sophie's response was a squawk, and some four-letter words, but ended with, "OK."

"And one other thing."

"Of course, I think I still have, oh, two or three officers left for you to borrow."

"This is one for you. Can you make a list of everyone who accessed the records of Pandy Melton's case in the last two weeks?"

Sophie didn't answer for a moment. It was a job anyone could have done, and she was a uniformed inspector, with enough work to keep three people busy. But she was also the only person he completely trusted in Melin Tywyll police. She would be discreet, and leave no traces of what she'd been doing. She wouldn't mention her search in passing to anyone else.

"No problem," she said in the end. "I'll do it as soon as I've sorted you out with some nice PCs."

Mal straightened his already straight tie and picked up his jacket. He ran up the stairs to CID, paraphrasing Shakespeare in his head *if it were to be done, it was well done quickly. Or more to the point, before it's too dark.*

Carey was in his office, door closed. Mal flung it open without knocking, but didn't go in. Standing in the doorway, he raised his voice, so everyone could hear.

"DI Carey. I've just been hearing an extremely worrying rumour about drug-growing at my house. I've arranged for two uniformed officers to conduct a search, and I'd like you to come too, and perhaps Abby could accompany us. I'll see you downstairs in twenty minutes. I would advise warm clothes and waterproof footwear. And a good torch." He heard his pompous tone and smiled inside. Daniel would go ballistic at the thought of Carey and co trampling all over his vegetable beds and polytunnels, and going into his precious woods, disturbing the wildlife but it was the price they had to pay. He planned to make Carey personally walk over all thirteen acres of land, then come back to the station to write a report about where he heard the rumour, and detailing the meticulous search that showed it to be false. He had every intention of ensuring that the report would not be finished until after the pubs had closed for the night. "Twenty minutes," he said again.

Out of the corner of his eye, he saw Bethan's lips twitch. Then her phone rang. She listened for a few moments and looked up, gaze flicking between Mal and Carey. "A member of the public has come in to report seeing the attack on Charlie," she said.

"You'll have to take the statement," Mal said. "DI Carey and DC Price may be gone for a while."

14

THE LEAST POPULAR PUB

D aniel thought the Red Lion was everything a pub shouldn't be. As he walked in, the few people already there looked round, then looked away, because he obviously wasn't very interesting. Like the Slater's Arms, and the wine bar, the walls of the Red Lion had been painted white, but there the resemblance ended. These walls had taken on the yellow tinge of the millions of cigarettes smoked in the pub since the paint was last renewed in about 1970. The smell of tar and nicotine had sunk deep into the walls, seeping out to greet every visitor. Also like the Slater's Arms, the Red Lion had received a consignment of dark wood tables. Again, they were crowded into a space too small to accommodate them all. Unlike the tables in the Slater's Arms, these tables were sticky with spilled beer. The beermats were stained, and some had doodles, or phone numbers. *Surely beer-mats are free?* Daniel thought.

Old photographs of the town were hung apparently at random around the pub walls. The glass in the picture frames needed cleaning, along with everything else in the place.

Daniel resolved not to drink enough to need the toilet. He noticed that the only vaguely newish furnishings were the curtains. They were thick and oversized. Perfect for ensuring that no light escaped into the street to alert any passing police officer that the pub was still serving drinks after hours. But at this time, it was quiet. There was a table on the far side of the room where he could talk to Eluned, and no one would be able to hear. It was vile, but perfect for his purpose.

He'd ordered a bottle of cider, assuming that the pipes from the cellar were cleaned less often than they should be, and as it arrived, so did Eluned. She looked round and said, "I'll have the same."

He would have recognised her even if they hadn't arranged to meet. As he'd said to Pandy, Eluned Bennion would be forever associated with shaving her head, aged seventeen. He remembered that her hair had grown back slowly, covering her head in soft down, like the feathers on a baby bird. She had that same hair now, and it suited her bold face and emphasised her big, dark blue eyes. She wore red lipstick, and her nails were painted the same colour, but those were the only nods to traditional femininity. Eluned was dressed in the same way as Daniel: jeans, thick sweater, waterproof coat, lace-up boots. She took her coat off as they sat down.

"Are the chairs as sticky as the carpet?" she asked, moving a half-shredded beermat to put her bottle down on.

"'Fraid so," he grimaced. They had both left the proffered glasses behind on the bar. "Tell me how you are, and aren't a policeman."

Daniel took a drink from his bottle of cider. "It's a long story. I was a policeman for fifteen years, and I left a few months ago. I was a detective inspector."

"OK." It was the sort of *OK* that meant *keep talking.*

"I was there when Pandy found your father. I thought he

might still be alive, so I tried CPR, but it was too late. I'm really sorry."

"You tried. I'll be honest, I don't really believe it yet. I got here yesterday and no Dad, but that was pretty normal. I haven't been home for a long time. It's not that I don't get on with my parents, more that they don't get on with me." Eluned took a drink. "I'm going to get some crisps. They can't spoil crisps, can they? Do you want some?"

Daniel nodded. He'd seen that the pub offered food, but couldn't imagine anyone in their right mind eating anything cooked here. Eluned showed no sign of grieving for her father, he thought. She was shocked perhaps, because murder was always shocking, but he got no sense that she was about to cry. When she got back from the bar, she confirmed it.

"I probably seem heartless, Daniel, but I hadn't spoken to my father in years. Mum sent me Christmas and birthday cards, and I sent them to her, but that's pretty much all the contact we had. She rang me to say he'd been killed--murdered--and asked me to come, so I came. I don't know why she wanted me, but here I am."

"What happened between you and your dad?" Daniel asked, although he had a good idea of the answer.

"He's a homophobe. Sorry, he *was* a homophobe. Not like an out-there sort of homophobe. Not rude, just made sure that he never asked my girlfriends round, where he always made Rhys's girlfriends super-welcome. I mean, I knew he disapproved, and he knew I knew, and in the end, I couldn't be bothered. I met Maraid, and we applied to be wardens up in Shetland, and we've been there for a few years now."

"Pandy says you were a good friend to her when she got divorced." Daniel felt bad for asking about the divorce, and the violence that went with it, when Pandy clearly didn't want to talk about it. But he wanted to know.

"That bastard. Her parents died you know, in the Tsunami in Bali, and that Melton just sucked her up in the aftermath. She's such a sweet person. But it's like she's got a sticker saying *Take advantage of me* on her forehead." Eluned stared at Daniel. He put his hands up to ward off her unspoken accusations.

"I'm worried about her. Her little girl is staying with some friends of mine. I've promised to keep her allotment ticking over, and I'm going to ring all her yoga clients in the morning and cancel all her classes for the next week. I'm also trying to get her to see a doctor, but I'm not sure that's going to happen."

"She found my dad, right? And that's what's caused all this?"

Daniel took a deep breath. "This needs more cider." He bought them another bottle each and told Eluned the whole story, including Pandy's persecution by Carey.

"He's the laziest cop who ever lived. Find a suspect and then make the evidence fit. Somehow he knows about Pandy's ex, and he's using it as leverage to get her to keep going back to the station to answer the same questions. That's how people finish up confessing to stuff they haven't done... But that's not all. She's said that Cerys would be better off without her, and I don't like where that leads. Fair play, she says she changed her mind, but it's still frightening."

Eluned was as good a listener as Pandy herself, Daniel thought, remembering how easy it had been to talk in front of the fire at the allotment. He saw Eluned thinking about what he'd said, and trying to decide whether to tell him something about Pandy. Her face cleared as she made up her mind.

"You remember the accident—at the New Year's raft race?"

Daniel shook his head, then a vague memory drifted into his mind. "Someone died? And we never had the raft race after that? We must have been, what thirteen or fourteen?"

"Pandy was on that raft. So was my brother Rhys, and a guy

called Dylan something. It was his girlfriend who died. I ought to be able to remember her name, but I don't. I didn't know her, or Dylan. Their raft hit another one and they all tipped into the water. The girl drowned. It was awful. Rhys was in shock. Pandy tried to kill herself. One of those things they call *a cry for help.*" Eluned's tone expressed what she thought of downplaying a suicide attempt. "But if Pandy didn't kill Dad, who did?"

"I was going to ask you the same thing," Daniel said.

Eluned must have been thinking about it, but her face showed no answer. "I have absolutely no idea. I didn't like him much, but he wasn't abusive. Ask Rhys when he gets here, but I think you'll get the same reply. Dad was just an ordinary bloke. Obsessed with his allotment. A bigot. Liked a pint now and again. Talks about his grandchildren according to Mum. Doesn't approve of young people. Reads the Daily Mail."

"Tell me about Rhys. I don't remember him very well."

"He didn't kill Dad, if that's what you're asking. I Skyped him in Australia, so he's got an alibi."

Daniel shook his head. "No, that wasn't what I meant. You said grandchildren. Rhys has a family?"

"A wife and three kids. I don't think he meant to emigrate, but he met Lucy and she got pregnant, and he got a good job, and he never came back. I think, though I may be wrong, that he went to Australia to get away from here after the accident. It was his last year of uni, and he went as soon as he graduated."

***

The woods were dripping with moisture, and the ground underfoot was slippery from recent rains. If Mal hadn't known how much attention Daniel paid to his trees, he'd have been worried about the creaking and groaning noises, as the wind got stronger with the darkness. As it was, everyone but PC Jones was starting to weary, and Mal didn't like the look of DI Carey: red-faced and sweating under his borrowed waterproofs.

He wouldn't miss Carey if he dropped dead of a heart attack, but at the same time, he didn't need the aggravation.

They had started by the house. Mal had shown them the two polytunnels and the raised beds, and the almost cleared area around what they called their 'lawn': a roughly trimmed meadow giving a fantastic view across the valley below, though not on a February evening. He showed them around the outside of the house, and into all the sheds. But not the house. "I was told that the alleged cannabis was being grown in the *grounds*," he said, looking Carey straight in the eye. "Isn't that right, DI Carey?" PC Jones had to turn away and cough.

Then Mal led them into the woods, telling them to spread out and "investigate every patch of ground."

At one point, PC Jones deliberately found himself next to Mal and whispered, "Dope plants need light and heat."

Mal patted his arm. "But it must be true, PC Jones. Daniel is growing dope in the woods. Everyone says so." They shared a small smile. Mal had worked with PC Jones for a long time. The man was gloriously fat, but could keep going all day, unlike the skinny Kelley, who was beginning to fade, along with his mentor. Abby was visibly tiring too, but Mal wasn't letting any of them ease up until Carey called the search off. Which he finally did at eight o'clock. They'd actually been outside the smallholding for the last half hour, but as the boundaries weren't visible on the ground, the only person who knew it was Mal.

"There's nothing here," Carey said, leaning against a convenient tree in his weariness, "and I'm ready for a pint." Kelley nodded enthusiastically, but Mal shook his head, and resumed his most pompous tone.

"Sorry, but it's back to the station, I'm afraid, no pubs for us, even if we are technically off duty. We need this report written up asap, before the rumour spreads any further, and people start talking about *no smoke without fire*. DI Carey, you take the lead on that, with Kelley and Jones to put the map together. This is a potentially serious matter, and I want it done and dusted by tonight, so that we can get back to Hayden Bennion in the morning."

Mal knew this was only one battle, and that the war would continue. *But it's a battle you're going to remember, you piece of shit.*

He took Abby aside and told her to go home.

BACK AT THE POLICE STATION, Bethan had left Mal a statement from the witness to the attack on Charlie Rees. It wasn't helpful, except to confirm that the assault had probably been abandoned when the attackers saw they were not alone. One of the attackers sounded as if it could have been PC Kelley, but it could equally have been any other thin man. The others were just figures in the darkness.

There was also a note from Sophie: "Ring me."

"DI Carey did not access the domestic abuse files last week," she told him when he rang. "In fact, no one accessed those records in the last two weeks."

"Thanks. I think." Mal wasn't sure how that information fitted with anything else.

"Did you have a nice walk in the woods?" Sophie asked, sounding innocent.

"It was a very serious matter." Mal said, equally innocently.

"PC Jones enjoyed himself very much, and hopes he gets to do it again soon," she said and he heard her laugh as she ended the call. But it wasn't funny, not really.

Mal moved from the chair behind his desk to one of the sofas allegedly provided for 'informal meetings'. He slipped his shoes off and put his feet up, moving the sofa cushions so that his head was supported. It had been fun tormenting Carey by making him trail round the soggy woods in search of cannabis they all knew didn't exist. It had kept Carey away from Daniel, giving him time to work on the case. But now Mal needed to think. Carey didn't like him, or Daniel, or the way CID had been run. He didn't like gay people, or women, or people of colour, especially in positions of authority. He was lazy, a bully, and at least a borderline alcoholic. But was that enough to explain his behaviour?

15

SAD HOMECOMINGS

I t was too late for Daniel to see anyone else from his list, and neither he nor Eluned wanted to stay in the Red Lion longer than they had to. They left through the bunch of smokers crowded on the pavement by the door. The Main Street was narrow here, so the pavement was only wide enough for them to walk in single file towards the car park. Daniel offered Eluned a lift home but she shook her head.

"I'm in no rush to get back, and it's not actually raining." The smell of rain was in the air though, and they were hit by gusts of wind as they walked. Daniel thought of his trees, and of the creatures who depended on them. He made a mental note to check the Community Allotment in the morning to see that everything was still standing. Maybe he could catch up with Lizzie and Beth to find out if they really had been growing illicit substances.

The Land Rover was buffeted by the wind as he drove home, and he was glad to turn up the steep track to his house. There was no sign of Mal's car, though it looked as if he'd been and gone from the tyre tracks and footprints. There seemed to be a lot of footprints, but Daniel put the observation aside for later.

He got the fire going, made himself some cheese on toast and washed an apple. Then he texted Mal.

Daniel: *What time are you coming home?*

Mal: *Late. Don't wait up.*

Daniel understood that Mal was keeping the spotlight off him and his investigation into Hayden Bennion's death. He hadn't said so, but he hadn't needed to. But he wasn't going to be able to keep it up for long. Daniel needed to find out who killed Hayden as quickly as possible, and all he knew so far was that it wasn't Pandy.

He cast his mind back to the night of the murder. The only cars left in the car park had been his own Land Rover and Pandy's Bongo. Even through his almost-dozing he'd been aware of cars leaving the site, and he was sure that no vehicles had left for a while before they found the body. Had there been many other cars parked there during the day? He thought not. In fact, he hadn't seen more than a few cars in any of his visits, suggesting that most plot-holders lived close enough to walk there. He found his list of committee members, and began to look up addresses.

But why would a committee member kill Hayden Bennion?

Why would *anyone* kill Hayden Bennion? Hayden had been unfriendly, and his daughter didn't like him very much, but there didn't seem to be enough there to drive someone to murder. He'd apparently spent all his free time at the allotment, to the annoyance of his wife, but again, that wasn't a motive for murder. And he refused to believe that an argument at the Allotment Society AGM led to a man's violent death. What else did he know about Hayden? That he'd worked in the timber yard, but he'd been retired for long enough for any work-related disputes to have been forgotten surely?

He wondered briefly about the raft race accident. Something about Eluned's references told him that it had had a profound impact on her and her brother, as well as on Pandy. He would have known about it at the time, but couldn't remember the details. He opened his laptop and began googling. There was nothing. But his mother would remember. He looked at the time, and picked up his phone.

"What's up, love?" his mother sounded panicked, which is when it occurred to him that it was an hour later in Spain than it was in Wales.

"Nothing Mam, I know it's late, but I wanted to pick your brains."

He heard his father in the background, and his mother explaining in an exasperated voice.

"Pick my brains about what?"

"Do you remember the New Year's Day raft race?"

"Of course. And that terrible accident. That poor girl who died. Why do you want to know?"

Daniel explained that he'd met Eluned and Pandy and that the accident seemed to have stayed with them both. "What happened to everyone else, do you know?" he asked.

"Pandora. She was a nice girl. Bag of nerves though, always was. She lost her parents in that awful Tsunami. Didn't have a lot of luck. But you say she's back in Melin?"

"She is, and she's in trouble. I'm trying to help her. Do you remember Eluned's family?"

Daniel heard his dad in the background "Eluned Bennion? Shaved her head…" His mother laughed. "Poor Eluned's never going to be allowed to forget it. Her brother went off to Australia."

Daniel allowed his impatience to get the better of him. "What about the girl who died? Who was she?"

"Merren, Davies, I think. Her parents moved away. They got religion or something. I don't know what happened." There was an altercation in the background. "Your dad says it was the other lad who was called Davies — Dylan. Here you talk to him." Daniel heard his father's voice.

"Dylan Davies. They lived over the back of our old house. They moved away after the accident, but I heard Dylan had died not that long ago. But don't ask me who I heard it from because lord only knows. That's ex-pat Spain for you. Gossip morning, noon and night."

Neither of his parents could remember the surname of the girl who died, but he could find out. Maybe along the way he'd work out why the accident seemed so important.

***

Mal managed to keep DI Carey occupied writing his report until just before pub closing time. Perhaps Carey would get his pint, perhaps he wouldn't. Mal didn't care either way, and he'd used the time to get through a mountain of his outstanding paperwork. He'd also read the pathetically thin case files on Hayden Bennion's death. There had been no follow up on any of the forensic evidence from the scene of the crime, no attempt to talk to Bennion's family beyond offering condolences and asking if Bennion 'had any enemies', and no attempt to establish who else had been on the allotments on the evening of the murder. But there were pages and pages of interviews with Pandy. There were also interviews with people who had witnessed the altercation at the AGM, and with a David Jones, who had seen (though not heard) Bennion arguing with Daniel. There was nothing in the files about people growing cannabis either at the allotments or on Daniel's smallholding. The only solid piece of evidence was Hector's autopsy report, and that pointed away from Pandy. Clearly neither hints nor direct instructions were going to make Carey do a proper investigation. His mind was made up. But it was time to go home. Before he could, his phone rang.

"Could you look something up for me?" Daniel asked. "The

inquest report into the accidental drowning of a young woman on New Year's Day 1999, here in Melin."

Mal looked at his computer. It was updating itself with many spinning wheels and the occasional whirring noise.

"Tomorrow," he said. "I'll be home in twenty minutes."

MAL PARKED outside the house for the second time that day, but this time he was going to stay; to crawl into bed next to Daniel and fall asleep. Flora gave him her usual loud welcome home, so he let her run in the garden for a minute before he went in. The two of them went upstairs to where Daniel was reading in bed.

"Hi gorgeous," Daniel said.

Mal sat down wearily on the side of the bed and started taking his clothes off, throwing his shirt towards the laundry basket, and missing. "What's this inquest all about then?"

Daniel put the tablet he'd been reading from down onto the floor.

"When I was growing up, there was a raft race on the river every New Year's Day. Not on the rapids, the bit above them, where there's a good current but not much in the way of obstacles. You know, where the canoe club is?"

Mal nodded, finished getting undressed and slid into bed.

"Well, when I was about fourteen, there was an accident. One of the rafts turned over and a girl drowned. They didn't hold any more races after that. No one can remember much about the girl who died, but the odd thing is that Pandy was on that raft, and so was Rhys Bennion, Hayden's son. They were both in their last year at uni, and they were a sort-of couple. I don't know whether it's got any relevance at all, but it keeps coming up in conversation. I don't remember much about it, but Pandy was really badly affected, and so were Eluned and Rhys Bennion."

"Stranger things have been important," Mal said. "I'll send you everything I can find. Now, let me tell you how I spent the early part of this evening..."

"You took Carey and Kelley into my polytunnels?" Daniel said. "I'm going to have to have them ritually cleansed of evil. I'll need a lot of sage. And probably the woods too. And my toolshed? I hope you checked that they didn't steal anything."

"PC Jones was right behind them all the way."

"You didn't take them down to the hide? Not now we've seen the badgers?"

"No way. Carey has no idea where the boundaries are anyway, so if that's where you've been growing your weed, it's still safe."

Daniel propped his head on his elbow. "Let me get this straight. there's a rumour going round the station that I'm growing dope. And you brought Carey and three others up here, in February, to search for it."

"Yup."

"But even you must realise that the reason cannabis factories are inside, is that the plants need a lot of heat and light? And there isn't much in the way of heat and light in north Wales in February."

"Yup."

"So you basically made everyone search for something that couldn't exist. And all the searchers knew it couldn't exist. Except Kelley, he's stupid enough to think cannabis grows in the dark."

"That's exactly right. I'm so glad you understand. Then I made Carey write a long and detailed report, with maps, explaining everywhere they looked. Because Carey isn't a completely stupid man, unlike Kelley. He told people that it would make sense for you to be growing a bit of weed, because it's a painkiller, and you've been injured. He almost had Bethan convinced. If the rumour made it to HQ, well, you know what would happen."

"But you are also a deeply wicked man who takes pleasure in making his enemies stumble around in the cold and dark in search of non-existent dope farms."

"That too." Mal pulled Daniel towards him and switched the light off. They both felt the soft thump as Flora jumped onto the bed and snuggled down to sleep.

16

IT'S ALWAYS A DOG WALKER...

M rs Joanna Richardson (she insisted on the Mrs) walked her two chocolate Labradors every morning before her husband went to work. She didn't have a job outside the home, so she could have walked them at any time, but she had spent most of her married life trying to avoid her husband in the early morning. Mr Richardson was one of those men who woke up in a bad temper and slowly calmed down over the day. By the time he came home, he was mellow and charming. In the evenings, Joanna remembered why she had married him. But she made sure that she was out of the way while he made his breakfast, had his shower and got himself into the car. This morning it was cold, and damp, but last night's wind had dropped. Joanna slid her hands into soft leather gloves and attached the dogs' leads to their collars.

The dogs didn't care about the time of day or the weather. They would have gone for a walk through the bombing of Coventry, Joanna thought. They were Instagram-perfect dogs, but not too bright, and sometimes Joanna wondered how it would have been if she'd chosen a rescue dog, something cute, cuddly and smart. *A companion.* But Labradors need long walks, and they kept her fit. They suited her image, and now they had done as much calming down as chocolate Labradors ever do, they helped her start conversations with interesting-looking strangers. They were well-behaved when she went to do her charity work. She had no complaints about them.

Her route took her from the oldest part of Melin Tywyll where her house—The Old Rectory—was set behind a high wall next to the parish church. It must originally have had a much bigger garden, but that had been sold long before and was now covered with smaller houses. From there she walked through the town centre, past the revolting modernist abhorrence that was the police station and on to the cattle market. On market days, she and the dogs would see the animals arriving and being unloaded into the auctioneer's pens, the whole area smelling of their droppings and the air full of their cries. After that her route wound its way through the back streets until she came to the steep steps leading down to the bridge.

From there, the river path was the best part of her walk, downstream following the white water as it crashed over rocks through the canoe slalom course. At the bottom of the course, paddlers had to get through a final wave that seemed to turn back on itself, and then the river became calm again. She'd seen an otter there, more than once, so she always paused to look, and this morning was no different. She saw movement and colour in the water, and stopped. It wasn't an otter. It was a woman, with long hair, wearing red clothes.

Joanna told herself that it was a mannequin. Or a bundle of rags. But the truth was that she knew what it was from the first moment she saw it and she felt nausea rise in her throat. She pulled the dogs to the nearest bench, sat down and dialled 999 on her phone. Then she prepared herself to wait. She didn't know how long the woman had been in the river, but Joanna wasn't going to leave her now. She felt tears running down her face, and for the first time, both dogs leaned against her as if to offer comfort. She stroked their silky heads and told them that everything would be fine.

***

Hector looked up from the body, which was still dripping water onto the path beside the river. Uniformed police had been quick to raise a tent and tape off the scene, and others had gently pulled the dead woman from the river. Abby Price sat with Joanna Richardson and her dogs, taking down an account of her horrible discovery. All Hector could think about was the little girl, getting ready for school at his house, happily unaware of her mother's death.

"It's definitely Pandy Melton," he said. "And all the signs are that she drowned." He fished gently in the pocket of Pandy's coat, and pulled out a mobile phone and a small purse. He handed them to Bethan Davies, who slipped them into evidence bags.

"I don't need to check her ID," Bethan said. "She's been in and out of the police station all week. I hope fucking Carey is pleased with himself. Bastard."

Hector slipped in surprise. He didn't know that Bethan knew any swear words, let alone used them. "You're assuming she jumped?"

"Because that sad excuse for a detective wouldn't leave her alone. He might as well have pushed her in himself." Bethan turned away from the body, and Hector saw the flush of anger on the tips of her ears. She walked out of the tent and began stripping off her paper suit. He stood up and followed, calling for the men from the mortuary to bring the body bag and the stretcher. This was an autopsy he didn't want to do, and before that, phone calls he didn't want to make.

Hector: *Ring me once you get home from taking the girls to school.*

Sasha: *What's wrong?*

Hector: *I'm fine, but please do as I ask. H x*

He got a thumbs up in reply. She would cope, because that's who she was, but her heart would break as she did it. His already had.

Abby Price had her arm around the woman who'd found the body, leading her and two brown dogs back up the path towards the police cars on the other side of the bridge. The woman looked shaken and pale. Hector had seen things caught in the wave at the bottom of the rapids. They turned over and over, until they were either sucked underneath to finish up who knew where, or something flung them out into the stillness beyond. He didn't need much imagination to picture Pandy's body rolling in the cold, soulless water, making no impact on the river as it flowed impassively towards the sea. A body in the ground would leave an impression. The plants and insects would be disturbed. Not this water.

He walked towards the bridge where he had parked his car. Sophie Harrington was talking to a man in a high viz jacket. Two uniformed officers were removing traffic cones from the bridge to allow the mortuary van to leave with Pandy's body. Their voices drifted towards him in the morning stillness.

"They're saying suicide, poor cow."

"Poor cow nothing. Fucking man-hater she was. One less to worry about."

"Steady on, Kelley, the woman's dead."

"No, mate, listen. I know her type ..."

Hector thought of the little girl innocently enjoying her school day, unaware of what was waiting for her. He saw red.

Whatever Kelley was going to say next was cut off by Hector grabbing the back of his collar and pulling. Hard. Kelley staggered and gurgled, his air supply restricted. Hector kicked the man's ankle and Kelley fell inelegantly onto his arse on the tarmac, Hector still holding his collar. Fighting was not Hector's regular practice, but he had been to public school, and anger gave him strength. He yanked Kelley's collar again. "*You* listen, you piece of crap. That woman was a *mothe* ..."

This time it was Hector who didn't finish his sentence. Sophie had his arm, and her face in his. "Dr Lord, *Hector*, step back. Step back now!"

The rage lifted enough for Hector to let go of the collar after a final yank, leaving his fingers swollen and throbbing as the blood rushed back. He felt his heart race and heard buzzing in his head. He suddenly needed to sit down. Sophie felt like a rock next to him.

Kelley gasped for breath and his head fell forwards. The other PC helped him to his feet.

"That's assault, you ... Saw that," Kelley was still struggling for control of his breathing. He shrugged off the other uniformed officer's hand. "You... All saw..." He looked towards Sophie, still gripping Hector's arm.

"I am sure Dr Lord meant you no harm PC Kelley, and will apologise," Sophie said, with steel in her voice. Hector felt her grip on his arm tighten. He took a steadying breath.

"I...ah...sincerely apologise for my actions. Overcome by events. I really am very sorry."

Kelley's mouth opened, but Sophie was quicker. "Thank you, Dr Lord. Now, lads, the cones if you please. Kelley, my office before you go off duty." There was a moment of stillness; a frozen tableau of the man in the high viz jacket and the two uniformed policemen staring at Sophie gripping Hector's arm. "Cones. Now." And the pieces began to move again.

Hector called Mal.

"The body in the river is Pandy Melton. I think she drowned. There are some cuts and bruises, but all post-mortem. Your sergeant is calling it as suicide. Too much pressure from that dickhead Carey. From my perspective, it's too soon to say."

There was a long silence at the other end. Then, "Thanks, Hector," and Mal hung up. Hector thought he would go home. Meet Sasha and tell her in person, let them ring social services together, decide what to do together. He hoped Pandy had nominated someone to care for Cerys in case of an accident, but he feared that she hadn't. All he knew was that it couldn't be James Melton.

***

Mal parked next to the Land Rover outside the tin shed on the allotments. He made his way gingerly along slippery paths, following handmade wooden signs to the Community Allotment. Daniel was lifting a large piece of black plastic from an area of dark, bare soil, and laying it down on a grassy bit. The exposed side was covered in clumps of soil, and so was Daniel. Flora lay on an old sack, her lead hooked round a fence post. Mal noticed that Daniel had his hair tied into a bun on top of his head. It looked cute, but he didn't suppose that's why Daniel had done it. Daniel was singing to himself as he wrestled the plastic.

"Hey," Mal called.

"Hey, you too." But Daniel's face betrayed that he understood that Mal hadn't come for a cup of coffee or a chat.

"You'd better sit down," Mal said, seeing the pile of plastic chairs in through the open shed door.

"Don't tell me you've come to arrest me."

"It's worse than that." Mal made his way to the shed, avoiding the slippery plastic, and brought one of the chairs out. "Sit."

Daniel sat, looking worried.

"A woman walking a dog early this morning found a body in the river below the rapids. We've identified it as Pandy Melton. Hector says that it's definitely her, and that he thinks she drowned." Then Mal wrapped his arms around Daniel, squatting awkwardly on the muddy ground to hold him close. "I'm so sorry, love, I know you liked her."

Mal saw Daniel's eyes begin to shine with tears, and felt his attempt to hold back a sob. "Everyone liked her. Everyone *decent*. She was so kind, Maldwyn. She wouldn't hurt anyone, I don't think she had it in her. And her little girl..."

"Bethan thinks she killed herself because Carey bullied her."

Daniel sat up so quickly that his forehead caught Mal's chin. Mal bit his tongue and tasted blood.

"She didn't kill herself. I don't know how she came to be in the river, but she didn't kill herself. I don't care what anyone else says. I was with her yesterday--I took her over to see Cerys. We talked all the way, about how she'd thought about suicide. Like, really thought about it, and decided to live. If it wasn't an accident, then someone murdered her."

"Dan, people change their minds."

"Nope. She had thought it all through, pros and cons, and made her mind up. She was going to force Carey to charge her or stop his harassment, bring Cerys home and get her life back on track. Ask her solicitor, he'll tell you the same. She'd made an appointment with the doctor for some meds for panic attacks. You can check that too. She was planning her future. I'm here because she wanted to keep this project going. *Check*, dammit, Mal. *She didn't kill herself!*" He was shouting now, and heads were beginning to pop up around them, like meerkats on the grasslands. "She taught yoga, and meditation, and she did reiki healing, and she volunteered at Women's Aid and the food bank. She had no money, but she did all that stuff..."

Mal saw that Daniel was barely holding it together, but he still had to play devil's advocate. Part of him *wanted* to prove that Carey had driven this good woman to her death, so he could get rid of Carey once and for all, but most of him wanted to console Daniel. "I will ask—no, *tell*—Hector to look for *any* sign of it not being suicide. But Dan, look at me. I'm going to let the rumour stand. OK? Because I want Carey scared. Not because I don't believe you."

Daniel nodded through a haze of tears. "Come with me to go and see Hector and Sasha later?"

Mal had no idea how he was going to be able to find the time, but he said yes anyway. He heard a noise, and looked round, expecting to see Flora trying to escape. Instead, he saw two women, clearly a couple from their intertwined hands.

"Is it true?" the taller one asked. "Pandy's dead?"

Mal stood up and nodded. "I'm sorry, but yes. Were you friends of hers?"

One of them nodded. "Pandy was going to borrow our caravan next weekend, to take Cerys and Arwen for a break. She needed to get away for a bit. The fascist cops were driving her to a breakdown. It's on the beach on Anglesey — the caravan. Sorry, I'm gabbling."

The shorter woman tried to smile. "I think that is one of the fascist cops, Lizzie."

"Detective Chief Superintendent Maldwyn Kent, fascist cop at your service," Mal said with a slight bow.

Daniel interrupted. "See, Pandy was making plans."

Mal ignored him, and focussed on the two women. "Would I be right in thinking that you were accused of growing illegal substances on your plot?"

Lizzie nodded. "Yup, PC Plod's big boots over everything, and no surprise, no dope."

"Leaving aside the fascist nature of the police service, why do you think someone reported you for cannabis growing?" Because Mal was beginning to have some ideas about Adam Carey, and was starting to wonder if Carey was trying to distract him, and if he was, what was he trying to distract him from. What was Carey up to that he didn't want Mal to see?

17

LAST MAN STANDING

Hector Lord enjoyed his work. Like most people he had days when he would just as soon roll over in bed and go back to sleep, especially if he could wrap his arms around his beloved Sasha, knowing Arwen was safely asleep across the landing. This morning was one of those mornings, except Sasha had already gone downstairs, and he could hear her quiet voice talking to the two little girls. They'd told Cerys about her mother's death when she got home from school the day before.

Cerys had looked as if her world had ended, sobbing into Sasha's chest, her heart breaking. They'd had to tell her more than once that it was true, that Pandy wouldn't be coming back, that the doctors wouldn't be able to work a miracle. In the end, she'd asked, "Did my dad kill her? He used to say that he would."

Hector felt his heart breaking, imagining how Cery's short life had already been blighted, and the sorrow that was just beginning. "We don't know yet, Cerys. But we are going to find out,"

Later, in bed, listening out for the sound of crying, Hector had said fiercely to Sasha "We must keep her here, keep her safe."

"It's not that simple."

"I *know that*. But where else is she going to go? Can we at least *try*?"

"Of course we can."

Hector was comforted. With Sasha on his side, he thought mountains could be moved. But now he had to get up, get ready and go and carry out the autopsy on Cerys's mother. He could have asked a colleague to do it, but he'd promised Daniel and Mal. It wasn't that other pathologists wouldn't do a good job, but they wouldn't be looking to prove it wasn't suicide. He felt responsible for Cerys. His instincts told him that Pandy wouldn't willingly have left her daughter, but instincts weren't evidence.

***

Ladies and gentlemen, we have arrived at London Heathrow. Please remain in your seats until the seatbelt light is turned off. The temperature outside is fourteen degrees Celsius and local time is 8am. Thank you for flying with us today, and best wishes for your onward journey.

Rhys Bennion couldn't remember feeling this bad the last time he'd done the almost twenty-four hour flight from Sydney. And he still had to hire a car, and drive for five or six hours to north Wales, where his mother would be alternately angry and crying, and he'd be expected to sleep in his old room, with its lumpy single bed and draughty windows. Then when he'd been to his father's funeral, he had the whole journey to do again. It was costing a fortune, he was using up time he didn't have to spare and he was missing his youngest daughter's birthday. *How is this my life?*

Rhys told himself to get a grip, and joined the slow shuffle

off the plane and into the Arrivals hall. It would be good to see
his sister, anyway.

***

Mal received another message to call on the ACC Crime
about twenty minutes after he had sat down behind his desk.
He's going to tell me that the Hayden Bennion case is closed. Half an
hour later, he sat outside the ACC's office wondering what
Carey had in common with this man. When he was still sitting
there five minutes later, he started making calls. First to his
secretary to ask for a copy of the inquest report into the raft
race accident. Then to Abby to get a list of all the allotment plot
holders, and mark off who had been at the acrimonious AGM.
Then to Bethan to ask her to think about where and when she
had heard the rumour that Daniel was growing pot, and to find
some kind of report about the tip-off to search Lizzie and Beth's
polytunnel. "And while you're thinking, find out the whereabouts of Pandy Melton's ex-husband. Check if he's allowed to
see the child at all." He was scrolling through the list of information he needed when he was finally called in.

He had been right about the Hayden Bennion case. "It's
never good when someone takes their own life, but I think we
can draw a line under Hayden Bennion's murder. No need to
waste any more time on it."

"I'm going to wait for the pathologist's report, sir. The
coroner will want to know that we have tied up all the loose
ends before we make our report." Mal's voice was authoritative.
The ACC had been flying a desk for so long that he had probably forgotten that there would have to be an inquest into
Pandy's death, and that the coroner would certainly require
some evidence as to the cause of that death.

The ACC's face flushed with embarrassment. "Of course
that's what I meant. Now what's this about taking four officers
to search the woods by your house?"

Mal had no intention of discussing the search with the ACC. Even he wasn't stupid enough to think they were going to find a cannabis farm in the north Wales woods. "Can I ask a question, sir? It may seem personal."

"What?"

"Are you married, sir?"

"How is that your business, Kent?"

"It isn't. I was just curious. A theory, that's all."

"Keep your curiosity to yourself in future."

"Sir." Mal put his hand in his pocket, setting off the ring tone on his phone. "Excuse me, sir." He looked at his phone. "The pathologist would like to see me if we've finished here?"

The ACC waved him away irritably, the woodland walk forgotten in his outrage about being asked about his marriage. Nonetheless, Mal stopped by the civilian secretary's desk on his way out, and gave the woman his best film-star smile.

She didn't return the smile. In fact she looked irritated at his interruption. "What is it? I'm not in the mood for doing people favours today."

"All I want to know is whether your boss is married."

"Did you ask him that?"

Mal nodded.

"Then I'm surprised I didn't hear the shouting. No, my boss is not married. He was. He is now divorced, and..." she leaned closer to him, over her desk. "We do not speak of it." She leaned back and laughed. "I have no idea what happened, but he hasn't a good word to say about his ex, and since they split up some of his comments about women are borderline harassment. Actually, they're vile and offensive, and I'm looking for another job. He was mostly OK before, but now? No thanks. Why do you ask?"

Mal shrugged. He had the beginnings of an idea, but that was all it was. He decided and see what Hector had found.

· · ·

HE FOUND Hector turning over a pile of damp clothes on a bench in the lab: a thick wool jacket with a padded lining, a red hand-knitted sweater and a woolly hat. There was no sign of Pandy's body. Hector looked up when Mal came in and then went back to the garments.

"This is what Pandy was wearing," he said. "And a skirt, leggings, boots and so on. Underwear."

"OK," Mal said. He didn't want to think about Pandy choosing her clothes on the morning of her death.

"The thing is," Hector said, looking closely at the coat, "that when a body goes through those rapids, it's going to get pretty bashed about."

"OK," Mal said again. He didn't want to think about that either.

"Pandy was wearing lots of thick clothes, so they protected her quite a bit." Hector stood up and moved away from the bench. "Imagine that, for whatever reason, you've fallen in the Afon Ddu, and you feel yourself being swept away down the rapids. What do you do?"

"Panic?"

"Apart from panic."

"Try and grab something to hold on to, I suppose."

"That's what I thought, and what my assistant thought, too. So I looked at Pandy's hands, expecting to see bruises and lacerations from grabbing at tree branches and so on. There are none. What do we deduce from that?"

"Either that she was wearing gloves, or she was unconscious or dead when she hit the water."

"Exactly my assumptions, although I would add a fourth possibility, that she was alive when she entered the water but hit her head immediately, knocking her unconscious before she could try to save herself. So, let's go through those things one by one. First, gloves."

Hector went back over to the bench and felt in the front pocket of the jacket, producing a pair of woolly mittens, as damp as the rest of the clothes. They gave off a wet sheep smell. "I don't know why I put them back in her pocket," he said, laying them next to the pile of clothes. "Next, was she dead when she entered the water? No, she drowned. Water in the lungs proves it. I can check whether she drowned in the bath or a swimming pool and someone brought her dead body and threw it off the bridge, but my working hypothesis is that she drowned in the river."

"So, unconscious then?" Mal asked.

"Unconscious. And that's where it gets interesting." There was a pause. Hector ran his hands over his face. "I can't believe she's dead. Her daughter is in our house, and what I find could make a huge difference to her life. If her mother committed suicide by jumping off that bridge, Cerys is going to feel it for the rest of her life. Not that she won't be traumatised however her mother died, but suicide, it's kind of worse, do you see?"

"That Cerys wasn't enough for her mother?" Mal said. "Though it's more complicated than that, as I'm sure you know."

"I think," said Hector, as if he had made his mind up about something important, "I think that someone hit Pandy on the back of her neck and pushed her over the parapet of the bridge into the river. If this was anyone else, I'd write up my report saying exactly that, send it off, go home for a beer and wait for my day in court. But I am so desperate for it *not to be suicide* that I don't trust myself. I want a second opinion, from someone not involved. I've asked a colleague to come up from Aberystwyth tomorrow and we'll go through it together."

"Preliminary findings inconclusive?" Mal asked.

"Preliminary findings homicide," Hector replied. "The same as Hayden Bennion: bashed and drowned."

***

Rhys Bennion stopped at the first services he came to on the M4. He bought himself coffee and a bacon roll, taking it back to the hire car to eat. Drizzle clouded the windscreen, but given that the view was of a car park, he didn't bother to clear it. Once he'd finished his roll, he got his carry-on suitcase open and rummaged around for his phone so he could ring his sister.

"I'll be about five hours, depending on the traffic," he said.

"How's Mum?"

"Same, same. But listen, Pandy Melton was found dead yesterday."

"Pandy? Our friend Pandy? What's going on?"

Rhys felt the prick of tears in the back of his eyes. His father's death had been a shock, but he hadn't cried about it. He supposed that he would, at the funeral, or when he saw his mother. They'd had so little to do with each other for years. He'd invited his parents to visit them in Australia, but he knew they wouldn't make the trip. Pandy, though. He hadn't seen her for years either, but the news of her death was somehow worse than learning about his father. Pandy had been his first real girlfriend, the first woman he'd slept with. He knew from Eluned that she'd been divorced, and that she was having some problems with her ex, but the last direct contact they'd had must have been... his mind went blank from trying to work out the dates. He thought about the Christmas holiday all those years ago. The four of them making a barely functioning raft, and Dylan's girlfriend, Merren, insisting on painting flowers on the barrels they used. She said they were only going to do the race once, and they should make a show. Rhys could see her in his mind's eye, creating wilder and wilder designs, until the raft looked like the back room of a florist's shop. She had enjoyed herself, laughing and threatening them all with her paintbrush. Eluned had joined in with that bit, he remembered, still angry that she was too young to join them in the race, but wanting to be a part of it. Everything had changed after the race. It suddenly hit him that of the four people who'd climbed on to the flower covered raft that chilly morning, he was the only one still alive.

18

INVISIBLE BRUISES

Sasha looked at the social worker, Heidi something-or-other, who was tucking into one of Sasha's cherry cakes with obvious pleasure. This was the third social worker she'd met in the last 24 hours. The first had been her friend Veronica, who she'd called as soon as she learned of Pandy's death. The second had brought a series of endless questionnaires for both her and Hector covering everything from their health (good) to their criminal records (none). This woman, who didn't look old enough to have finished school, let alone be a qualified professional, wanted to ask her about her relationships. The woman had longish fair hair that had probably started out carefully styled, but was now beginning to sag, along with the rest of her. Sasha was tempted to add extra sugar to the coffee, but she offered "more cake, or I can make you a sandwich." The look of longing on the woman's face told its own story of missed lunches and supermarket ready meals. Sasha put a bowl of soup in the microwave, and then in front of her guest, and made a cheese sandwich to go with it.

"Now tell me what you want to know, and I'll talk at you while you eat."

Heidi ate hungrily, but not before asking how Sasha and Hector met, who Arwen's father was, whether they planned to get married, how they parented together, and many more, all from a printed list. Sasha grabbed the list and started answering the questions in turn.

"I met Hector over lunch with some friends. One of them had been shot, but it's OK, he's better now. We'd been looking at wedding dresses for my sister. Hector and I bonded over some images of the brain with Alzheimer's disease.

"Here's the thing. Hector and I have two things in common. One, we both love the study of the human body. He likes dead ones, and I'm still making up my mind. I'm doing a degree. Two, we've both come out of abusive relationships. Arwen's biological father was into coercive control. He doesn't know where I am, he never knew I was pregnant, and he's never going to find out. Hector took up with a guy who liked to hit people, but that's his story to tell. We both know a bit about what Pandy was going through, and we're starting to see what Cerys's father did to her, too. We just want her to be safe. If that means daily visits from a social worker, fine. I'll feed whoever turns up—cake, sandwiches, soup—whatever." Sasha hadn't realised how badly she wanted Cerys to stay with them until she'd started speaking. The thought of the little girl having to start again somewhere new, or worse, go back to her father, made her want to beg Heidi for an instant, positive decision.

"Look, Cerys and Arwen are already best friends. She's stayed with us before. It's as easy to take two girls to school, or feed two girls, as it is to look after one. When we get married, they can both be bridesmaids. And if that sounds like I'm getting desperate, it's because I am."

Heidi finished her soup and sandwich and her eyes flickered towards the cake. Sasha pushed it, and a knife, towards her, then put the used dishes in the dishwasher.

"You need to know," Heidi said, "that Cerys's father has

applied for custody. Good practice guides us to maintain familial relationships, as having the best long-term outcomes for the child."

"What if the kid's father murdered her mother?" Sasha wanted to grab the cake and throw the policy-spouting moron out of the house.

Heidi nodded slowly. "Well, that would make a difference, certainly. But we don't yet know that's what happened. For now, we're minded to leave Cerys with you and your fiancé, but there's a long way to go before anything more permanent."

***

Mal saw the stack of files and notes on his desk and felt as if he was walking into chaos. He knew that it was an unreasonable way to feel, and that the chaos was in his head, and outside in the world. Keeping his surroundings neat and polished was one way of imposing order. He knew what he was doing, and why he was doing it, but the untidy pile of paper still irritated the hell out of him.

The documents in question were the investigation and inquest reports into the raft race accident. He gathered them all up, shuffled them together neatly and put them in his briefcase and rang Daniel to ask if he had time for coffee.

"I'll order it now," Daniel said, and Mal could hear the familiar sounds of their favourite cafe in the background: background murmuring, the clatter of crockery and the *oooof* as someone opened the ill-fitting door with their shoulder. Five minutes later he sat down opposite Daniel, two coffees balanced precariously on a tiny table. Daniel tried to move in his chair, and the table wobbled alarmingly, splashing coffee into their saucers. Around them, people, were conversing in Welsh. It slowly dawned Mal that he could understand most of what was being said. Since he'd spoken in Welsh to Carey, he had started using the language a little at a time, every day, and not just to Daniel. His outburst to Carey had shaken something loose in his mind and he was losing his fear of the Welsh language. Was he finally settling into small town life?

"I always thought the people in this cafe were just gossiping," he said. "But most of them are talking about politics."

"Why do you think we always come in here?"

Mal shrugged. "Because they let you bring the dog? Because they do good cake?"

Daniel looked at him with pity in his eyes. "I thought you were supposed to be a detective. Look at the noticeboards: Green Party meetings, yoga, vegan cookery, even the Community Allotment. This is the place for us alternative types in Melin to get our caffeine and sugar fix."

"I just follow your lead, as ever. If this is the cafe you go to, this will be the cafe I go to."

They smiled at each other and it felt nice. Cosy and domestic. A couple meeting each other for coffee, like people whose business wasn't murder. People who were planning to get married. Daniel reached over and squeezed Mal's hand. "Why did you want to meet?"

"I've got your inquest files, and I've talked to Hector. He doesn't think Pandy's death was suicide, but he's getting a second opinion tomorrow. He thinks Pandy was killed in the same way as Hayden Bennion, although in completely different circumstances. No surprise that the ACC wants it to have been suicide and the Hayden Bennion case closed."

"You're not going to close it though?"

Mal shook his head. "Not if I can help it. I believe Hector. Pandy was murdered. Two people connected to those allotments, both dead within a few days of each other. I can't pretend it doesn't set alarm bells ringing."

"And the accident at the raft race. They were both connected to that. Rhys Bennion says that Hayden provided the wood for the raft, so there's a connection. There's something there, I'm sure."

"There's something else too. We can't get hold of Pandy's ex-husband. I asked Bethan to try and contact him, and she can't. I mean, obviously she will, but she hasn't yet. If Pandy was murdered, James Melton has to be the prime suspect. He threatened her in open court, and got sent down for it."

Daniel had found a pen from somewhere and was scribbling on a napkin. It was something he did when he was thinking. Mal knew that the words would be meaningless to anyone, possibly including Daniel himself.

"What I want to know is," Daniel began, "how did Carey know to use the threat of James Melton? Because he was completely evil, Carey I mean. He almost broke the door down, and was aggressive before there was any need to be. He's straight in there with *Come and answer our questions or we'll tell your violent ex where to find you.* He even suggested that he would arrest her and make sure James Melton knew where Cerys was. It was completely over the top. And he had to have got the information before he turned up at Pandy's house."

"There before you, Dan. Well, almost. I asked who had been accessing the records of the injunctions on James Melton, in the weeks before the murder, and the answer was no one."

They both considered the implications of this. Daniel spoke first. "Do we think Carey knows James Melton? Or is that a conspiracy too far?"

Mal's phone buzzed with a text message.

Sasha: long story short, social services say that Pandy's ex is applying to the courts for custody of Cerys. H and I will oppose. We're applying to be temporary foster carers. We have very temporary 'custody', emphasis on Very Temporary.

"Maybe not such a far-fetched idea," Mal said, turning the phone so that Daniel could see the message. "I assume Sasha is telling me this so I can furnish her with all the details of James Melton's misdeeds. Which I will."

Daniel had a sudden flash of envy of Sasha, and her ability

to add to her family. The thoughts were outrageous, and rational Daniel knew no one wanted to gain a child like this. To be jealous was to wish Pandy dead, and he didn't. His emotions must have shown on his face.

"What's up?" The coffee was gone, and Mal should have been back at work. Daniel picked their coffee cups up and took them over to the counter.

"Two more, please," he said and went back to the wobbly table. "Hector and Sasha will get permission for temporary care of Cerys. And that's right, Maldwyn, it is. But..." He blinked hard as the tears started, surprising him with their suddenness, and the intensity of the sadness that produced them.

Mal held Daniel's hand, not moving as their new coffees arrived. "But you're thinking about your own need for a child. And if I know you at all, feeling guilty about it."

"You do know me. It just came at me out of the blue. Sorry."

"Dan, if you decide you want children, we'll look into having children. See, that was easy. Now, if we could sort out who killed Hayden Bennion and Pandy, ideally in the next day or two, I'd be a happy man."

***

Daniel unpacked the files from Mal's briefcase and started reading. The story was a tragic one, but not complicated. The raft race was held every year, and although there had been capsizes and crashes, any injuries had been minor. The canoe club had checked the course for obstacles before the race, the St John Ambulance people were in attendance, and there were always plenty of spectators and officials with towels, blankets and hot drinks. No one under sixteen was allowed to compete. Prizes were given for well decorated rafts, for crossing the finish line first, or because the organisers felt like it. The event was a light-hearted, if chilly start to the new year. As he read, Daniel remembered that his parents had taken him to the race when he and Megan were small, and there had always been pictures in the local paper.

Daniel read the eye witness accounts from the day of the accident, catching his breath when he saw a statement from Miss Pandora Nicholson. All the accounts were the same. Two rafts had collided, and as the rafters had tried to push themselves loose, Pandy's raft had tipped up, throwing all four of them into the water. After that, things got confused. People from other rafts tried to help. Pandy was pulled onto another raft, Dylan and Rhys made it to the bank on their own. In the melée, it took everyone a few minutes to realise that only three people had been rescued.

I saw a girl get pulled out of the water and I thought it was Merren, Dylan Davies' statement read. *Then when I looked again she wasn't there. It was a raft with all girls and I was confused. We had got out of the water OK. It was freezing cold, but I never felt in any danger. I saw Rhys and Pandy and I assumed Merren had got out too, that I just hadn't seen her.*

Merren's body was found very soon afterwards. The autopsy found that she had a head injury, probably from being struck by one of the rafts, and that she had drowned. The coroner ruled that the death was 'a tragic accident'.

Daniel found the original autopsy report. Merren's head injury was a blow to the back of the neck at the base of the skull. Hector's words came back to him. *Bashed and drowned.*

19

AS IF HE KNEW

Three people had died in the same way. Hit on the back of the head and then drowned. But that was all the deaths had in common. Merren's death was an accident; Pandy's death *might* have been an accident. The only definite murder was Hayden Bennion. Daniel turned it over and over. The three were connected to the raft race accident, but only Pandy and Merren had been on the raft. Hayden Bennion may have been a spectator--particularly as his son had been on the raft--but so were hundreds of other people.

Daniel could imagine the scene: a day like today, cold and damp. People wrapped up in woolly hats, scarves and mittens, wearing waterproof coats and wellies against the wet grass. The river brown and turgid, but flowing faster than it appeared, so all the rafters had to do was stay afloat and away from the banks—paddling was optional. Most people would be on the side of the river away from the town. That side was flat, used as a park, football and rugby pitches, but it was often soggy underfoot. When the river burst its banks, this was where the water went first. On the other side, the land was also flat for a few yards then rose up towards the town. The river walk was on that side. From his reading of the investigation reports, it was on the town side that Pandy, Rhys and Dylan had got out of the river. Whether this was significant, Daniel didn't know. He wanted to talk to Rhys, to ask him for his recollections, but he had no excuse to barge in to a house mourning a husband and father. And he wanted to find out what had happened to Dylan Davies. Eluned had said that he'd died, but that was all. There were just too many things he didn't know.

***

Mal was looking at DI Carey's personnel file. Carey had been married twice, and divorced twice. He didn't know what to do with that information. Was it significant or not? He turned his chair away from the desk so he could stare out of the window, but despite the view of distant hills, nothing much registered. On the other side of his office door, he could hear people talking, the bang of doors on the floor below, and the hum of the inadequate heating system. He let it all blur into one background buzz, and thought about what Daniel had said about Carey's behaviour. *Aggressive when he didn't need to be. Knew about Pandy's ex before he arrived.* Everything was telling Mal that Carey had decided on Pandy's guilt before he'd gone to question her. He re-ran the events in his mind.

Daniel found the body about six o'clock. He'd taken Pandy home less than an hour later, and Carey had brought Pandy in for her first interview before nine. He *must* have known about Pandy's ex before the murder was even discovered. Which suggested that Carey had information that he planned to use against Pandy, and the murder was the excuse he needed to use it. Or did Carey routinely collect information like this *just in case?* No, that wouldn't fly. Carey was from north Wales, but not from Melin Tywyll. He couldn't be very deeply entrenched in the local gossip because he simply hadn't had time.

None of it fitted with Carey's lazy approach to investigation. It fitted with his bigotry—Pandy was exactly the kind of person who would push all his buttons. But the person who hated Pandy most of all was James Melton. Melton had threatened Pandy in court, and now he was trying to claim custody of their daughter. Mal spun his chair round back to the desk and rang Bethan.

"Any sign of James Melton?"

"Not so far, sir."

"Can you find out what connections he has in this area? Here, Wrexham, the coast? When they were married, they lived in Liverpool, and Pandy didn't come back until after the divorce. I want to know if Melton has any friends here."

Specifically, whether he has a friend called Adam Carey.

***

Rhys Bennion pulled into the drive of his old home and switched the engine off with relief. His memories of the narrow winding Welsh roads had been horribly accurate, and he was shattered. The house was a dull red brick semi-detached with a bay window at the front, on a street of almost identical houses. The front gardens had almost all been paved over for car parking since he'd been there last, and more of the street trees were gone. He thought of the steadily rising temperatures in his adopted homeland, and wondered whether anyone here would get the message before it was too late. He saw the front door begin to open and his heart sank. Please let it not be his mother.

Thankfully it was Eluned. She smiled at him and they hugged.

"Jesus, I'm dead on my feet," he said.

Eluned carried his bag and led him into the kitchen, unchanged by the looks of it. "Mum's having a lie down. We keep getting the neighbours round chattering on about the police finding out who did it so we can have 'closure', whatever that means."

"It means they can stop worrying about it, I guess."

Eluned put the kettle on and found the biscuit tin.

"Is that the same biscuit tin we had as kids, or does she get another one the same every year?" Rhys asked. "I'd forgotten how much I hate this place."

The kitchen was clean and deeply unfashionable. The colours were a bright yellow and royal blue: tiles and curtains featuring blue bowls of lemons. Yellow napkins were folded on the counter top, and a blue casserole dish stood on the stove. Everything matched. From the smell, he thought his sister had been making some kind of vegetable stew. He hoped for dumplings. It felt like dumpling weather. Rhys thought this kitchen was aiming for the bright and sunny feeling of his own kitchen in Australia, only without the actual sunshine, and he counted his blessings again.

"It's not so bad here. Not all the time anyway. I met an old schoolfriend, Daniel Owen. He wanted to know about the raft race--you know, the accident."

"Because of Pandy?"

"No, because of Dad. Daniel found Dad's body."

"Dad wasn't even *there*."

"I couldn't remember the name of the girl who died. How awful is that?"

"Merren Jones. I'll never forget it. It's like you burble along thinking you're safe, and the world is an OK place. Then something like that happens and everything changes. Why did Merren die, and not me, or someone off another raft? It's completely random. Someone's life taken away for no reason." He'd never said anything like that to Eluned before. She'd been fifteen when the accident happened, and he'd been about to graduate from university. It had felt like they were from different generations. They'd built their relationship over email and Skype when he didn't come back from Australia and she moved further and further away from home. She'd seen his family over the internet, and he'd 'met' her partner, and seen the birds they monitored.

"Is that why you moved away?"

"One reason. Every time I saw a river, or heard one, the memory came back. Not like PTSD or anything, just not being able to forget. Australia seemed like the logical choice."

"You sound like a proper Aussie when you say that." They smiled at each other.

"I am a proper Aussie, Eluned. I'm not a Welsh boy any more." Despite himself, Rhys yawned. The endless journey was catching up with him.

"You should talk to Daniel Owen. He was a friend of Pandy, and I think he knows what's going on in the police."

"I'm the last one, you know. Merren, then Dylan and now Pandy. I'm sorry, Eluned, you didn't need all this. I'm knackered, I'm missing Ellie's birthday, and when you told me about Pandy, it all came back. I think I'm going to go and have a lie down of my own. But I will go and talk to your mate if you want me to."

***

Bethan knocked at Mal's office door, even though it was already open. He waved her in.

"I've been thinking about the dope-growing rumour, and looking into James Melton like you asked," she began. Mal thought she looked uncomfortable, and he had a fair idea about why—Bethan was a rule-follower. He wasn't supposed to be a hands-on investigator any longer, but he was acting like one, without going through the chain of command. She was giving him the benefit of the doubt, but only because they had known each other for a while, and because she knew he was a rule-follower too. Except when he wasn't, like now.

"There's something wrong here, Bethan. I don't know what it is, but I'm going to find out, and to do that I need to be able to trust people. That's why I asked for your help. Because I do trust you." He hoped she would see that he meant his words and that they weren't empty flattery. He did trust Bethan. She didn't lie, and she knew Melin Tywyll as well as Daniel did. "But if this makes you uncomfortable, then I won't ask again."

Bethan moved in her seat, making herself a bit more comfortable. He caught a whiff of her perfume, and heard the rustle of her jacket lining against the chair. He watched her face and saw the tiniest relaxation of the muscles around her lips.

"Can I ask you a question, sir?"

"Of course."

"Why did you drag DI Carey and Abby up to your house to search for cannabis? Abby told me you made them walk for miles through the woods, even though there couldn't possibly be any cannabis growing outside at this time of year."

Decision time. Mal chose to take a chance.

"Do you want a good answer or the truth?"

"Don't tell me anything that I might have to report."

Mal smiled. "I'll risk it. I think DI Carey started that rumour about Daniel growing dope. The notion that it's good for pain and therefore OK made it credible, even to people who know Daniel—like you." Bethan blushed slightly. "But round here, people would have come to their senses in a day or two. Not so at HQ. Once the rumour reached them, I'd have been suspended, or at the very least investigated. You know all that. If I'm right and DI Carey started the rumour, it would have reached HQ straight away."

"You wanted to stop it before it got any further."

"And it worked." Mal grinned. "I'm sorry to have put Abby through an evening tramping through soggy woods in the dark, but I'm not a bit sorry that DI Carey had to do the same. But pleasant as it was to take revenge on DI Carey for trying to cause trouble, I want to know why he did it."

"Because he's a bigot? People talk about how much they liked working for DI Owen, and DI Carey must know that," Bethan offered. "He's a racist, he hates gay people and he certainly doesn't think much of women. So he saw the chance to have a pop at you and DI Owen, and took it."

"That's what I thought. But he could have done it any time. Why wait until now?"

Mal watched Bethan as she worked her way through the implications. She'd been a detective as long as he had, and a police officer for longer. Her skills might be organisational, and she avoided intuitive leaps or gut feelings like she would avoid a runaway train, but she was no one's fool. He wanted to know whether she would see the same pattern that he had.

"Because Carey wanted you and DI Owen out of the way of the Hayden Bennion murder case? But that makes no sense. Why would he want to do that?"

"There's more." Mal told Bethan what Daniel had said about Carey's aggressive behaviour towards Pandy on the evening of the murder. Bethan looked confused.

"It's like he had a suspect lined up, before there was anything to suspect her of," she said. "As if he knew the murder was going to happen."

20

COUNTING THE TILES

aniel decided that another sojourn in the Lion was more than he could bear, so he agreed to meet Eluned and Rhys, in the Three Horseshoes, close to where he lived. An easy walk for him, and he could take Flora. He had barely settled into a pleasant corner table, close, but not too close, to the fire, when Eluned and Rhys arrived. Daniel stood up to welcome them, and offer to get drinks. Rhys was almost his height, though much broader and heavier, tanned from life in a sunny country, with receding hair and the look of a man who has spent far too long on an aeroplane. Flora looked at the newcomers hopefully, then settled back down to sleep when no treats were forthcoming.

"You want to know about the raft race?" Rhys asked when they were settled, his Australian accent vying with the Welsh.

"I know the basics," Daniel said. 'What happened and when, but I don't know much about the people involved. I met Pandy a few weeks ago, and she never mentioned it, but from what Eluned told me, it had a big impact on her life."

"On everyone's life," Rhys answered. "I never really came home again after it happened. Went back to uni, finished my degree and set off to see the world. I started in Australia, and didn't get any further. I made one visit home with my wife, while Josh was still a baby, and after that we had more kids and we couldn't afford it. I told Eluned earlier, I couldn't forget Merren's death, and everything here was a reminder. Then I heard about Pandy." Rhys shook his head, as if despairing at what the world had come to.

"What can you tell me about Merren and Dylan?" Daniel asked.

Rhys took a deep breath, and a drink from his pint.

"Don't know where to start really. Dylan and me were mates from school, and we always got together in the university holidays. We hung out with Pandy and a couple of others. Pandy and I were sort of going out, like, not exclusive, but we always seemed to finish up together when we were both here. It was different for Dylan and Merren. They'd been together for a year, and it was pretty serious. She was in the year below us at school but they didn't get together until after they went to uni. They were both at Aberystwyth, doing different things, and met at a party."

Rhys stopped, clearly remembering those days. He took another drink and carried on. "I don't know whose idea it was to do the raft race. Once it was suggested, it took on a life of its own. Because this was probably the last year we'd all be together in Melin at New Year. We blagged the barrels from some other rafters who had too many, I got Dad to give me a load of waste wood from the timber yard and we sort of tied it all together. It was a raft, but only just. Merren insisted on painting it with flowers and butterflies and things. We used up any bits of paint we could find. We had a crazy couple of days between Christmas and New Year putting it all together in Pandy's garden. Pandy's mum kept bringing us drinks and mince pies and stuff. You know her parents were killed in the

2004 Tsunami? Pandy almost went with them, but she had a new class to prepare for, and didn't want to be a gooseberry."

Daniel nodded, thinking that Pandy must have had survivor's guilt from the raft race, and then again from her parents' deaths. Perhaps it was not surprising that she dedicated her life to spiritual practices and educating children about how to make things grow. Or maybe that was cod psychology, and he should stick to things he knew about. He backtracked a bit.

"Pandy had a new class?"

"She trained as a primary school teacher, didn't you know? She taught at a school in a poor area of Liverpool, and someone had left, so she was taking over their class."

"I wouldn't have guessed," Daniel said, remembering how anxious Pandy had been, and how she praised him for the children's activities he'd organised, when she must have had years more experience.

Eluned finished her pint and stood up to go to the bar for more. "That bloke she married knocked all the stuffing out of her. She lost all her confidence. Said she wasn't going back to teaching in a school. Bastard." She pointed her glass at her brother and then Daniel.

Rhys shook his head, "I'll drive back."

Daniel nodded, and asked Rhys what had happened after the accident.

"Everyone disappeared. I went back to uni, and lost touch with Pandy and Dylan. It was like I didn't want to talk to them and be reminded. We probably should have stuck together, if only for Dylan's sake, but we were twenty, twenty-one, and didn't know how to behave. Or maybe that was just me. Mum told me Dylan's parents moved away, and then later, I heard that Merren's mother had become a vicar. I only found out that Dylan had died because someone said something on Facebook about it to Eluned. Neither of us felt we could start being nosy and asking for more information at that point."

Eluned came back with the drinks.

"I should have made an effort to stay in touch," Rhys said. "I wanted to forget Melin Tywyll, and rivers and everything to do with them. Then we started having babies..."

The atmosphere around the table was subdued. Daniel wanted to know more about Dylan Davies, where and why his family had moved away, and more about Merren's family. He sensed Rhys and Eluned had told all they knew, but he did have one last question. "This is going to sound insensitive, but what about your parents?"

"Dad went off me when I started going out with girls," Eluned said. "I hoped Mum would be on my side, so to speak, but she wasn't. There weren't any big rows, we just had less and less contact."

"I was the golden child," said Rhys. "I provided grandchildren, only they wouldn't come to see them. They wanted us to come here. Have you any idea what it costs to fly a family of five from Sydney to England? But fair play, we do Skype a lot, and Mum and Dad both took an interest in the kids, and the kids know they've got grandparents in Wales as well as in Australia. Dad probably didn't want to leave his precious allotment for a trip down under."

"But you came now?" Daniel asked.

"You kind of have to, don't you? I couldn't leave it all to Eluned. Mum's a bit of a stranger to be honest, but she's still my mum."

***

"So now you see why I want to know about James Melton, and whether he's got any connection to this area." Mal studied the 'teak' laminate on his police-issue desk. Men were supposed to like lots of dark brown furniture, at least in magazines, but he'd inherited this from his predecessor, who had left on maternity leave, and looked unlikely to return. He had come to prefer light and colour after spending time with Daniel. Though they would prise the keys to his glossy black car from his cold, dead hands. He tuned back in to the moment. Bethan looked shell shocked by the implications of what they were discussing. "I'll find James Melton," she said. "By the time I've finished, I'll know everything about him, including what colour his pyjamas are and what he had for breakfast. Charlie's back tomorrow, and he can do some of it."

"Be careful," Mal said. "You know Charlie was attacked on his way home from the wine bar. What you don't know is that earlier in the evening, Daniel and Charlie had a meeting in the wine bar. They were seen together by PC Kelley, who as we know is DI Carey's best mate. It could be a coincidence, or it could be something else. To be on the safe side, let's assume it's not a coincidence."

If possible, Bethan looked even more shocked. The colour had drained from her face, leaving her normally olive toned skin almost yellow. "Are you thinking that DI Carey was involved in *killing* Pandy, because..." her voice trailed off. She sat up in her chair. "Because," she said in a stronger voice, "I know a lot of people thought Pandy was a hippy do-gooder with her head in the clouds, but she was a gentle soul, who had every bit of rotten luck going. She didn't deserve this." The colour was back in her cheeks. "But that doesn't explain who killed Hayden Bennion."

And that was the problem, Mal thought. Taken to its logical conclusion, if Carey was involved—somehow— n killing Pandy, he must have been involved in killing Bennion, or at the very least, he must have known that Bennion was going to die.

"Isn't this all getting a bit Area 51, or QAnon?" Bethan asked.

"DI Carey is really one of the lizard people." Mal answered and their smiles broke the tension. "I don't know. Yes, Carey is a bigot, and he's a terrible DI. But I'm not ready to convict him without evidence."

"I'll look for it, sir."

"No, Bethan, *I'll* look for it. You get in touch with James Melton, and arrange an interview, but not here. Find out as much about him as you can. He wants custody of his daughter, so he's been in contact with social services here in Melin. Start with them. Actually don't. Talk to Inspector Harrington about the domestic abuse report on Pandy Melton."

***

Bethan read and re-read the report, until her eyes blurred. James Melton has essentially imprisoned his wife, tracking her movements throughout the day. She was expected to phone him at break times and immediately school finished each day. Any missed calls or lateness earned her a beating, or threats of one. Social workers had been called repeatedly by Cerys's teachers and doctors. The police had been called by Pandy's workmates and her doctor. She'd spent time in hospital, and the hospital had called the police. But Pandy was too frightened to take the help on offer. A statement from Cerys simply said: "Dad said he was going to kill Mum, unless she did what he said. When she did what he said, it was OK. I was scared when he got angry. I thought he would hurt Mum."

But what made Bethan want to throw things was the way Pandy had tried to leave. She took the report into the Ladies toilets because she didn't want anyone in the CID office to see her with it, or to read how Pandy had tried to kill herself and Cerys, and how Cerys had rung 999 when her mother lost consciousness. She sat on the broken chair by the basins and read the pages of legal argument, and psychological reports, police and social services reports, interviews with witnesses, and finally the findings of the court that sent James Melton to prison. Not for the way he treated his wife and daughter, but for his persistent swearing and ranting at the judge. He was taken away by court officers, vowing to kill Pandy as soon as he was released. By the end, Bethan was shaking, cold with sweat and with the dampness of the room seeping into her bones. Her body was stiff with tension. To drag herself away from the horrors, she breathed in the disinfectant, soap and the remnants of her colleagues' perfumes and hairsprays. She listened to the dripping tap, and the one overflowing cistern, and counted the tiles above the sinks.

Then she put the reports into their folder, put them under her arm and went to knock on Mal's door for the second time. He looked as though he hadn't moved.

"Sir, isn't it just as likely that DI Carey has it right? That Pandy killed Bennion because he behaved like her ex, trying to control the Community Allotment, and her? And then she killed herself? She's got previous, and she tried to kill the child."

Mal looked at her, and his face softened. She was always aware of his good looks, but they became part of the wallpaper after a while. But when he really looked at her, she was struck by his beautiful eyes and the way the hint of five o'clock shadow framed his face. *He should have been an actor.*

"Daniel and Hector both say it wasn't suicide."

"Both have been wrong before, sir."

21

DIVORCE IS A THING

Daniel stood in the quiet polytunnel. It had creaked and groaned a little in the high winds the day before, but now it was warm, and slightly humid, the only sounds those Daniel was making as he checked his grapevines, felt the temperature of the soil and decided not to begin planting out. *Nature always catches up.* The forecast was for more storms, and even snow. *Give it a bit longer.* He had promised to keep the Community Allotment going with Lizzie and Beth's help, and he would go there tomorrow. For now, he needed his fingers in his own soil.

Flora snuffled at his feet, sticking like velcro as dusk and her dinner time approached. He left the polytunnel, carefully closing the door and sliding the bolt home, and went to check on the other one. There was still chard and kale in the raised beds, and the very last of the purple sprouting broccoli. He decided on the broccoli for dinner, in cheese sauce, with roast potatoes, and whatever root vegetables were left in the fridge. If Mal made it home to eat at a reasonable hour, fine; if not, it would heat up.

Thinking about his garden and cooking helped him relax.

He was aware of a part of his mind mulling over the Bennion killing and the raft race accident, but he left it alone to mull, and concentrated on the here and now. On the sound of the owls in the woods, the smell of the earth and the scent of rain on the breeze. He wasn't ready to go inside, so he sat on a strategically placed log, with his hands full of produce and the dog on his feet. It was cold, but now the wind had dropped, not too cold to give himself five minutes to look at the sky, and the growing shadows in the valley below.

If I had children, I wouldn't need to keep worrying about what to do with my life.

It was a thought he had been pushing away for a while. He felt that he understood his women friends who talked of the 'biological clock ticking'. At the same time, he questioned himself. Was he trying to avoid making decisions? Was it fair to bring a child into a household where one member worked almost non-stop? He didn't know, but not thinking about it wasn't working either.

He wished he could have talked it over with Pandy. He loved Sasha, but things had a tendency to be black and white for her: make a choice and take the consequences. Pandy had seemed to understand that for Daniel, everything was in greyscale. Thinking about Pandy brought Dylan Davies's death to the forefront of his mind. A puzzle he could get to grips with, maybe even solve. He would try by himself, and if he had to, he would take advantage of one of his friends. But he would find out how and when Dylan had died. He took the dinner ingedients into the kitchen, collecting his laptop and setting it up on the kitchen table.

When Mal got home, Daniel was scribbling notes from the laptop screen. The oven was belting out heat, and the sink was full of pots and pans.

Daniel looked up. "Dylan Davies drowned," he said. "The coroner ruled it murder by person or persons unknown. He lived in Birmingham. There had been a series of gay-bashings, and he was walking late at night in an area where gay men had been attacked, so the police hypothesised that this was another in the series. He was found the next morning in the canal. There was no suggestion that he was gay, or had been to any of the gay venues. He was on his way home from a colleague's leaving do. Dinner should be ready soon."

"Hello to you too," said Mal. "How was the rest of your day?"

Daniel put his finger in the top of Mal's waistband and pulled him closer. "I may have been obsessing, but I've made dinner as well. So don't grump."

Mal ran his fingers through Daniel's curls, and bent down to whisper into Daniel's ear. "I'm not grumping."

A hot wave of desire swept over Daniel and he ran his hands over Mal's thighs and arse. "Show me how not grumpy you are."

Mal helped Daniel to his feet and kissed him gently, holding Daniel's face in his hands. Daniel felt their bodies melt together, heat tingling to the ends of his fingers. Mal's arousal, was obvious, and then the kiss wasn't gentle any more. Mal's muscular body was hard against his own, and he wanted to feel it skin to skin. He pulled his own sweatshirt off and started undoing Mal's tie and shirt buttons, running his fingers over Mal's chest to find the nipple ring, playing with it until Mal's breath was coming in gasps, and Daniel could feel him tremble.

"Hang on, let me help..." Mal lifted his shirt over his head and dropped it onto the kitchen table. Daniel bent to run his tongue over Mal's nipples, while his hands flicked open the button on Mal's trousers and pulled the zip down, and pushed them down to his ankles. Then he began tormenting Mal, nuzzling against his erection through Mal's boxers, as Mal ran increasingly urgent fingers through Daniel's curls.

Suddenly Mal stopped.

"What?" Daniel asked.

"I have another plan." He stepped out of his trousers, picked Daniel up bodily and carried him into the living room, dumping him unceremoniously onto the sofa. "Get your clothes off and stay there."

Daniel shivered, and not from the cold. Mal came back with a towel and lube. "I am so done with you torturing me. It's my turn."

***

"Tell me again about Dylan Davies?" Mal said, as they sprawled half-dressed on the couch afterwards, pretending not to notice as Flora edged her way onto Mal's lap.

"He drowned. In one of the restored canals in the centre of Birmingham. You know, the posh bit with all the nice flats and coffee bars. The attacker or attackers must have got lucky, because it's usually pretty busy. The police said he might have been attacked in a side street and then dumped in the canal, unconscious. Is this setting off any alarm bells for you? Bashed and drowned?"

"Maybe."

"Three of the people on that raft have died in almost the same way, along with the man who supplied the wood to build the raft. I told you, Hayden Bennion gave the rafters the wood from where he worked at the timber yard."

"But..."

"I know all the 'buts'. Except I don't believe them. I believe Hector, and I would put money on Dylan Davies having been hit on the back of the head before being pushed into the canal to drown."

Mal decided that there were things he should share. "But what you don't know is that Pandy almost killed herself and Cerys three years ago. Cerys called the police, and that's what got them away from James Melton. She was very lucky to be allowed to keep Cerys afterwards, and there was *a lot* of psychiatric help and social services observation. It would be fairer to say that James Melton blew it in court, by swearing at the judge and threatening to kill Pandy repeatedly. Also, Cerys was an amazing witness for a child. Very clear that her dad was a violent monster. Even with Hector's testimony, it's going to be hard to prove that Pandy didn't commit suicide, given the pressure Carey put her under. I'm sorry, love, but we're still left with only one death that is unequivocally a murder."

"Hayden Bennion. But if you were convinced that Pandy was murdered, would you look into Dylan Davies?"

"I'll look into Dylan Davies anyway. Only you have to think about an alternative to your raft race scenario. Our killer, or killers, might be much closer to home." Mal talked Daniel through his conversations with Bethan.

***

Rhys Bennion had driven himself and Eluned back to the family home, both feeling guilty about having left their mother with yet another neighbour, and the Valium prescribed by her GP. As Rhys had predicted, his mother alternated between anger and grief. Missing his father, while at the same time berating him for never having been around, for spending his time *at that bloody allotment.* No one knows what goes on in a marriage except the people in it, Rhys thought; unoriginal, but true. He wondered why his mother had put up with being abandoned for a bunch of old geezers talking about fertiliser and the diseases of onions. He also wondered whether why his father had preferred the allotments to a comfortable, home.

"Did Dad always spend his life at the allotment?" Rhys asked Eluned, when their mother had gone to bed. "I remember him going there a few times a week, but he was around here too. We got taken on outings, went on holiday as a family, that kind of thing. Or am I misremembering?"

Eluned sipped from the whisky Rhys had bought from the duty-free shop on his endless flight. "He did the garden here too," she said. "Built a climbing frame and a swing. And a sand-pit. Lots of lawn, and a football goal for you and your mates. He took the goal away when you stopped being obsessed, and put that bench and table in. Said my friends and I could have a gossip spot in the summer. So yes, he must have been here. But looking at the garden now, he hasn't been around much lately."

"It's February though. No garden looks good in February."

"Ours does. And we're in Shetland."

Rhys gestured with the whisky bottle, and Eluned put another splash into her glass.

"Do you think he started spending all his time there after we left? Another victim of the accident?"

They sat and drank in silence for a while.

"I'm not going to feel guilty about it," Eluned said decisively. "I was still here after you went to Oz, and it was his choice to disapprove of me. Mum had choices too. She looks like crap now, but she didn't always. Think about when we talk on Skype. She looks fine, better than me most of the time. If he drove her mad, she could have left. So could he. They aren't destitute—selling this place would make enough for them each to get somewhere of their own."

Another silence, then Rhys spoke, his voice a little slurred from the whisky. He wasn't used to drinking much, not with three kids in the house. He imagined his sister and Maraid, with a bottle between them each evening as the wind howled outside. That was all there was to do in Scotland, right? "People their age get divorced all the time. It's a Thing, apparently. At least we know Dad didn't have another woman. There wasn't room in his life for anything except the allotment, by all accounts."

The idea that their mother might have another man came to them at the same time, and at the same time they shook their heads and rejected the thought.

"Except," said Rhys, "she takes care of her appearance,

wears nice clothes, and if he left her all day, every day ... no, this is nonsense."

Nonetheless, it was nonsense he couldn't get out of his mind as he tossed and turned in his lumpy bed, regretting the last glass of whisky. *Maybe I should tell that detective? Maybe I should ask Mum?*

22

ME TOO

Bethan was in the CID office long before anyone else arrived. She stopped for a coffee on her way, from the cafe on the High Street. She didn't approve of disposable cups, so she took her own, one she'd bought in Marks & Spencer's. She started the day by dusting her own desk and Charlie's, which was at right angles to hers. Then she booted up her computer, and put her phone on to charge, just in case. There was an email from DI Carey saying that the morning briefing was postponed until eleven. The office was cold, and she got her spare fleece out of the drawer, put it on and warmed her hands on the coffee cup. She recognised that she was trying to soothe herself after the previous day's speculation. *My job is to get an interview with James Melton, and find out what he's been up to. When Charlie comes in, that's all he needs to know.*

And that was what she told him when he arrived. "I'll get onto social services, find the name of the solicitor and hopefully get something set up. You start finding out everything you can about the bloke. We don't even know what he does for a living."

Charlie lowered himself carefully into his chair, obviously

still stiff and sore from the assault, though the cuts and bruises were fading.

"Keep getting up and walking round," Bethan told him. "If you sit still for too long, you'll seize up."

"Yes, Mother," he said.

She laughed and picked up the phone to Clwyd Social Services.

"I need to contact Mr James Melton," she said after she'd introduced herself. "He has applied for custody of his daughter Cerys, and I'd like to talk to whoever is dealing with the case." She heard the rattle of fingers on a keyboard.

"That would be Heidi Potts. She's on extension 3405."

Bethan scribbled the name and number. "Can't you put me through?"

The answer came by rote. "Re-dial substituting the extension for the last four digits." The line went dead.

Bethan was not surprised that extension 3405 was went unanswered. There was a beep, as if there might have been voicemail, but no message.

She rang the main number again, and got the same unhelpful reception. No, there was no one else who could help. No, she had no idea when Heidi Potts would be back. No, she didn't know how Bethan could leave a message.

"I am investigating a murder," Bethan said through clenched teeth.

"I'm sorry to hear that," the bored voice said, "but I still don't know where Heidi Potts is."

Bethan didn't know Veronica, the social worker who lived with Sophie Harrington, personally but she needed to speak to a real person, or at the very least be able to leave a message for one, so she rang Sophie and asked for help. Sophie harrumphed down the phone. "All the social workers have mobiles. That woman you spoke to must have been stopped for speeding, because she's supposed to give the numbers out. Hold on, I'll get it for you."

How do people get help from social services when they need it? Half an hour after Bethan had started, she finally got to speak to Heidi Potts. Thirty seconds into the call, she regretted bothering. The social worker seemed to be one who believed the police were the enemy, and their motives always suspect.

"I don't want to arrest James Melton," Ms Potts. "I simply want to talk to him. With or without his solicitor, at a police station close to his home."

"Are you implying that Mr Melton has done anything that would jeopardise a relationship with his daughter?" Heidi sounded defensive, despite Bethan's assurances.

Bethan bared her teeth, and bit back *other than driving her mother to try to kill herself?* "I'm not implying anything, Ms Potts. I have simply requested to meet with Mr Melton. If you aren't able to give me his contact details, perhaps you would be kind enough to tell me who his solicitor is?"

With a great deal of audible huffing and puffing, Heidi Potts disclosed that Melton's solicitor was a Mr Pilkington, of Pilkington and Corning. When she looked it up, Pilkington and Corning was a London-based firm, with offices in the City.

"Why would James Melton have a London solicitor when he lives in Liverpool?" Bethan asked the largely empty office.

"If it's Pilkington and Corning, I can tell you." Charlie replied, pointing at his computer. Bethan walked across and looked over his shoulder. On the screen was the bottom of a web page, the bit which told you how to contact people and who designed the site. It read

LEGAL ADVICE:
  Pilkington and Corning, Solicitors
  Suite 14, 342 Armitage Lane

SE1 4NH

WEBSITE DESIGN:
  J Melton & co
  jmco.net.co.uk

"WHAT'S THE WEBSITE?" Bethan asked, and Charlie scrolled back up.

MENTOO: *a place for men to take back their power*

Do you think women have had things their way for too long? Is it time for fathers to be considered equally in divorce and custody cases? Or for a man's earnings to belong to him, rather than the wife he's kept for years? Shouldn't men have rights to their own children, instead of courts automatically favouring mothers?

*READ on to see if meNtoo can help **you**.*

"DEAR GOD," Bethan said.

"You're not wrong," Charlie replied. "There are pages of it. Loads of statistics and case studies, all about men who've been screwed over in divorces, or lost access to their kids. And then this bunch offers to help, with a few success stories thrown in —faces blanked out and names changed. There is even a scheme for blokes who haven't got any money to apply for a grant to pay their legal costs. I looked for a list of donors, but there isn't one. And the only contact is either via the solicitors, or via their website contact form. No email address, no phone number."

"So there's no way of knowing whether this is a front for the solicitors to drum up business, or a real organisation?"

"Nope. But I did look at the solicitor's website, and no prizes for guessing who designed it. J Melton and Co also has a website, and they do have contact details. The same ones we've been using to try to get hold of James Melton in Liverpool."

"I think it's time we talked to the Detective Super. But close that tab first and clear your search history."

Charlie gave Bethan an enquiring look, but did as he was asked.

There was a crash and Abby Price stumbled through the door, somehow managing not to drop the cardboard tray of coffees and pastries she was holding in one hand. She had a shoulder bag over the other arm, which had caught on the door handle.

"Bloody thing," she said, putting the tray safely down on the nearest desk. "Sorry Sarge, I know it's a paper cup, but I thought you wouldn't mind this once." She handed one cup to Bethan, and after sniffing the lid, another to Charlie. "Lots of sugar for you, Charlie-boy. No cupcakes though, you'll have to do with the last of the cinnamon rolls."

"Thanks Abby. What have we done to deserve this?" Bethan asked, sipping her coffee, and wondering about the effect of a cinnamon bun on her figure, before deciding to eat it first and worry later.

"*I*," said Abby, with some emphasis, "have just finished interviewing all the allotment committee members, and all the plot holders who live within walking distance of the site. *All* of them. A few of them even have alibis. I have drunk a lot of disgusting tea, and I was ready for something nice."

"Have you found anything, though?" Charlie wanted to know.

"I have found that Hayden Bennion was considered a bit weird, even for someone who spends all his time on an allotment. A few people said he could bore for Wales about his grandchildren—but he's never seen two of them, because they live in Australia and he won't leave his allotment for long enough to visit."

"Hardly a motive for murder, though," said Charlie.

"I don't know. Apparently he talked about them *constantly*. *Is* there anything else more irritating than talk about people you're never going to meet? Unless they're on the telly. Anyway. There was a David Jones too. He gave me the creeps. Kept asking me if I was married and saying how *important* marriage and family are. I couldn't wait to get out of *there*. And that lesbian couple who were supposed to be growing dope. They were pretty odd, but not creepy, unless you think wearing the same clothes and having the same haircut is creepy. They had an alibi, so it doesn't matter." Abby had managed to eat her bun and drink her coffee while sharing this information. Quite how she'd achieved this feat, Bethan wasn't sure.

"DC Price. Playing favourites, I see."

Abby all but screamed, leaping backwards and knocking the dregs of her coffee onto the desk.

"Sir," she gasped, "you gave me a shock."

"Calm down, officer," said Carey with a smirk. "I'm sorry to break up the mothers' meeting, but *does* anyone have anything to report? The briefing is a little late this morning, but His Queerness will be in attendance, and we don't want to keep him waiting."

The silence that greeted this was painful. In the end, it was Bethan who took a deep breath and grasped the nettle.

"I would rather you didn't talk about Superintendent Kent like that, sir. I have always found him to be an excellent officer, and I think he deserves our respect."

"I'm guessing you like the male model look then, sergeant? Has anyone got anything to report, or not?"

Bethan had blushed a deep red. Carey's casual bigotry had always been directed at civilians in the past, but now he was turning on them.

"We'll report at the briefing," she said. "Excuse me." Bethan needed to get out of Carey's presence before she lost her temper, or worse, cried. Abby followed her to the Ladies, and they looked at each other in shock.

"He keeps patting me," Abby said.

"Our foremothers stabbed men like that with hat pins," Bethan replied. "I'm thinking of buying some."

Abby laughed, which is what Bethan had hoped for. She didn't *want* to be mother here; she had two grown boys. But she would stand between Carey and the two DCs if she had to.

***

Mal sensed the strained atmosphere between Carey and the others as soon as he arrived in the briefing room. It wasn't as if things had been great before, but Bethan sat as stiffly as a shop-window mannequin, Abby looked frightened, and Charlie wasn't sprawling over three seats, or looking at his phone. Carey looked as he always did: like someone who was being forced to deal with his inferiors and didn't like it.

Bethan didn't wait for Carey to speak. "We haven't been able to make contact with James Melton, sir, but we do have his solicitors' details, and we'll be contacting them straight after this. Melton appears to be involved in a men's rights organisation, focussed on child custody disputes and what they perceive to be unfair divorce settlements."

Carey muttered something under his breath.

"Adam? Something to contribute?" Mal asked blandly.

"I said, what the fuck has this got to do with anything?"

Mal raised an eyebrow.

"Sir," Carey added, lip curling.

"I think it's what we call a *lead*. James Melton went to prison for persistently threatening his wife in court. Now his wife is dead. I think that makes him a person of interest, don't you?"

"The silly bitch killed herself. She murdered Bennion, then jumped in the river. She's got a history. Cunt."

"Either you moderate your language, Adam, or I'm going to have to ask you to leave. The evidence suggests that Mrs Melton may have been murdered." Mal said. He wondered where Carey had acquired the confidence to behave like this in front of so many witnesses. It worried him. Carey had no filters when it came to his thoughts, but in a group, he could usually manage to keep his vileness to his expressions rather than his words. Now it looked as though all bets were off.

They limped through the rest of the briefing, Carey contributing nothing, except for a few disdainful snorts. When Mal wrapped it up, Carey was out of the door before he could be stopped. Mal heard him head downstairs, for the exit, rather than upstairs to CID.

"Charlie, would you mind seeing if you can find out if DI Carey is having a smoke, or whether he's left?" Mal asked.

Two minutes later, Charlie was back with the news that Carey had got into his car and driven off.

23

LEADING NOWHERE

Mal was not so desperate for DI Carey's company that he wanted to send out a search party. He thought, perhaps fancifully, that the police station felt lighter without his sneering presence. Back in his office, he stared unseeingly out of the window again. Again, it was raining, the drizzle blowing like smoke across the hills and forests in the distance. Closer to, the trees lining the car park were as black as if they had been burned. Litter lay in front of the recycling bins, either because they hadn't been emptied, or because there was too much recycling for the collection period. In the rain, bits of cardboard adhered, soggily, to the tarmac. A Coke can rolled silently across the ground. He could hear the quiet buzzing of the light over his head, and his own breath. Daniel's meditation exercises were beginning to rub off on him. He heard himself whisper *this moment, this breath.* Except he didn't want to *notice* his dislike of Carey, he wanted to work out what it meant.

Carey obviously had an agenda, and presumably he would reveal it in his own time. If he didn't reappear without a good reason, Mal would have grounds for disciplinary action, and that would be fine. In the meantime, it looked as though he, Mal, would be running the murder investigation himself. He tried to draw the threads together in his mind.

Firstly, Carey's theory. Pandy had killed Hayden Bennion for reasons that seemed good to her, and then she'd killed herself. In support of that theory was its neatness, and Pandy's history of mental ill health. Against it were Daniel's certainty that Pandy had thought about suicide and rejected it, and Hector's autopsy findings. Hector's 'second opinion' should be confirming his findings (or not) later today. That would be far more conclusive than Pandy's friends insisting that she wasn't suicidal. In his experience, no one was ever suicidal according to their friends and family. He did wonder whether Pandy had the bodily strength to have murdered Hayden Bennion. On the other hand, she had discovered the body, and it was right next to her van, where her fingerprints and DNA would not be questioned.

Or she killed Bennion, and her own death was an accident?

Secondly, the raft race accident. Mal knew himself to be a plodder, a logical, linear, list-maker, and a follower of procedures. By contrast, Daniel was intuitive, and his intuitions were often right. It could be a complete coincidence that three of the four people on the raft were now dead, and so was the man who had supplied the wood to build it. Or, there might be someone targeting those people, twenty years later. He made a note to find a person to talk to in Birmingham to see if they could cast any further light on Dylan Davies's death. It also occurred to him that if there really was someone murdering raft-racers, Rhys Bennion could be in danger. His second note was to see how they might keep him safe.

Thirdly, James Melton. On paper, Melton was the obvious suspect. He'd threatened Pandy so regularly that he'd been sent to prison for it. He was connected with an organisation whose existence promoted the interests of allegedly oppressed husbands and fathers. Their online presence suggested that they believed in legal action rather than violence, but James Melton was a violent man — Mal was prepared to take Pandy and Cerys's words for that, over any denial from Melton. Daniel's description of Pandy's terror at the thought of her ex-husband finding out where she was hiding had the ring of truth.

Finally, and most disturbing: Carey himself. There was no escaping the idea that Carey must have gone to Pandy's house with the intention of using the threat of James Melton to intimidate her, and the clear implication was that he had the threat ready before the murder had been committed. The unpleasant little toad probably had the strength to kill both Bennion and Pandy, and he certainly intended to create a diversion by accusing Daniel of growing cannabis. He had friends in high places — Cowlishaw by report, and ACC Bowen by the way he tried to shut down the enquiry.

Conspiracy theories are not my thing. But if they were, I'd be looking for a membership list from meNtoo.

Mal felt ridiculous even entertaining the idea, but was it any more ridiculous than the idea that the competitors from a raft race twenty years ago were being picked off one-by-one? There was only one way to find out. He called Abby, Charlie and Bethan into his office. Three leads, three officers, leaving him with Carey. He outlined his ideas, sent Abby to liaise with Hector, and his 'second opinion', asking her to check about the possibility of an accident as the explanation for Pandy's death. Bethan already had the bit between her teeth about James Melton, and he gave Charlie the job of finding more about Dylan Davies, explaining Daniel's raft race theory. As he expected, Charlie liked the idea of trying to prove Daniel right. When they'd gone, he rang Sophie and asked her to put the Bennion household on a regular patrol. Then he went back to staring out of the window. It was time to call in favours, and he wasn't sure where to begin.

There was a sudden *ping* from his phone, announcing a text from Abby.

DC Price: Did you see that I've finished interviewing all the plot holders and committee members? I forgot to mention. Sorry.

***

Hector found himself in a space both familiar and strange. It was his own autopsy suite, but he wasn't doing an autopsy. Instead, Chris Mills, the pathologist from Aberystwyth, was poring over sections of tissue Hector had taken from Pandy's body and murmuring 'mmmmhmmm' to himself. Chris was completely engrossed, clearly unaware that he was making a sound. Tatty jeans poked out from underneath his lab coat and his feet were encased in mismatched sports socks and a pair of crocs in a purple camouflage pattern. The coat itself had seen better days—clean but patterned with old ink stains. Hector's colleague had long hair, tied back; not by design, Hector thought, but because he forgot to get it cut. An odour of cigarette smoke hovered near where Chris worked. But he was a terrific pathologist.

The microscopes were set up on a lab bench, next to a dog-eared notebook, covered in impenetrable scribbles. Hector perched on a lab stool, sipping from his mug of coffee and waiting for Chris to finish. It looked like taking a while. As he had done ever since Pandy's death, he let his mind wander to Cerys, and the possibility of being able to keep her with them. That he and Sasha could provide a home for the child was not in doubt—if social services would agree—but he had no idea how they were going to manage the practicalities. Sasha was juggling already, and would need more lab time to finish her degree. He knew she would give it up for the children, but that was hardly fair, given that she had spent most of the last ten years working as a cleaner before finally getting to follow her dream of studying biomedical science. He sighed, and Chris looked up from the microscope, realised that Hector wasn't trying to attract his attention and went back to work.

There was a tentative knock on the door. Hector slid off the stool and went to see who was there.

"Hi, Abby, come on in," he said. Chris looked up again. "This is DC Abby Price. I'm guessing she's here to see if we've got any news."

Abby nodded.

"We haven't, not yet." Chris went back to scribbling.

"Come and have a coffee," Hector said to Abby who nodded again, this time a bit more eagerly. Hector's coffee was excellent. He'd bought himself a top-of-the-range machine when he'd realised how far it was to walk from the mortuary to the Costa Coffee by the hospital entrance. He led the way to his office and asked Abby to take a seat.

He thought Abby was probably modelling herself on Bethan Davies. Hair in a neat braid, tasteful skirt suit and low-heeled shoes. But Bethan had been working the look for decades, and Abby was too young and enthusiastic to pull it off with conviction. Hector imagined she went everywhere at a run, like a puppy excited to go for a walk, jumping up and down, tail wagging. He hated the thought of her having to deal with the odious Carey after working as part of Daniel's team. He sighed again as he set the coffee machine to work.

"Is everything OK, Dr Lord?" Abby asked.

Hector turned from the machine and smiled. "Yes, fine. I was hoping Chris would be finished by now, and we'd have something to show you."

"Well, thoroughness is good, I guess."

***

Charlie was also talking to a pathologist, a grumpy one, who was taking Charlie's questions personally. "I made my report, Constable, and I don't have anything to add to it."

Charlie held the telephone away from his body, listening as the man sounded off abut police officers who didn't understand what they were reading.

"I do understand the report, sir," Charlie said. "I was just asking whether, in your expert opinion, the victim was unconscious before entering the water." He hoped that the flattery might get the pathologist to speculate. It didn't. He had already talked to the DI who'd headed the investigation into Dylan Davies' death, and gleaned nothing new. She had repeated the information they already had: that there had been a string of gay-bashings, and this was assumed to be part of the series. "Though this was the worst, obviously. No one else finished up in the canal, or died."

Charlie decided to extend his brief to interviewing Alan Davies' parents. Perhaps they would have something to add. He worked out that it would take a couple of hours to drive to the Warwickshire town where they lived, less if he pushed it a bit and got lucky with the traffic. Bethan was surprisingly enthusiastic when he suggested making the trip.

"This case has been hanging round like the flu. If you can close off one lead, that's progress."

"Any movement on James Melton?"

"Waiting for the solicitor to ring me back. Story of my life."

***

Twenty years living in a well-heeled Warwickshire town had done nothing to mute the Davies' Welsh accents. Charlie could have been walking into any of his relatives' homes, albeit the house must have been new when the Davies' moved in. There was a signed photograph of the Welsh rugby team, too much furniture, a surfeit of well-dusted china and a lot of pictures of a man who Charlie assumed was Dylan.

"He wasn't gay. Whatever the police said. He had a lovely girlfriend, Sienna. She was heartbroken," Mrs Davies said. She did not ask him to call her Bronwen. Charlie had barely had time to sit down and say yes to a cup of tea, before Dylan's mother began to criticise the Birmingham police, not for failing to arrest their son's killer, just for associating him with the attacks on gay men.

"I don't think the police are saying that Dylan was gay," Charlie protested, "I think they meant that his attackers might have thought so."

"Well, they were wrong."

If that's important to you, thought Charlie, let's go with that. It was important enough for Dylan's mother to go on about it for another ten minutes, before Charlie could ask about their move away from Melin Tywyll after the raft race.

"Oh, that lovely girl," Bronwen Davies said, adding that, once again, the existence of Merren Jones proved that Dylan was as straight as a die. Charlie tried to conceal his frustration by drinking his tea.

"Is that why you moved?" he asked? "Because of the accident?"

"However did you get that idea?" This time the speaker was Dylan's father. "I got a job as the headteacher at a school here. I'm not saying we weren't glad not to be reminded about poor Merren, but we had planned to move before the race. Dylan went off to university, and we spent the Easter holidays house-hunting, and then moved in the summer."

"Did any of you stay in touch with people in Melin?"

"Of course," they answered in unison. "Though Dylan's friends never bothered much," Bronwen Davies continued in an aggrieved tone. "But he made plenty of new ones here."

Even allowing for his parents' naturally rose-tinted spectacles, Dylan Davies had been a successful sales manager, with a flat in one of Birmingham's trendy new blocks. He had travelled widely, been engaged once (his fiancée cheated), and was in the process of settling down with 'the lovely girlfriend' when he was killed.

Charlie had one last question. "Did you see anyone from Melin around the time Dylan was killed? Or had Dylan mentioned seeing anyone?"

They looked puzzled.

"Only our relatives. Is that who you meant?"

"I meant from the time of the accident."

They both shook their heads. "That was a long time ago, sergeant. Water under the bridge."

Charlie flinched at the cliché, which was a bit too apt for comfort, but made no comment about the promotion.

24

THE OLD TEAM

The case had run into the sand. Stalled. Gone dead. All the leads led to dead ends. Mal went in search of Daniel, and found him at the first place he looked, dressed in his rainbow gardening jumper, thick trousers, work boots and a woolly hat covering his curls. The raised beds looked newly tidied, and Daniel was in the process of painting little signs saying things like "Potatoes here", "Raspberry Canes" and "Community Allotment" with a pointing finger. Each had a stake, and Daniel being Daniel, each was going to be covered with a coat of waterproof varnish before being planted. He looked up from his work and grinned. "The fascist cops have come to visit again. Should I make a sign saying "No drugs here"?

"No. You should come somewhere warm and let me tell you about my disaster of a case."

"I've got blankets. And executive seating." Daniel pointed at the plastic chairs.

Mal visibly shuddered. "Sweetheart, it's about minus ten degrees, and I'm in work clothes."

Daniel got out his phone. "According to my app, it's not

even freezing. And Hector cleaned those chairs personally, in the teeth of disapproval from one of the old guard. But seeing as you are a wimp from south Wales, go home and light the fire, and I'll be with you as soon as I've put everything away. Half an hour, tops." Mal walked gratefully to his car, and turned the heating up high. Back at home, he lit the fire as instructed, made a pot of coffee and dug out the sandwich toaster from the back of one of the cupboards. He sliced bread and cheese, buttered the bread and left it all ready. By the time he'd finished, he could hear the Land Rover growling its way up the slope to the house. He was going to break all the rules, real and self-imposed, to see whether Daniel could drive a wedge into the mess of this case to open it up, or at the very least provide an intelligent sounding board.

Daniel brought the smell of cold earth in on his clothes. He stripped the hat, sweater and boots off in the back porch, and came into the kitchen in his jeans, thick socks and a long-sleeved T shirt. Mal stepped up close and kissed him, his face cold, but his tongue warm and welcoming. He felt himself growing hard, and ran his hands round to grip Daniel's arse. Daniel pushed him away.

"I'm still aching from last night, you pervert, and I'm much in need of a hot shower."

"Let me help. I'm cold too."

"Only if we get to drink the coffee while it's still hot."

"Promise," said Mal, not meaning it. They used the shower to warm up in every sense, and came back downstairs relaxed and happy. The coffee was still hot, though that was mostly a tribute to Mal having wrapped the pot up in a towel before they'd left it. He made the toasted sandwiches, and they sat on the sofa, leaning against each other, eating melted cheese, wincing as it burned their mouths.

"Thank you," said Mal, snuggling closer.

"For what?"

"For being you. For putting up with me."

Daniel kissed him. "*Croeso*. Now tell me about this case," he said, breaking off the kiss. "Before we finish up in bed and no work done at all."

Mal got up to put another log on the fire, and their plates back in the kitchen.

"I shouldn't be here," he said. "I should be running that disaster of a police station, writing strategies, maintaining discipline, monitoring progress across all our work, filling in endless fucking forms, and signing reports, but here I am trying to find out who killed a not very interesting bloke at the bloody allotments. And I can't even do that. Your theory about the raft race might hold water, excuse the pun, but the police who investigated Dylan Davies's death can't get beyond the gay-bashing, and Dylan's parents leaving town was nothing to do with the accident. Hector and his mate are still debating what happened to Pandy, and even Bethan can't get James Melton to an interview. Then to top it all off, Carey's gone walkabout."

"Fuck," said Daniel. "No wonder you need my help."

***

Rhys Bennion sat at the scrubbed farmhouse table in his mother's kitchen as she fussed around making sandwiches for their lunch. Exactly as he remembered, sandwiches were made from two thinly buttered slices of brown bread, then either cheese or ham, topped off with some sweet pickle. They would be served on one of her blue and yellow plates, with either a blue, or a yellow paper napkin. Dessert would be a piece of fruit. The sandwiches were never tasty, but he had kept quiet all through school, because most people had the same. Fuel, not food for the soul. The bread was brown because that was the 'healthy choice'.

"Did you know," he said, "this kind of brown bread is just white bread with food colouring?"

For the first time since he came back, his mother smiled a genuine smile.

"Really? And I've been serving it all these years, thinking it was better for you all. It's white bread for me from here on in."

"Blimey, Mum, what's next, ready meals?"

"I tell you what's next, boyo, takeaways, fish and chips, pot noodles. *Anything* I don't have to make from home grown veg."

Rhys stared at his mother. She had never once complained about the produce his dad brought home. She had complained often and at length about the time spent on the allotment, but never about the fruit and veg. He reached over and held her hand. For all the efforts she made with her appearance, his mum would soon be seventy; an *old woman*. He felt a rush of warmth for her.

"Come to Australia, Mum," he said. "Get some sunshine. Meet your grandkids in the flesh."

"I'd like that. I could maybe go with you, when you go home. If that's possible. If there's somewhere for me to stay. I could help out a bit." She sounded hopeful, but unsure of the reception to her suggestion.

The kitchen door opened and his sister came in, flopping down next to him at the table.

"Mum's thinking of coming to Australia for a visit," Rhys said.

"And maybe Shetland too, when I get back," his mother added. Now both of them stared at their mother. She looked down at her sandwich making.

"Marriage is like that," she said in a low voice. "For better and for worse. Your Dad was a good man, and a good father when you were growing up. But he changed. Got obsessed with that allotment and his committee. He decided he didn't approve of gay relationships, and once he'd made his mind up, he wouldn't change it, silly old fool."

Rhys noticed that there were tears in his mother's eyes. He

pulled a tissue from the box and passed it to her. She blew her nose and took a deep breath.

"Don't get me wrong, I'll miss him, but I won't miss his stupid rules. I've been thinking about it all since he died, and after I stopped with the Valium the doctor gave me. I want to spend time with my children. I can't help thinking about that poor soul David Jones, you remember, Merren's dad? He lost his wife a few months ago."

"When did you see him?" Rhys asked.

"Day after your Dad...you know... He kept saying how lucky I was to have my children, and I think he was right."

She put the sandwiches on three plates, and they sat down to eat, more at ease in each other's company than Rhys could remember since he'd left for university.

***

Daniel loved the way Mal smelled. He always had, since the first time they met. It wasn't just the cologne, though that was nice, it was something about the familiarity of Mal's skin. His boyfriend had changed out of his work clothes, and was now dressed in black jeans and a black roll-neck sweater and underneath would be a black long-sleeved T shirt and black briefs. The thick sheep-coloured woolly socks on his feet were completely out of place. Daniel looked at them and smiled inwardly. "Love you," he said to Mal. "But I still think I've got this case right. It's the accident."

"So how do you explain Carey, and James Melton?"

"I don't. I keep coming back to the one thing all the victims have in common, and it's that raft race. Dylan Davies wasn't gay. Never mind that his parents protested too much, there's no evidence at all for him being gay. He wasn't attacked coming out of a gay bar, he wasn't with a bunch of other men, he wasn't beaten up, like the other victims of the gay-bashers. No, I think he was attacked by the same person who killed Pandy and Hayden Bennion, and it's something to do with the accident.

Someone connected to Merren Jones. What happened to her parents? Do we know?"

"There's a David Jones on the allotment committee." Mal said.

"There's a David Jones on every committee in Wales."

Mal sighed. "I'll get Bethan to find out about *this* David Jones." Daniel watched as Mal got his phone out of an impossibly tight jeans pocket. "Bethan, could you or one of the others find out about a David Jones who's on the allotment committee? Specifically, whether he had a daughter called Merren who died in a raft race accident twenty years ago?"

Daniel couldn't hear the answer, but it was long and interrupted by several mmm-hmmms. After much too long, Mal ended the call.

"What?"

"Abby interviewed David Jones. She said he gave her the creeps. He talked about the importance of marriage and family all the time. He lives a few minutes' walk from the allotments. But whether he's *that* David Jones, we don't know. They're going to find out and ring me. What we do know is that James Melton has agreed to be interviewed, in Liverpool, tomorrow." Mal sighed. "I should go back to the office, but I'm awarding myself half an hour off to worry about Adam Carey. Would you care to join me?"

"Only if you ring Hector first for the results of autopsy number two."

"Abby will ring me. Be patient."

Daniel poked Mal in the ribs, eliciting a loud yelp. Then he cuddled up again. "I wonder whether the bloke Hector talked to at the community allotment afternoon was the same David Jones? Because Hector said he was creepy. He's the one who donated the chairs—the executive seating. *And* if it's the same bloke, he's had a go at Lizzie and Beth too."

"Half an hour. That's how long I've got. You've already

solved Hayden Bennion's murder, now I need you to think about what I should do about Carey." Daniel felt Mal kiss the top of his head, and ruffle his curls.

This is lovely, but I have less than no ideas about Carey.

They were no further forward when Mal's self-appointed half hour ended, and he changed his slippers for work shoes and socks. "What are you going to do this afternoon?" Mal asked.

Daniel shrugged. "Wait to hear something, I guess. Work in the garden. Think about Carey. Make your dinner. Read my wedding magazines."

In the event he put his wellies on, and took Flora for a long and muddy walk in the woods. His mind disconnected from police work as he took in his surroundings, though he knew his subconscious was worrying away at the problems. He'd made some paths in his woods, and left the rest to nature. Flora had been trained to keep to the paths, to avoid disturbing any small creatures, and Daniel had the sense of life beginning to awaken from the winter. A few of the trees were showing the first signs of new growth, tightly furled leaves waiting for some warmth and sunshine before they could open. The hollies were the only green amongst the tangles of trees and scrub. Daniel knew that they would lose their prominence later in the year, as the deciduous trees came into full leaf. For now, they were the stars of the show. The first primroses were coming into flower. In a couple of weeks, their yellow faces would cover the ground in between the trees. It was overcast, cold, and damp as well as slippery underfoot, but Daniel didn't care. Walking in the woods, observing the changes, always cleared his mind. It calmed his soul. Thoughts of the case came crowding back in as he rounded the corner by his polytunnels and saw the house. His overwhelming feeling was of having missed something. Something important.

He let himself and Flora into the porch, then sat down on the bench where they took their boots off, and rang Mal.

"I don't think I *have* solved your case, love," he said, not bothering with any pleasantries. "There's more, I know there is."

"First too late, Daniel. We've just picked up David Jones outside Rhys Bennion's house with a crowbar in his hand. He's confessed to the lot."

25

HAVE CROWBAR, WILL TRAVEL

David Jones was a small man who should have looked smaller surrounded by the trappings of his situation. His clothes had been replaced with a grey tracksuit, the same colour as his last remaining strands of hair. The only thing of his own that had been left to him were his spectacles: thick lenses, wire rimmed and not yet unfashionable enough to be trendy. But far from looking cowed, he looked defiant, puffed up with his own importance. He had a lawyer, and two police officers were hanging onto his every word. The seats might be uncomfortable moulded plastic, the desk bolted to the floor, and the carpet stained with many years' worth of spilled tea, but David Jones was holding court.

Jones been found 'lurking' outside the Bennion house by PC Morgan, doing his regular drive-by.

"I've never seen anyone look more suspicious," Eluned had told Bethan. "Once I got him in the car he started talking and I couldn't make him stop. I was a bit worried, like, about the crowbar, but he dropped it on the floor, good as gold."

Mal looked at the man across the table, and cursed silently. Bethan had begun the questioning, gently, clearly determined not to upset an apparently elderly and distressed suspect. But she needn't have worried. David Jones was desperate to tell his story, words pouring out in torrents of hatred for the "swine who stole my girl's future". He'd been lucky with his lawyer, a keen young graduate called Barney Jackson, who kept suggesting that Jones had the option of not answering every single question, and insisting on breaks for tea, food and the bathroom. None of it had any impact on David Jones, who wanted everyone present to know that he had killed three people, and would happily have killed another had the police not stopped him. He leaned forward over the table, brushing the strands of hair back across his bald head.

"There is no way Merren should have been on that raft. *No way.* She didn't want to go, but that boyfriend, he made her. Told her she was soft. What's wrong with soft, I say? Nothing. *He* got out of the water, didn't even go and look for her. Didn't care, see.

"Those others, that Pandy, no better than she ought to be, carrying on with that Rhys. And now look at her. Divorced with a child. Only to be expected from that sort."

Bethan asked: "Can you tell us about Hayden Bennion, Mr Jones?"

"He encouraged them. Gave them wood. Believe me, the world's a better place thanks to me. A much better place." Spittle flew from Jones's mouth as he spoke, banging the table with his hand for emphasis. Behind the thick glasses, Mal could see wide eyes, their gaze demanding belief and agreement.

"Mr Jones," Mal began. "Your daughter Merren's death was ruled an accident…"

"It was no *accident,* do you hear me? No accident." Jones's voice rose as his passion built, and the solicitor put a hand on his client's arm. "Perhaps a short break is in order," he suggested. Mal agreed readily.

"I need to get something from my office," he told Bethan, wanting to avoid conversation. Once there he rang Daniel, imagining him curled up on the sofa, glass of wine in hand, Flora pretending that she wasn't on Daniel's lap, and in the background, the stove bright with orange flames. "It's exactly like you said," he told Daniel. "Resentment that others lived when Merren died. He says Dylan forced Merren to go on the raft, that Hayden encouraged them by giving them wood, and he didn't have anything good to say about Pandy."

"So why now? After twenty years?"

"That's *my* question, remember. We haven't got that far yet. But he's a sad case. He doesn't look strong enough to kill anyone."

"Something's not right about this, Maldwyn. I know I've spent days telling you that it was all to do with the accident, and I think it probably is, but something's not right." Then in an abrupt change of direction, "Have you located Carey yet?"

"Not a peep." Mal knew that he *should* have been trying to find out where Carey had gone. "It's so peaceful without him."

"It's just weird that he disappears the same day that David Jones appears acting suspiciously and confesses." There was a moment of silence, then " Oh, I don't know, and it's not down to me any more."

Mal could hear the frustration in Daniel's voice. He understood it because he felt exactly the same way. David Jones was glad those three people were dead. He had wanted to kill them, but had he done it? Faced with a neatly tied confession, Mal wasn't sure.

***

Sasha looked through the rain on her windscreen at the long, low school building, waiting until the last possible moment to get out of the warm car and join the gaggle of mothers, and some fathers, round the school gates. She had been trying to make friends among the group, but it was hard going.

Her schoolgirl Welsh wasn't up to much more than *hello* and *thank you*, though Arwen was picking it up with no apparent trouble. It was a pleasant school, newly built, with wide corridors and spacious classrooms. There was plenty of space outside for the children to play, although she couldn't imagine any of them had wanted to go out today. The clock on the dashboard ticked over another minute, and Sasha pulled her scarf more tightly round her neck, feeling the rough wool irritate her skin. The matching hat was in her pocket, and she put it on. Gloves she would manage without. Both the girls would be bringing collapsing backpacks with things falling out and she would need to use both her hands, unobstructed by clumsy mittens or gloves. She pulled the keys from the ignition and got out of the car. Even with hat and scarf and her warmest coat, the cold was painful. The rain that had seemed no more than drizzle from inside had already begun to soak the car seat before she got the door closed.

And Daniel wants kids?

The bell rang from inside the school, and Sasha took her usual position by the chain link fence where Arwen and Cerys would be able to see her. She didn't want either of them feeling abandoned. She spotted Arwen with the rest of her class. Her backpack was spilling some kind of paper, and her coat was only half fastened. Mittens dangled unworn on strings at the end of her sleeves. Arwen was too old to run to her mother, but Sasha's heart still jumped a little when she saw her daughter, and she couldn't stop the smile.

"Where's Cerys?" she asked, hoping that the two girls hadn't fallen out. Arwen's face fell. "She's gone with her dad. He came to collect her at lunchtime. She didn't want to go with him, but the teacher said she had to. Will she be coming back, Mum?"

"Let's go and find out, shall we?" Sasha's voice betrayed none of the panic she felt rising up her throat, making her want to run to the nearest dark corner and throw up. She scooped

Arwen's backpack off her daughter's shoulder, packed it properly and fastened it. Then she took Arwen's hand and began to work against the oncoming tide of children, back towards the school.

"I need to see the headteacher," she told the receptionist who let her in. "It's urgent, and it's important. I think one of the children has been kidnapped." As she said the word, Arwen clutched at her hand. The receptionist didn't look impressed.

"Don't make me call the police," said Sasha.

A smooth voice came from behind her, "Can I help?" Sasha turned round. A man she recognised as the headteacher was looking at them both with a concerned expression. "Arwen, isn't it? And you must be Arwen's mum." The smile was oily. A politician's smile. A slim, dark-haired man dressed in cords and a sweater, an attempt at informality that Sasha found unconvincing.

"I also have responsibility for Cerys Melton." Sasha thanked whatever urge had made her put the paperwork from social services in her bag. "As you can see from these documents. But my daughter tells me that Cerys was taken out of school by her father, who has an injunction preventing him from coming into the town, and who does *not* have custody."

"Perhaps this would be better discussed in my office," the headteacher said and led the way behind the reception desk and into a small, plain office. He went behind the desk and sat down, waving Sasha into a chair.

"Could I see those papers please?"

Sasha passed them over, and the headteacher studied them carefully. Then he opened a drawer in his desk and produced a similar set of papers. "Your responsibility appears to have been superseded," he said, showing her the documents. "Mr Melton came here accompanied by a police officer, because of the injunction you mentioned, but you see that the signatures on these two papers are the same." He pointed them out. "I imagine when you get home, there is going to be a very contrite message from social services on your answering machine."

I very much doubt it, you slimy bastard.

"I don't suppose you remember the name of the police officer who came with James Melton?" she asked, matching his fake smile with one of her own.

Back into the drawer he went, producing a business card this time.

"A Detective Inspector Carey," he said, turning the card towards her.

***

Mal and Bethan resumed their seats opposite David Jones. The older man looked a bit calmer, but still much too cheerful for someone facing a murder charge. His solicitor's expression betrayed that he at least knew what was at stake. The room was warm, one of the only warm places in the glass box of a police station, and the odours of past interrogations filled the air; sweat, dusty carpet and despair.

"Mr Jones." Mal's gaze included the solicitor. "You know that you are here voluntarily?"

Jones nodded, and looked as if his tirades were about to start again. But Mal got in first.

"For the tape, Mr Jones is nodding. Mr Jones, you told us earlier that you had killed Hayden Bennion, Pandora Melton, and Dylan Davies and that you intended to kill Rhys Bennion. You told us this was because they contributed to the death of your daughter Merren. Is that correct?"

"They didn't *contribute to her death*, they killed her. *That's* what's correct."

"Thank you, Mr Jones." Mal kept his voice slow and steady, hoping that if he stayed calm, Jones would follow suit. From the solicitor's face, he hoped so too.

"Your daughter Merren died twenty years ago. I know you

still feel her loss, but could you tell me why you say you killed these people now? After so long?"

The question hung in the air, then Jones began to weep. Silent tears ran down his face and dripped onto his knees. "My wife died. I couldn't do anything before. She was a priest. She said we had to forgive. Then she died. So, you see, I didn't have to forgive any more."

Bethan produced some folded tissues from her pocket and passed them to Jones, who clutched them in his hand, but did nothing to wipe his tears. For the first time since he'd seen David Jones, Mal thought that this pathetic man might really have killed three people. His reverie was broken by a knock at the door. Charlie put his head in.

"A moment, sir?"

Mal got up and followed Charlie into the corridor. He would usually be annoyed at being interrupted, but he didn't think Jones was going to change his story.

"Two things, sir, one, Abby's back, with the new autopsy findings, and a call from a social worker called Heidi Potts. James Melton collected his daughter from school today, and he got away with it because DI Carey went with him."

26

HOW FAR TO LIVERPOOL?

Mal went back into the interview room. "I'm going to have to leave this for a while," he said. "A matter has come up that needs my urgent attention. Could I ask you to wait for me, Mr Jones, and I'll see that you get something to eat and drink."

Jones nodded, Mal suspended the interview and beckoned the solicitor.

"This could take a while, but I'm not ready to charge your client."

"Or let him go?" Barney Jackson replied.

"Or let him go." Mal confirmed.

The solicitor went back into the interview room as Bethan came out. Mal heard the rumble of voices from behind the door, as presumably Jackson explained the situation. He didn't think there would be much pushback from David Jones. The man wanted to tell his story, and the police were the only ones listening. It would have to wait.

"My office, in five minutes," he said to Bethan and Charlie, "and bring Abby."

The five minutes was to ring Daniel. It wouldn't be enough,

but it would have to do. He looked at the phone in his hand, listening to it ring at the other end. Daniel sounded out of breath when he answered.

"Sorry, my phone fell out of my pocket. I had to dig it out of the sofa cushions. What's up?"

"Two things. James Melton has kidnapped Cerys, and took Carey with him to the school to provide cover. Can you go and hold Sasha's hand? Second, I'm re-thinking whether David Jones did kill those people. I just can't tell. He wanted to kill them, and he's glad they're dead. I've got to go."

"Of course. I'm going now. Bastards. *Bastards*"

As he ended the call, Mal heard Bethan, Charlie and Abby arriving outside his office door. He got out from behind the desk to open it and let them in.

***

Daniel grabbed the car keys out of the dish by the back door. Flora looked at him mournfully.

"I'm not leaving you behind, you silly animal," he said. Together they made their way around to the front of the house, with its big windows looking over the valley, and on to the bit of hard standing where the cars were parked. On a day like this, he would have been happy to drive Mal's Audi, with its heated seats, and efficient windscreen de-mister. But only his Land Rover stood in their parking spot. He opened one of the back doors for Flora, who scrambled her way into the dog basket on the back seat. The rest of the space was filled with Daniel's gardening tools, bits of wood left over from the Community Allotment, wellies and spare waterproofs. It all smelled of mould. Daniel made his usual resolution to clear it all out. Soon. He started the ignition, knowing there was no point in trying to leave until the engine had warmed enough to keep the windscreen clear. He looked behind him. Flora had curled into the tiniest possible ball, having plenty of experience of the inefficiency of the Land Rover's heating system.

At any other time, the route to Sasha and Hector's house on the other side of Melin Tywyll would be a delight. High hedgerows full of flowers, glimpses of rolling hills through the gateways. In the distance the higher hills, and the forestry coating some of them in dark green. There was a section along the river, usually with roadworks, as the council tried valiantly to stop the endless collapse of the road into the water below. But today, all was gloom and grey drizzle. He still flicked a glance through the gateways as he passed, and he spotted a few early daffodils in the hedges. The high hills were shrouded in mist. But all he could think about was Cerys, a pawn in her father's desire for control, whatever the consequences for his daughter.

When he arrived Sasha seemed remarkably calm, but Daniel told himself not to be surprised. She would be concerned to play it cool in front of Arwen, he thought.

He hugged her, and she clung to him for a moment, blinking and swallowing hard as she pulled away. "Coffee?" she asked, her voice tight and higher pitched than usual.

As usual, the kitchen was warm and bright, the table covered with Sasha's books and notes, laptop turned on to show what looked like the inside of a mouth, all red and vibrating. Daniel didn't ask. The sound of a television came through the open door to the hall.

"Arwen is watching cartoons," Sasha said. "And when that stops working, I have other methods of taking her mind off things. Go and say hello."

Daniel followed the noise to the cosy sitting room, dominated by a large TV playing something brightly coloured with American accents. Daniel thought he should have recognised it, but he didn't. Arwen was entranced. He reached over the back of the sofa and tickled her ribs, making her squeak in shock. "Ow! Uncle Daniel, go away, this is the good bit."

Daniel went. "I've been sent away," he told Sasha, back in the kitchen. "What have you got to take *your* mind off things?"

"I tried to get her interested in a Harry Potter film," Sasha said, "so I could watch it with her, but she wanted one of those Disney princess things, and I hate them. Even the good ones. Only getting Cerys back will take my mind off getting Cerys back. Coffee?"

The question was moot, because Sasha had already assembled mugs and coffee pot and the kettle was starting to boil.

"I'll take any home-made cookies, too. Or cake. Schoolwork not doing it for you then?"

"Can't concentrate. Can't stop thinking about that awful man walking into school and calmly kidnapping Cerys. I don't care if he is her father. The idiot headteacher took him at face value, never checked, just let him take the kid because he had a few bits of paper and a tame cop."

"Pandy said Melton could be charming, and Eluned Bennion said the same thing. If he had kept his temper in court, he'd probably have got custody, or at least joint custody. Because at that point, Pandy was pretty unstable. I didn't tell you that, obviously. Did you see the papers giving him the right to take her?"

In answer Sasha took her handbag from the floor, and produced half a dozen sheets of paper stapled together. "This is what we got," she said, passing them to Daniel. "What the idiot headteacher showed me looked like the same set, just with James Melton's name instead of me and Hector. But I only had a quick look. The signatures look the same — Heidi Potts and a squiggle for the Director of Children's Services. Heidi Potts is the social worker we've been dealing with."

"And Heidi Potts didn't sign the other set of papers?"

"Nope. I love the phrase 'incandescent with rage' but I've never heard it in action until I spoke to Heidi."

"Because whatever happens, anything bad will be blamed

on the social workers," Daniel said. Cerys's abduction had turned his filter off. Social services had a duty of care, and so did the school and none of them had done their jobs. He might be being unfair, but right now, so what?

Sasha poured the coffee, and tidied her books to one side of the table. She closed her laptop, still on the disturbing image. Then she went over to one of the cupboards for the biscuit tin, and pushed it in Daniel's direction.

"Do you know where this James Melton bastard lives?" she asked.

"Liverpool. That's where they lived when they were married, and he still lives there. But that's all I know. Why?"

"Because if I knew where he lived, I'd go and get her."

"Wasn't there an address on the fake papers?" Daniel didn't react to the *go and get her* part of what Sasha had said.

Sasha blew on her coffee and shook her head. "I saw the name, and the idiot headteacher showed me the two sets of signatures. How long would it take to get to Liverpool from here?"

"Couple of hours tops I should think, depending on whereabouts in Liverpool. It's a big place." *Was he even thinking about this? Yes.*

"All we need is the address. Then we could go. You and me. The last people anyone would expect. Cerys was scared of him, her father. She asks all the time if he killed her mother. I can't stop thinking about her, all on her own with that monster." Then Sasha did something Daniel never expected to see. She put her head down on the table and sobbed.

"We'll get the address," he said, with no idea how they were going to do it.

***

Mal sat at his office table with Charlie, Abby and Bethan. Mal was still wearing his roll neck and black jeans, while the other three were more formal. Of them all, Mal thought he looked least like a police officer, and today, he didn't feel much like on either. He had a perfectly good suspect, happily prepared to confess, with an excellent, if skewed motive and who had every opportunity to commit the crimes. That was the plus side. On the minus side, his DI was last sighted helping to abduct a child from her legal (if temporary) guardians. "Where are we up to?" He sighed. "Abby, you start."

"They think it was murder," she said. "Dr Lord and Dr Mills, I mean. They agreed that Mrs Melton drowned, and they agreed that she had been hit on the back of the head before she was in the water, and most probably while she was on the bridge. Hit with something like a crowbar, or a heavy spanner, something like the iron bar used on Hayden Bennion. Neither of them thought she jumped. They talked at me for ages, and then said it wasn't up to them to solve the mystery, all they could do was give us the facts."

"But they didn't think suicide was likely?" Mal asked.

"By the end of it, I was losing track of the technical stuff," Abby said, "But no. Not suicide."

"Years of training and experience, and that's the best they can come up with?" Charlie was scathing. "She was hit on the head and then drowned. Wow." Mal thought he felt Bethan kick Charlie under the table.

"OK, what about James Melton? Charlie, what do we know?" Mal asked and Charlie got out his phone to read his notes.

"A social worker called Heidi Potts called. Absolutely tamping. Social services are supposed to be looking after Cerys Melton, and she's been staying with Dr Lord and his wife, under their supervision. So, James Melton and DI Carey turned up at the school and said they had the paperwork to take her, and they showed some documents and off they went."

"You've spoken to the school?"

"Spoken to the headmaster." Charlie looked at his notes. "A

Mr Minchin, and I have the papers that they said gave them the right to take Cerys out of school. Before you ask, Minchin didn't ring social services to check, because, as he said, there was a senior police officer present, as well as a letter signed by the Director of Social Services."

Mal turned to Bethan. "We've got Melton's address?" Bethan nodded. "We'll ask Liverpool colleagues to go round there as soon as we've finished here."

"What if she's not there?" Abby asked. "Because surely he wouldn't take her back to his house. Not with fake papers."

"If she's not there, we'll look somewhere else." Mal said repressively.

"What about the DI, sir?" said Charlie. "Helping in a kidnapping."

"We don't know that," Mal said, although he was pretty sure that he did know. "DI Carey could have been acting in good faith. He could have been fooled just as much as this Mr Minchin."

There were looks of incredulity from around the table and a loud snort from Charlie.

"Evidence. We don't have any evidence that the DI was knowingly involved. I will contact ACC Bowen, and you, Charlie, will go to DI Carey's home to see if he's there. If he's not, tell me, and start looking for his car on the ANPR cameras."

Like I should have done when he drove off this morning.

"Bethan, can you go back to David Jones? Get as much detail as possible from him about the mechanics of the murders. *How* did he kill those three people? Because I'm not yet convinced that he did. Abby, go and look at all the forensic evidence from the first murder. Is there anything that puts Jones at the scene? You interviewed him. Talk to his neighbours. Can anyone give him an alibi, even a partial one? Go and get on with it, people. I need to start making calls."

27

NO ONE OF THAT NAME HERE, MATE

Charlie wasn't thrilled by the idea of trying to find DI Carey. If Carey had been 'acting in good faith' then he was stupid as well as a bigot, and he would have something else to hold against Charlie if it was Charlie who located him. If Carey was bent, then Charlie would be the unpopular cop who found out about it. He hadn't forgotten Mal's arrival in Melin Tywyll, fresh from uncovering corruption in his previous job. To say that he hadn't been popular was an understatement. He wasn't all that popular *now*, but at least he was respected as someone who got the job done.

And he's a bloody sight better than Adam fucking Carey.

Charlie's car was like his flat. Small, untidy and smelling of socks. Which Charlie knew perfectly well, and chose not to change. It was always better to travel in someone else's vehicle. Let them worry about the price of petrol, keeping track of mileage, and filling in expenses claims. Nope, a messy car meant no one wanted a ride in it, including him, if he was honest. He gathered up handfuls of takeaway containers and chocolate wrappers and shoved them in the nearest bin. He brushed the crumbs off the driver's seat, and threw his spare clothes into the boot. It still didn't smell any better, and he vowed to get one of those dangly air fresheners next time he bought petrol. He sighed and started the engine. Carey only lived a few minutes' drive away—like everyone else in Melin Tywyll—and he couldn't put it off any longer.

The address seemed familiar, and when he got there, Charlie realised that Carey lived on the same street as the Bennion family. The house was dark, and looked tired and un-lived-in. Charlie walked up the overgrown drive, thinking *no car* and noting the way that the gutters sagged, and the bottoms of the garage doors had rotted. He rang the doorbell, but could hear nothing inside, so he knocked on the door and rattled the letterbox. Still nothing. He looked up and down the street, and saw no one. He sighed and headed for the side gate. It was swollen with moisture, and he worried it would break before it opened, but open it did, and Charlie set off down the path to the back of the house. He was not surprised to find more empty windows and dark rooms, and to get no answer to his knocking at the back door. He went back to his car, trying his best to close the side gate as he went.

At the police station he knocked on Mal Kent's door. "Sorry, sir, there's no sign of DI Carey at his house. There's no car either," he said when Mal called him in.

"See if you can track the car then."

"Sir."

But none of the ANPR cameras had picked up Carey's car on any of the routes out of town. Charlie contemplated going back to Mal, but decided against it. Instead, he went to knock on Inspector Harrington's door.

"Ma'am," he began, already having second thoughts. "We are trying to contact DI Carey. He's not at home, and we can't find any trace of his car..."

"You want uniforms to keep an eye out?"

"Yes, ma'am. He lives on the same street as the Bennions, and I know there have been extra patrols there." He took in the mess in the inspector's office, revelling in the idea that someone so untidy could be promoted.

There's hope for me yet.

"Good thinking, Rees." Sophie looked at the clock on her wall. "Why don't you go to the break room? PC Kelley should be there now, and I think he's a friend of DI Carey." Charlie felt his heart pound in his chest. No way did he want to front up Kelley, not after suspecting Kelley was one of the blokes who'd broken his ribs. The same thought seemed to strike Sophie. "I'll take a walk down with you."

***

Mal phoned ACC Bowen, only to find him absent. His disaffected secretary had obviously decided that Mal was on her side. "He's gone for a long lunch at the golf club with the PCC, and if the past is any guide to the future, lunch will segue into early evening drinks, then late evening drinks and a cab home."

I really do need to get hold of him urgently," Mal said.

"I don't think you do. Not to put too fine a point on it, he'll be well hammered by now. But I didn't tell you that."

Mal considered his options. Talking to a drunk Jack Bowen wouldn't achieve anything except the demand to *sort it out Malcolm.* Going over Bowen's head, and perhaps revealing why he hadn't spoken to Bowen himself, would make him an enemy for life. *So, cover my ass.*

"I'd like to leave a message for ACC Bowen, to be given to him as soon as he makes contact. As I'm sure he will, later this afternoon."

"Of course, sir. What shall I tell him?"

Mal summarised the abduction of Cerys Melton, with the apparent assistance of DI Carey. "We can't locate DI Carey, and we are becoming concerned," he said. "I will be liaising with colleagues in Liverpool about Cerys Melton, and we are making every effort to find DI Carey. The ACC should also know that we are interviewing a person of interest in the Hayden Bennion murder case." As he spoke, he was typing an email to Bowen with the same information. "I've put it in an email as well," he told the secretary. "How's the job hunt going?"

She laughed. "Don't worry about me. I'll make sure to record all the messages you've sent. He won't be able to claim you didn't keep him up to speed. Dickhead." The last word was spoken so quietly that Mal couldn't be sure he'd heard it. He thanked the woman courteously for her help and ended the call. Now for Liverpool.

His opposite number in Liverpool sounded harassed. Mal supposed they all sounded harassed. Police numbers had been dwindling year on year, and they were having to do more and more, with fewer and fewer resources.

"You want me to send someone round to this house, see if there's a little girl there and take the dad into custody, right?"

"Yes please," Mal said. "He's broken his injunction, and there's a power of arrest attached to it. I'll email the paperwork now. He is explicitly barred from having contact with his daughter; again the papers are on their way. But there's some-thing else." Until he mentioned Carey, the request was a straightforward one. He got similar requests from other forces frequently 'our villain is on your patch, can you bring 'em in please?' But 'our villain is on your patch, apparently being aided and abetted by one of our officers,' was a whole 'nother story. Still, it had to be faced. But he bit the bullet and explained the problem to the Liverpool officer.

"Oh, mate, that's bad," said the voice at the other end of the phone. "Is this Carey bent or just stupid?"

"God only knows," said Mal. "God only knows." He heard the cackle of Scouse laughter echoing in his ears long after he ended the call. But at least they had set the ball rolling to reunite Cerys with her best friend, and people who genuinely cared about her welfare. Which reminded him to share the news with Sasha. She'd be glad to know that something was happening to bring Cerys back. Even if, as seemed likely, Cerys and James Melton were not at Melton's house, they had started looking, and they wouldn't stop until she was found. But there was no answer from Sasha's number.

***

"Got it," Sasha told Daniel, waving a torn white envelope in the air. They were in Arwen's bedroom, which had become Arwen and Cerys's bedroom according to the new sign on the door. An extra bed had been moved in, but Cerys's clothes were still in a big suitcase, and her books in a pile on the floor. In one corner, a lone long-haired doll faced a group of stuffed animals. Behind the doll, a blackboard leaned against the wall. It bore the single word "lesson". Sasha saw him looking at it and smiled.

"It's a birthday card," Sasha said, handing Daniel the envelope. Inside, he saw a typical glittery rainbow unicorn card. He opened it to find a drawing of a house: a window on each side of the front door, two matching windows upstairs, and a chimney with a curl of smoke. The front door was coloured in red, and there were blue curtains lining the downstairs windows. Generic trees stood on each side of the house. It was a drawing by someone who knew what they were doing. Accurate, but simple at the same time, like in a children's book. The rest of the card was covered with elegant handwriting.

Happy Birthday to my darling daughter! You're in double figures!

I'm keeping your birthday present here, in my new house. Isn't it pretty? Would you believe that the address is Marmalade Lane? There is a beach not too far away. I would love you to be able to visit, and your mama too if she would like it. I miss you both very much.

All my love
Your Papa xxxxx

"He's allowed to write to her," Sasha said. "I picked up this card when I went round to collect her clothes and teddies from Pandy's house. It wasn't on display or anything, but I thought she might want it. She'd put it in her underwear drawer. Or that's where it was, anyway. Shut up, Sasha."

Daniel looked at the envelope. It had been put through a commercial franking machine, and the postmark had been torn away. The address was written in the same elegant handwriting. He wrote the card and the envelope then put it through the mail at work, Daniel thought. The handwriting was unmistakable, and Daniel imagined the envelopes coming through Pandy's letterbox, bringing horrible reminders of the man she had escaped. He gave himself a mental shake.

"Marmalade Lane, close to a beach, somewhere in or near Liverpool. Let's go and google."

To both their surprise, Marmalade Lane was a real address. Not in the city, but to the north, and very close to a beach.

"What are we waiting for?" Sasha asked. "Your car or mine?"

Second thoughts hit Daniel hard. James Melton was a violent man, who had somehow persuaded a serving detective to help him abduct his own daughter in defiance of the courts. This was a job for the police, and he wasn't the police. They didn't even have the full address, and he could hear Arwen's TV show in the background. Were they seriously proposing to take her on this rescue mission? He opened his mouth to say as much, but Sasha got there first.

"I know what you're going to say, so don't waste your breath. I'm going. You can either come with me, or stay here and look after Arwen. You've got ten seconds to decide."

"We'll take the Land Rover," he said, memories of folding himself into Sasha's tiny car making his knees ache. "The local police will probably beat us to it though. If we can find the address, they certainly can."

"So, we'll collect Cerys from the Liverpool cops. Now get that dog in the car, and your coat on, while I get Arwen organised."

Five minutes later, they were headed for the main road and Liverpool.

***

The Liverpool police might be harassed, but Mal was impressed with the speed with which they got back to him. His phone rang as he was headed down the stairs to the interview room to see how Bethan was getting on with David Jones. He heard the Liverpool accent and his heart lifted at the thought of Cerys safe, and James Melton under arrest. We can sort the rest out later, he thought. Except it wasn't like that.

"Wrong address, mate," said the voice on his phone. "That's an office block in the middle of town, and there's no James Melton on the list of businesses based there. Send us a picture if you've got one, and we'll hawk it round a bit, see if anyone in the building knows him."

Shit, shit, shit and double shit.

Mal felt everything around him fade, leaving only the knowledge of his failures. Failure to find Hayden Bennion's murderer, failure to protect Pandy, or find out who attacked Charlie, failure to deal with Carey, and now failure to keep a ten-year old girl safe from her own father. He was drowning in failure. One minute, he told himself. One minute of self-pity and then it's get-a-fucking-grip time. He let his eyes wander over the tired concrete stairs, remembering how he and Daniel had met here for surreptitious kisses, and out of the window at the grey clouds hanging low over the hills. He allowed his inner critic full rein until the minute was up. Then he told it firmly to get back into its box, squared his shoulders and ran up the stairs.

"Abby. Whatever you're doing, stop it. The address James Melton gave us is an office block. We need to know where he lives, and we need it yesterday."

28

ONE STEP BEYOND

C harlie had no experience of police canteens, but he imagined that they looked and smelled much more pleasant than the break room at Melin Tywyll police station. He had a mental image of a cheerful 'dinner lady' serving bacon rolls and meat-and-two-veg meals, along with copious amounts of tea. Talking to some of the longer-serving officers, Charlie learned that the break room should have been a canteen, but the food preparation area had been turned into the 'soft' interview room, and the only food preparation was done in either the microwave or the vending machines.

Three men jumped to their feet as Sophie and Charlie entered the room. Sophie Harrington had that kind of effect, Charlie had noticed. She never had to say "I'm in charge", but the words were out there somehow.

"PC Kelley, a word please," Sophie said, and Kelley followed them out of the room, and into the soft interview room next door. The room was used for interviewing rape victims, or children, or anyone deemed especially vulnerable. Instead of the usual table bolted to the floor and plastic chairs, there were comfortable sofas, and pictures on the walls. It was designed to comfort, not intimidate, but it wasn't working on Kelley.

Charlie had started his police career in uniform. He had met a few PC Kelleys during those years, and was forever astounded that they had been accepted in the first place. Policing is like everything else, he thought, you have to work at it, to learn what works and what doesn't. He doubted that Kelley had learned anything new since he'd finished his basic training, and worse, he didn't know why that was wrong.

Kelley was ordinary in lots of ways: watery blue eyes, close cropped brown hair, two days' worth of face fuzz that did nothing to enhance his sharp features, or to hide the acne he should have grown out of. Under his uniform he was a thin man, the sort of thinness that came from being underfed as a child. Charlie had arrested plenty of men who looked like Kelley, and from the frightened look Kelley was giving them both, Charlie wondered whether he would be arresting another one today.

"I'm sorry. I didn't mean it, OK? I didn't know ..." PC Kelley's voice was high and he was struggling to get his breath.

"Sit down, PC Kelley, Mark, and take a couple of deep breaths," Sophie said. Kelley dropped onto one of the sofas, as if his legs had been kicked from under him.

I know how that feels.

"Now then Mark, start from the beginning. What are you sorry about?" Sophie's voice was so calming, it was almost a purr.

Kelley looked down at the floor, his hands clasped together so tightly that his knuckles shone white. He mumbled something under his breath that sounded like "hitting DC Rees."

"Speak up please, Mark, and sit up straight," Sophie said, with a lot less of a purr.

"I said I'm sorry for hitting DC Rees. The other night. After the wine bar. I didn't mean him any harm, honestly I didn't."

Yeah, right. Sorry you got caught more like.

"So, you are telling me that you were one of the men who assaulted DC Rees in the street?"

Kelley nodded miserably.

"I think you *did* mean to harm him," Sophie went on. "But you were disturbed, and thank goodness for that. What I want to know is why? Why an unprovoked attack on a fellow officer?"

Kelley went back to looking at the floor.

"PC Kelley. I want an answer." The purr had completely gone from Sophie's voice, replaced by a tone that would have etched glass. "Now, please."

"I'll get the sack," Kelley said miserably.

"I think that's very likely, yes," said Sophie. "But it's guaranteed if I don't get an explanation in the next ten seconds."

Kelley looked up, and for a moment seemed almost defiant. "It's the queers, ma'am. DI Carey says they're taking over the police and there's no room for normal people any more. The DI said DC Rees was one of them too, and when I saw him in the wine bar, I knew it was true. DI Carey said we should be teaching people like that a lesson. Like the Khans. Kent said we weren't supposed to follow them any more. Taking over, see. Pushing us out."

Charlie realised that his mouth had fallen open and he closed it before anyone noticed.

"Let me get this straight," Sophie said, "You allege that DI Carey told you to attack DC Rees because he was gay?"

"Not exactly."

"Then what did he tell you to do *exactly?*"

All the fight had gone out of Kelley. His shoulders slumped and he rubbed the back of his neck with one hand. "The DI did me some favours, ma'am, sponsored me in the Con Club, introduced me to people. See, I'm not from round here. So I owed him. But he's right about the queers and the ni, um, the black people taking over. He said the Khans were drug dealers and we could prove it, only Kent said we had to stop. And that made him angry. He said he wanted me and a couple of his other mates to have a go at Kent's boyfriend, who used to have the DI's job."

"You agreed to this plan?"

"Like I say, I owed him."

Charlie began to see how the attack on him might fit with the murders. It was only the beginnings of an idea, but it was worth asking the question.

"Did DI Carey ask you to attack Daniel Owen on that particular day? Like not just *beat up the boss's boyfriend*, but beat him up on that actual day? And then, because you couldn't find him, you came after me? Is that what happened?"

"Yes," said Kelley, "But they say you're not a poofter, so I'm sorry."

As Sophie told Kelley that he'd be suspended, pending a full investigation, all Charlie wanted to do was laugh, except that his job was to find DI Carey.

"DI Carey is a friend of yours," Charlie began, "and we need to talk to him. He's not at home. Do you have any ideas about where he might be?"

Kelley scrunched up his face in a parody of a cartoon character thinking. Only it probably wasn't a parody, Charlie thought.

"He mostly goes to the Slater's or the Con Club. They've got a snooker table in the Con Club. He likes snooker."

"What about other friends in the police? Or girlfriends?"

"Girlfriends? Not bloody likely. He's paying two ex-wives already. Bitch one and bitch two he calls them. He says there's never going to be a bitch three. Tried to steal all his money, but he showed them. Bitches."

Charlie gave serious consideration to punching Kelley as hard as he could. He felt his hands curl into fists, and he even took a preparatory half-step backwards to increase the momentum of the blow. He was surely entitled to hit Kelley—Kelly had hit him. And he was fairly certain that Inspector Harrington wouldn't see a thing. But then Kelley spoke again, and the urge passed.

"The DI has some high-up mates at HQ from when he worked on the coast, so you might ask them. Those blokes are a bit out of my league if you know what I mean."

Anyone who can read is out of your league, Sunshine.

"Does he ever talk about friends in Liverpool?" Charlie asked, wondering whether Kelley knew where Liverpool was.

"Not friends, no, but he did go to visit a couple of weeks ago. Just before that bloke was killed at the allotments. He said where he'd been, like, when he got back. I don't think it was friends though. He didn't look like he'd had a good time."

***

Back in the CID room, Mal walked over to Abby. Peremptorily telling her to abandon a job he'd asked her to do, just because he'd had an unwelcome call, was unfair. "Sorry," he said. "That was harsher than I meant it to be. Did you find anything of any use?"

"Not from forensics, sir. Paul Jarvis says they haven't found much of any use. Lots of fingerprints on the van, mostly the second victim's, and a million smudges on the water barrel."

"Smudges?"

"I asked about that. Paul says that it looked as if someone had given the top of the barrel a wipe over, but you could see where the finger prints had *been* if you see what I mean. He says he reported it to DI Carey."

"There's nothing more he can do?"

"If there was, he didn't tell me about it, sir. But I did have a phone call from Rhys Bennion, the first victim's son. He wanted to know when they could arrange a funeral for his dad. I said we'd let him know. And he asked what had been happening outside their house. He'd seen David Jones arrested."

"You didn't tell him anything?"

Abby shook her head, "He wants to know if, and I quote, 'it's that creepy guy who's been hanging round'. I asked him for a description, and it did sound a bit like David Jones. Apparently, he and his sister have spotted someone at the end of their drive a couple of times, but whoever it was disappeared when they went to look. Maybe Rhys Bennion had a lucky escape?"

"Maybe he did," Mal said. It was starting to look as if there might be a case for David Jones to answer. But he wondered why neither Rhys nor his sister had rung the police to say that they had someone lurking round their house. Wouldn't anyone whose father had been murdered do that? He put the question aside to come back to later. "Now, see what you can do about finding James Melton, and if you can find a picture of him, so much the better."

Then Mal ran back down the stairs to the interview rooms and David Jones. He asked Bethan to step outside, and she did, looking worried.

"What's the matter?" he asked.

Bethan shook her head. "I'm not sure. It's all a bit strange. Can we get a coffee? Would that be OK? And something to get my blood sugar up?" Mal checked the time on his phone. Their favoured coffee shop was about to close, but there was time to get a take out. "Come on then, but we'd better be quick. I'll go, you suspend the interview."

Coffee and the last of a coffee and walnut cake on the table in front of them in Mal's office, Bethan began.

"I think David Jones killed Hayden Bennion. He describes everything too well. The camper van, the water barrel, that bit of iron railing that Dr Lord found, even down to the flaking paint. He says that Hayden was always at the allotments, and never spent any time with his family, that he'd driven his children away but he bragged about having grandchildren constantly. And then he goes on and on about how his daughter shouldn't have been on the raft, that the other rafters stole her from him, but his wife said they had to forgive."

"But he's not the forgiving sort?"

"I think he'd have been OK if his wife was still alive. She had cancer, and died quite quickly. They'd moved away to make a fresh start after the accident—lived in Bournemouth. He had a job at the council, and Mrs Jones decided to train to be a priest. He says they were always church-goers, but she didn't get 'the call' until after Merren died. Long story short, she got a job as a hospital chaplain, and he carried on at the council, and then she died, and he came back here."

"Why? He'd got his job, and they must have had friends, and their church?"

"The council was making cuts. They asked for voluntary redundancies, and reading between the lines, Jones was as good as told to volunteer. He says he started questioning his faith—his words—after his wife died, because what sort of God would take his daughter and his wife? I ought to feel sorry for him, but he's hard work. His job at the council was to help people find housing, but all he could talk about was how everyone he dealt with were scroungers and benefit cheats. No wonder they wanted to get shot of him. He stopped going to church, and after a while his church friends stopped going to see him. His family—brother and two sisters—live in Melin, so he came back." Bethan stopped to drink some coffee and eat some cake.

"Let me guess," Mal said. "His relatives all had their own lives, their own families and no time for him?"

Bethan took a last drink and nodded, swallowing.

"He got an allotment to keep himself busy, and make some friends. Only it didn't work out like he'd hoped. Instead of new friends, he ran into Hayden Bennion and Pandy. He says

Bennion didn't even realise who he was, or appear to remember the accident. I am *so* sick of the man. He needs psychiatric help, and if I have to spend much more time with him, so will I."

Mal grimaced along with her. He hadn't taken to David Jones either, even though he, like Bethan, thought he *should* be sympathetic to a man who had lost his daughter in a tragic accident, and was grieving for his wife.

"But did he kill three people?" Mal asked.

"That's the problem," she said. "If I had to gamble on it, I'd say that he *did* kill Hayden Bennion. He knows exactly what happened, his wife's death pushed him to the edge of sanity, and seeing Bennion and Pandy again brought all the feelings about his daughter back. I can see him hitting Hayden in a moment of fury. But I can't see him for the others. He *says* he killed them both, but he won't give any details. He talks about pushing Pandy into the river, but he's given me two different locations. He doesn't seem to know anything about Birmingham, and at one point he started to argue with me about the city having canals running through the middle. I honestly doubt he's ever been there. But there *can't* be two murderers in one small north Wales town, killing people in the same way, within a few days of each other. That's a step too far."

29

LOCUSTS MARK 2

By the time they had followed the tunnel onto the Liverpool side of the Mersey, Daniel was more convinced than ever that they were making a huge mistake. The trip had been easy, with little traffic. Even the rain had stopped. The first section was on familiar territory: winding roads through the Clwyd hills and valleys, then endless roundabouts and by-passes until they reached faster dual-carriageways and the M53. But it was going to start getting dark soon, and if the house on Marmalade Lane didn't look exactly like the picture, they were going to have to knock on doors to locate Melton. And then what? Yes, Sasha and Hector had legal custody of Cerys, but how would it look if they forced their way into Melton's house to kidnap her back? Hardly the actions of responsible foster carers. He tried to share his thoughts with Sasha, but she was having none of it.

"We find them. If he won't let her go, we call the cops. If he does let her go, we call the cops. Maybe the cops will get there before us. Good, then we can just take her home. Just keep driving."

He kept driving.

Sasha had bribed Arwen with her iPad, allowing her to play games and listen to music. When Daniel caught sight of her in the mirror, the iPad lay ignored on her lap, and she had a book in her hands. A Harry Potter by the thickness of it, and the look of the cover. They'd thrown a couple of cushions into the back seats, and Arwen had made herself a nest, oblivious to everything except the travails of Harry, Hermione and Ron. He had never been able to read on long journeys without getting car sick. But he wished he could be lost in a book right now, like Arwen. *Instead of being on this potentially disastrous trip that I should never have agreed to in the first place.*

Suddenly the city seemed to disappear behind them to be replaced by vast empty skies. On their left an endless beach stretched to the horizon with streaks of pink and purple across the sky, the precursors of sunset. Signs along the road warned of quicksand.

"I think we're there," he said. Sasha was staring at a map on her phone, and he began calling out the names of the streets as they drove.

"Next right, then second left should be Marmalade Lane," she said.

Many of the buildings on the seafront were low rise blocks of flats, which Daniel thought must have stunning views. Behind them were a mixture of bungalows and houses, mostly post-war, with a few older places mixed in. Marmalade Lane was exactly where Sasha said it would be. Daniel turned, and slowed down. They found the house at the far end of Marmalade Lane, looking exactly like the drawing, abutting a scrubby field with a few horses, and then what looked to be a golf course and farmland. Daniel kept going, finding his way into the golf club car park and stopping. The engine made its usual juddering and clicking noises as he turned the ignition off.

"What are you doing?" Sasha demanded, and Daniel felt

Arwen undo her seatbelt and wriggle her way between the two front seats.

"Are we there?" she asked. Can I have a sandwich now, please?"

"I need to think for a minute," Daniel said. "And this might be a good time to tell Mal and Hector where we are."

***

Mal stared at their empty plates and coffee cups. He trusted Bethan's interview skills. If she thought David Jones had killed Hayden Bennion and not the others, he would be inclined to back her judgement. But something niggled.

"Rhys Bennion called," he told Bethan. "He said that someone who sounds like David Jones has been hanging round their house for a couple of days. Lurking, then disappearing when they came out, according to Rhys. I'm thinking aloud here. Does that sound like the David Jones who killed Hayden Bennion in a fit of temper? Is it possible that Jones *witnessed* the murder of Hayden Bennion, and that's why he can describe it so well?"

Now it was Bethan's turn to stare at the table. Then she sat up straight in her chair and her voice was firm. "No. I think he did it. I think the CPS will agree to a charge, but only on the Hayden Bennion killing. And Jones needs psychiatric help, because I think the other two are wish fulfilment. He wanted to kill them, and they're dead, ergo, he must have killed them."

An alternative scenario was taking shape in Mal's mind. It was nebulous and he couldn't make all the pieces fit—yet.

"Arrest Jones on suspicion of murder, and get onto the CPS for a charging decision about Hayden. That way we get to keep him."

"You're not convinced though, are you, sir?"

"At the start of this case, I had a bit of an argument with Daniel." He raised his eyebrows and Bethan smiled. When Daniel had been Mal's DI, their arguments had been frequent, loud, and often took place in front of the rest of CID. "I know, hard to believe. Daniel said *no one is murdered because of a disagreement about gardening.* He was right. And it's making me wonder whether anyone is murdered because of a twenty-year-old accident. Jones got a plot at the allotments, and ran into two people who brought back bad memories. He didn't have to kill them; he could have given up his allotment and joined the bowls club instead. He came back to Melin. He must have known it would remind him of Merren." Mal sighed heavily. "But let's see what the CPS has to say."

As Bethan got up to go, there was a knock at the door. She opened it to Sophie and Charlie.

"I'll leave you to it," she said.

Mal got up and crumpled their paper plates and coffee cups, wiping the last few crumbs away with a paper napkin, and putting it all in the bin, with a mental apology to Daniel, who would have insisted on taking it over to the recycling bins in the market car park. He waved his new visitors into his office and to the chairs around the table. "OK," he said. "Tell me some good news."

"Well, not *exactly* good news," Sophie said. "But we know that one of the people who attacked Charlie was our very own PC Kelley, on DI Carey's instructions."

"Fair play," Charlie interrupted. "I was only Carey's second choice as punch-bag. Carey really wanted DI Owen. I mean *ex*-DI Owen."

"That makes me feel so much better," said Mal, trying not to let his fury at the idea of Carey targeting Daniel show on his face. Not after Charlie had been injured. "Now tell me the rest of it." At the end of the recitation, Mal summed up: "DI Carey befriended PC Kelley, who I think we can all agree isn't the brightest button in the box. He introduced him to the delights of the Conservative Club, and fed his prejudices about gays and people of colour and women. A cynic might think that Carey didn't want a friend, he wanted someone who would do his bidding. Because Carey already had plenty of friends, like ACC Bowen."

ACC Bowen who hasn't got a good word to say about his wife, just like DI Carey. And James Melton.

"And you say that Carey went to Liverpool and came back unhappy?"

Charlie nodded. "Sir, James Melton? And the *meNtoo* weirdoes? Could Carey have been part of that crewage? Because Kelley said Carey hated his ex-wives, and thought they were trying to rob him." Charlie seemed desperate to convince Mal of the connection, leaning forward, eyes bright. "I know it's a long shot, sir, but..."

"But it's worth looking into. Carey and James Melton know each other well enough to take Cerys out of school together. We *have* to locate James Melton. Abby's already on that, so Charlie, I need you to find Carey's ex-wives and ask them about their divorces. Did he use Pilkington and Corning as his solicitors?"

Charlie almost tripped over his own feet in his haste to get back to his desk and get some evidence for his theory. Sophie didn't move.

"My problem is," Mal said to her, "that we have a suspect in custody for the murder of Hayden Bennion, but I honestly don't think the motive holds up. On the other hand, I have Pandy Melton, whose violent husband had been threatening her, and trying to get custody of their daughter for years...and I have DI Carey throwing up distraction after distraction until we can't see the wood for the trees. Now Pandy is dead, Melton has Cerys, he's got Carey giving him cover, he's got solicitors on tap, and he's got a job he can do from anywhere with an internet connection."

"He's got what he wanted, and now he's going to take Cerys out of the country? And come back when his tame solicitors get the courts to give him custody?"

"Yes, dammit. Yes. But we don't know where the bastard is. He might have gone already."

***

Sunset over the expanse of sand was mesmerising. The streaks of pink got darker, the few clouds turned orange and the sun began, very slowly, to sink into the sea, turning it red, then black. The Land Rover was becoming chilly. Arwen was back in her nest, head in her book, but Sasha was vibrating with impatience.

"We should just go and knock on the door."

For what felt like the twentieth time, Daniel said, "If he denies that Cerys is there, there is nothing we can do, and he'll know that we'll call the police. He'll have time to get his lawyers in, and hide Cerys. Once it's dark, I can go and have a look. If Cerys is there, we can get the police to come, nice and quietly. We already know he's violent. Don't let's give him the chance to prove it. Give Arwen another sandwich. Have one yourself. Go behind a bush if you need to."

"It's nearly dark now."

"Nearly isn't enough. If I'm going to sneak round peering into windows, I want it *properly* dark."

They sat and waited in silence. Daniel turned the engine back on for ten minutes to warm them up. A few cars went in and out of the golf club, or along the front by the sea. Daniel saw a couple of cars stop as he had done, facing the water and the sunset. He got out of the Land Rover and snapped a couple of pictures on his phone, then climbed back in with a shiver. "Five more minutes," he said. "But you are staying right here until I get back. Promise."

"Yes, boss," Sasha said. He didn't believe her, but he knew she wouldn't put Arwen in any danger, and that had to be enough. When the five minutes were up, he walked back round to Marmalade Lane. The nearest streetlight was fifty yards away on the other side of the road, leaving the pavement by Melton's house in darkness.

This is such a stupid idea. But I'm here now.

He walked up the front path, praying that there wasn't a motion-activated light. There wasn't. None of the lights were on at the front of the house, so he let his eyes get used to the darkness and followed the faint glow of a paved path around to the rear. He stopped at the corner. To his right, windows were lit up and un-curtained, meaning anyone inside would see only their own reflections. Even so, it was hard to step forward and look through into the house. He saw a modern, well-fitted kitchen with grey units and a white marble island. Two men sat at on opposite sides of the island, one facing Daniel and one facing away. The man facing him was DI Carey and his face was puce with rage.

Daniel slid to the ground and inched his way until he was directly underneath the window. The sounds from within were of two men shouting, but it took him a moment to tune in.

"*Nothing's going to change it, my friend, you're in this as deep as I am.*"

"*I'm fucking done with this shit.*"

Daniel recognised Carey's voice. The other man must be Melton.

"*You're done with it when I say you're done. You help me at the airport, or you're toast. Your choice, Adam, your choice.*"

"*We had an agreement. You never said anything about leaving the country.*"

"*What the fuck did you think I wanted the kid's passport for? Wall art?*"

But Daniel could see no sign of Cerys. It was much too early for her to be asleep, and there were no other lights on in the house. He kept inching his way round underneath the windows, half listening to the row from the kitchen. An owl hooted from somewhere nearby, and underneath it, Daniel heard a much quieter noise. A child crying.

There was a building at the end of the garden, maybe a home office, or a guest annex. It was a new-looking building designed to look like a log cabin, with a wide deck, and floor-to-ceiling windows across most of the front. Curtains were drawn tightly preventing him from seeing inside. He circled the whole structure, and even the bathroom window was closed and obscured with a blind. That was where the crying came from, and that was where he found Cerys. He'd tested every door and window, but they were all locked. He could easily break in, but he was afraid that they'd hear from the house. Instead, he called softly through the window that they were coming to get her, and that things were going to be OK. His heart broke as Cerys sobbed, *I want my mum.*

"Cerys, *cariad,* it's Arwen's Uncle Daniel. Has anyone hurt you?

There was a moment of silence, then a whispered *no.*

"Can you open the window from your side?"

There was more sobbing, then another *no.* "He took all the keys. I looked."

"Have you locked the door?"

"Yes. But it's only a little lock. And he's too strong."

"Listen, *cariad,* I'm going away for a minute, and then I'm coming back to get you out. Aunty Sasha and Arwen are here to look after you and the police will come and get your dad."

"OK. Please be quick."

Daniel's heart raced as he ran back to the Land Rover.

30

SAND

"Cerys is there. She's OK and she's safe, but I want to go back to make sure she stays that way. You need to ring Mal and get him to call the cavalry."

Sasha nodded and pulled out her phone.

"And when you've called him, *stay here.*"

Daniel opened the back door of the Land Rover and scrabbled around until he found his heaviest set of secateurs—the kind that would cut through tree branches. He jogged back towards Marmalade Lane, flitting from shadow to shadow, not going round the house this time, but straight over the fence and into the back garden. He went to the bathroom window and tapped.

"The police are coming, Cerys. Can you be brave for a bit longer?"

"OK." But the voice sounded shaky. And then, "He's got a gun. He used to tell Mum he would shoot her with it."

Shit.

"Have you seen the gun?"

"No. But he said he had one. He *did.*"

"I believe you. I'm going to tell the police, so they're prepared."

He got his phone out and started texting:

Daniel: Cerys says JM has gun. She hasn't seen it

Mal: I'm telling L/pool now

Daniel: how long?

Mal: ETA 10 mins, ARU may delay

Daniel: when they get here, I'm getting her out

Daniel: or if anything changes in the house

Daniel: tell them to come quietly

Daniel: Carey and JM in kitchen at back of house

Mal: they know

Light flared across the lawn, lighting a rectangle of grass. Daniel saw a figure outlined in the kitchen doorway, black against the brightness. A voice shouted.

"We're going *right now*, and you're coming with us."

If he broke the window, Melton would see him before he could get Cerys away. If he waited until Melton went into the cabin, would he have enough time to get Cerys out before Melton got into the bathroom? And the million-dollar question...*did* Melton have a gun?

Before he could decide, he heard a hiss in his ear. Sasha.

"What are you doing?" she whispered.

"Trying to get Cerys out before..." he nodded towards the back of the house, "... sees me."

"Oi! Dickhead!" Sasha ran across the garden, heedless of obstructions, waving her arms, heading for the front gate. "Fucker! Child snatcher!" Melton started after her. There was something dark in his hand.

Daniel didn't hesitate. "Cerys, Get as far away from the window as you can. I'm going to break it." He waited until he heard the little girl move and then he swung the secateurs as hard as he could, once, twice, three times, until it broke. Then he told Cerys to stay back and attacked the shards of glass until there was room for her to escape.

"Come on, *cariad,* climb onto the toilet, and put your arms up." He took hold of her, silently cursing the missing fingers and the way their absence made everything more difficult. He carefully swung her up, and through the window and onto the ground.

Beside him, there was a swirl of movement, and Cerys was snatched from his grasp.

"Arwen! You shouldn't be here!"

"We're going to hide, Uncle Daniel. Come and find us when it's safe. Don't worry, we're good at hiding." And before he could grab them, they had disappeared into the darkness.

He heard a yell from the front of the house. He sprinted round in time to see Melton lunge for Sasha. She escaped by a layer of skin, and carried on yelling abuse. "Run Sasha!" he shouted, and rugby tackled Melton, almost knocking him down, and jarring his own arm on the secateurs he was still holding. But Melton was heavy with muscle and strong. He shrugged Daniel off, and rocked backwards to take a punch Daniel knew would knock him out.

"Police!" Daniel shouted, looking over Melton's shoulder. It worked. Melton paused for long enough for Daniel to swing the secateurs at his head. Blood spurted from his ear, and Melton screamed, clutching at his head. "Bastard," he gasped, stagger-ing, but somehow staying upright.

Daniel kicked him in the balls. Twice. "Don't move, or I'll do it again." Melton was groaning and cursing, writhing on the ground, his hands darting between his head and his balls, as if not sure which to protect.

Daniel was trying to get his breath to call Sasha when everything went dark. He thought he heard someone spit out the word *queer* and then stars swirled and he passed out.

He came around to feel Sasha pulling on his arm, "Wake up, for fuck's sake, wake up."

"I'm awake," he said. The world was still spinning and he could see at least three Sashas, all moving. He got onto his hands and knees, and shook his head, gently. Then he threw up, just managing to avoid his own hands and Sasha's body. It seemed to help. He tuned in to the groaning noise beside him.

"I kicked him in the ribs," Sasha said, and he saw that she'd pulled Melton's jacket down over his arms so he couldn't move. "But that other guy, the fat one, he's legged it down towards the beach."

"Call Mal, say no gun," Daniel got to his feet, gave Melton a last kick, and staggered across the road, forcing himself to break into a run, his head still spinning and his eyes telling him that the streetlights were all fuzzy. He kept misjudging his steps when the pavement dipped for driveways, so he ran in the road. He heard the sound of sirens and kept running. He tasted his own vomit and spat, but then he heard the sea, murmuring in the distance. More lights appeared, high and red, far away. Close by was the smell of the sea and the signs for quicksand at regular intervals by the low wall between the road and the beach. He saw a figure, a hundred yards ahead, no more.

"Carey!" he yelled, "Carey, it's over. Stop. Come back." The figure paused, looked back and carried on, staggering, and drifting towards the sea and away from Daniel. Daniel stuck to the road, running as hard as he could because he knew the sand would slow him down. He kept yelling, as he drew closer and closer, until the figure slowed, and stopped. Daniel hopped over the wall, and suddenly the figure was shouting to him.

"I'm stuck." Carey waved his arms. "I'm sinking. For God's sake get me out of here."

"Keep still. I'll call for help."

"I'm sinking, help me."

Daniel backed up towards the road as he rang Mal. "Carey's stuck in quicksand."

"Don't go near him. You've done enough. Let the bastard sink. Daniel. I need you to stay safe."

Two minutes later, the police surrounded Daniel like a swarm of bees, calling for the coastguard, the lifeboat crew, the fire brigade, radios crackling and buzzing, making his head ache. In the mêlée, Daniel slipped away, jogging back to Marmalade Lane.

Sasha was talking at high speed to two plain clothes officers. "I'm the one that called you in. Those men abducted a ward of court, against an injunction. I've got the paperwork to prove it. Chief Superintendent Kent will tell you. Now I need to find Cerys and my daughter." She caught sight of him. "Daniel, tell them."

Daniel knew he and Sasha must look at least as disreputable as the suspects the police had been sent to arrest. He took a deep breath.

"My name is Daniel Owen. Until last year I was a DI with Clwyd Police. I took medical retirement because I was injured. My friend Sasha has temporary care of Cerys Melton who is a ward of Clwyd social services. There is an injunction preventing her father James Melton from having any contact with her. He illegally removed her from school this afternoon. We traced him to this address, and immediately called for police help. Sasha's daughter Arwen and Cerys are hiding. We need to find them. It's cold and dark and they're only little."

A familiar voice said, "He's right. Let's find the girls and sort the rest out later." Mal showed the two officers his warrant card, and everything changed for the better. Daniel hadn't expected Mal to come in person, but here he was and *thank you, God, for bringing him.* Mal lifted his hands as if to put his arms round Daniel, and Daniel felt himself leaning towards him. Then he remembered that Mal was at work, and not on his own patch.

"*Diolch*," he said.

"*Coeso,*" Mal replied and Daniel grinned.

Daniel led the party into the back garden, and down to the log cabin.

"This is where they disappeared," Sasha called out, and there was a rustling in the hedge as the two girls appeared, shivering, hair standing out in spikes and clothes torn. They ran into Sasha's arms, crying with cold and relief.

It took a lot of fast talking from Mal for Sasha to get permission to take the girls home, in Mal's car. They took the blankets and Flora from the Land Rover.

Daniel knew that he was going to have to wait until Mal could leave. Mal did some more fast talking to keep the paramedics from insisting on Daniel taking a trip to hospital. He promised to watch Daniel like a hawk and wake him every two hours when he slept.

"Sorry, love," Mal said. "But you know you have concussion. Deal with it."

"You'd better be careful with my car," he said to Mal.

Mal growled.

Daniel stayed awake on the way home to Melin Tywyll on a mixture of chocolate and will power. When they got back, and into bed, he belatedly remembered Carey, stuck in the quicksand and wondered whether they'd got him out before the tide came in, and decided he didn't much. He asked anyway.

"They got him out."

"Good, I think." Then he got as close to Mal as he could and went to sleep.

31

AFTERMATH

T wo weeks later ...

DANIEL COULDN'T DESCRIBE the scent but it was unmistakable. He'd been back to his old secondary school on more than one case, but this was a primary, and newly built. Even so, it still had that same smell. He would have known where he was if he'd been blindfolded. As he wasn't, he admired the colourful 'mural' painted on a roll of paper on the wall. It told the story of the last dragon in Wales, complete with daffodils, Welsh flags, dragon hunters, and a decidedly handsome Chinese-looking dragon. The walls also held rolls of honour: Excellent Atten-dance Record, Excellent Reading Record, Being Kind to Others and so on. All had a list of names underneath. From where he was sitting, he couldn't see Arwen or Cerys's names, and he didn't want to go and look and miss his call.

He could hear singing from the main hall, accompanied by

a rather loud piano. From the nearest classroom, he heard a teacher tell the class to settle down. They didn't, or at least not until the teacher had threatened loss of games time. He imagined other groups reciting their times tables (did they still do those?) or practising joined up writing on one of those books where the body of the letters had to fit in between two lines, with only stalks and tails allowed above or below. Or did they bother with handwriting any more? Had it been replaced with texting?

"Mr Owen? Please come through." As he stood up, Daniel felt his stomach heave with nerves. He took a deep breath and let it out slowly and told himself to relax. He was ushered into a small, rather plain office, contrasting with the studied casualness of the man in front of him. Daniel couldn't tell which was the real man; the one who made such an obvious effort with his clothes, or the one whose office reflected no personality at all. The man held out his hand, and Daniel shook it, giving him points for not reacting to the missing fingers. A middle-aged woman stood up and held her hand out too. She reminded him of Bethan. Very well put together.

"Sit down, please, Mr Owen. As I'm sure you know, my name is Steve Minchin, and I'm the headteacher here at Ysgol Dewi Sant, and this is Ceridwen Protheroe, our Chair of Governors. Now then, Mr Owen, could you start by telling us why you want to be a teaching assistant?"

Daniel took another deep breath and told them about his nephew and niece, about Cerys and Arwen and about the Community Allotment.

***

Charlie was holding court in the CID room. Bethan and Abby sat at their desks, coffees in hand. Mal was handing round a box of cakes. The last one was a ridiculous rainbow cupcake which he ceremoniously placed in front of Charlie.

"Congratulations, future Sergeant Rees," Mal said, and Charlie blushed bright pink.

"I never thought I'd pass, not first time," he said. "Now all I need is a job."

Mal thought he had a very good chance of getting one. Bethan had passed her inspector's exams years ago, but had no desire to leave Melin Tywyll for promotion. But ACC Bowen owed Mal, big time, and Mal was going to call in the debt. Bethan to DI, Charlie to sergeant and at least one more DC, as well as more uniformed officers for Sophie. It would mean keeping quiet about Bowen being involved in *meNtoo*, and about him being drunk and incapable while they were trying to locate a missing child, but he was prepared for that. Bowen was going to fuck up again, so Mal would get another chance. But in the meantime, Melin was going to have enough staff. He was tired of running just to keep still.

"Sir, what's going to happen to DI Carey?" Abby asked.

"I think he'll be allowed to resign." There was an outbreak of protest. Mal held up his hand to quell the noise. "I'm no fan of DI Carey, but James Melton *was* blackmailing him. He was using the free legal services Carey had from Pilkington and Corning as leverage. Once Carey had started passing Melton information about Pandy, he was compromised. I can live with Carey getting his pension as long as I don't have to see him again. And don't forget that he's going to be giving evidence against James Melton, at least on the child abduction." *And that will buy me even more favours.*

"But he should be prosecuted for perverting the course of justice at the very least," said Charlie. "Because if he didn't kill Hayden Bennion himself, he knew who did, and I bet it was him who wiped the fingerprints off the water barrel."

"I refer you to my previous answer, Charlie. Perhaps more to the point, I understand that both his ex-wives are returning to court to ask for more money for themselves and their chil-

dren. I don't think Carey will be living the high life, pension or
no pension."

"His house is going up for sale, and he's been asked to leave
the Conservative Club," added Bethan. Mal didn't wonder how
Bethan knew these things; she just did, and she was always
right.

***

Rhys Bennion pushed the laden trolley towards the Qantas
check-in desk. His modest suitcase had the clothes he'd
brought with him, and a couple of small gifts for his family. His
mother's cases contained presents for her grandchildren to
make up for all the Christmases and birthdays she'd missed. In
vain, he had pointed out that Australia had plenty of shops, and
that there was no need to bring the entire contents of the John
Lewis toy and electronics departments with her. She smiled
and kept adding things which she claimed would take up no
space and weigh nothing. As Rhys heaved the cases onto the
conveyor, he hoped the excess weight bill wouldn't be more
than the price of their tickets.

Once they were through security, he bought them cups of
tea and scones with jam and clotted cream. "No clotted cream
where you're going, Mum, so make the best of it while you can."
She ate with pleasure, and it did his heart good to see it.

"Was that David Jones really trying to kill you?" she asked,
between sips of tea. "I kept meaning to ask you, and then
forgetting in all the excitement. It's not like I don't care, it's just
that we've been so busy."

Rhys thought about what Daniel had told him and Eluned
the day before.

"We don't know how James Melton knew about the accident, and David Jones's obsession with it," Daniel had said. "We
think Pandy must have told him about the accident when they
were married. David Jones and his late wife were both on Facebook in mutual support groups for people who have lost a

child. There's a bit of crossover between bereaved parents, and divorced parents who've lost custody of their kids. If you search for 'parents who've lost a child' you get both. James Melton is a web designer. He knows his way round social media. He made the connection."

"That's the bloke who killed our dad? And blackmailed this DI Carey to put the blame on Pandy?" Rhys had asked.

"Honestly?" Daniel had said, "Opinion is divided. My old sergeant is convinced David Jones killed him. My partner is equally convinced it was James Melton, and I tend to agree with him. David Jones has confessed and James Melton is denying it. The Crown Prosecution Service are happy to charge Melton with Pandy's death, but not your father's. David Jones won't be fit to stand trial any time soon. But the blackmail bit is right. I'm afraid you may never know. It's possible that James Melton will admit he did it once he gets to trial, but it's equally possible that he won't."

"Do you think David Jones meant to kill Rhys?" Eluned had asked.

"I think he wanted to. I think by then he'd deluded himself that he'd killed your father and Pandy, and Dylan Davies. But he hung around your house, and did nothing. That's one of the things making me think he didn't kill your dad. It was all in his head. The other thing is that DI Carey seemed to know that someone was going to be murdered at the allotments, probably your dad, because then either Pandy or David Jones would be in the frame. He seemed to know *before* it happened. There's no relationship between Carey and David Jones. If David Jones did it, it was on the spur of the moment, and Carey couldn't have known in advance."

"And what about Dylan Davies?" Rhys wanted to know. "Did James Melton kill him?" Rhys knew he was going to feel guilty about not staying in touch with Dylan for a long time to come. The least he could do was remember that he'd been killed too.

"Melton's got a solid alibi for Dylan's murder. Birmingham police are convinced that Dylan was in the wrong place at the wrong time. It's still an open investigation."

Rhys came back to the here-and-now of flight departure calls, the sound of wheelie suitcases running over industrial carpet and the hiss of the coffee machine in the I behind them.

"No, Mum, I don't think he was trying to kill me. Not really. He's in a psychiatric ward, and that's where he'll be for a while."

"Well, you should be safe in Australia at least," his mother said.

"Mum, in Australia, even the trees are trying to kill you."
***

Daniel was back in Sasha's kitchen, eating cake and drinking coffee, with his legs crossed at the ankle, in what Sasha called his Sebastian Flyte pose, though he doubted that Sebastian Flyte would approve of his hand-knitted Fair Isle socks. There was the usual jumble of textbooks and papers on the kitchen table, and the sound of a herd of migrating wildebeest upstairs.

"I hope you didn't go to the interview in those jeans," Sasha said. "They are positively obscene."

"I wore a suit. Not my best, but the next one down. And a tie. I looked very smart."

"Smart enough that they gave you the job, obviously."

"I know. Go me. I'll be making almost half as much as I did as a probationary constable fifteen years ago. It was pretty competitive apparently, according to my source in the school office."

Sasha leaned forward across the table. "You're going to finish your work day at the same time as Arwen and Cerys finish school."

"Probably a bit later. I expect there will be clearing up to do."

"But roughly the same time."

Daniel nodded and took another piece of cake.

"And you *like* Arwen and Cerys."

Daniel nodded again, "I do, very much."

"They'll be going to Big School next year, on the bus."

"That generally happens once they turn eleven, yes."

Sasha banged the flat of her hand on the table, knocking a pile of papers onto the floor. She pulled the cake plate out of his reach.

"*Why are you being so annoying?*"

Daniel laughed, then choked on a cake crumb. He coughed, and Sasha gave him a glass of water, and he coughed some more.

"Serves you right," she said.

Daniel looked her in the eye. "Yes, Sasha, I will look after Arwen and Cerys until either you or Hector get home. I won't even charge you for it."

"Good," she said. "Now listen up, because I've got a real problem."

"Arwen and Cerys aren't a real problem?" They both listened to the sounds of mayhem from the girls' bedroom.

"They are very well-behaved little girls," said Sasha primly, as something heavy fell on the ceiling above their heads followed by girlish yelling. Sasha opened the kitchen door and shouted up the stairs to tell the wildebeest to be careful.

Silence reigned.

"*That's* when you should worry," Sasha said to Daniel. "When they go quiet. No, this is a different sort of problem."

"I'm all ears."

"Hector wants to get married. To me. I want to marry Hector. The problem is that I'm already married. To Arwen's father. He doesn't know about Arwen, and I don't want him to know. I don't want him to know where I am, or even that I'm still alive. He mustn't know. But I have to get a divorce, and I don't even know where he lives."

"That *is* a different sort of problem."

The kitchen door crashed open and two identically dressed ten-year olds hurtled in, wondering aloud if it would be tea-time soon. The problem was going to have to wait.

32

WEDDING MAGAZINES

 week after that ...

THE SUN WAS SHINING and the trees were showing off their new greenery. Across the valley, lambs ran about, jumping on anything higher than themselves, forming gangs and then scattering to poke violently at their mothers' teats. The sound of the tiny voices floated towards the house. Daniel had cleaned the cobwebs off their deckchairs and set them up, with cushions, on the 'lawn'. The chickens had followed him, and were investigating for grubs in the new grass, ignoring the bowls of expensive pellets back in their run. Daniel sank into one of the deckchairs and patted his knee. Flora looked at him as if he was mad and rolled around in the grass, wriggling with pleasure. Then she stood up, shook herself all over and flopped onto Daniel's feet. Behind him, Daniel heard Mal come down the steps from the house, bringing the smell of hot coffee with him. He pulled the empty deckchair towards him, so that it touched his own. Hand-holding was definitely on the agenda.

"Is it really warm enough to sit outside?" Mal asked.

"Go and get a fleece you big wimp, but give me the coffee first. I don't care how cold it is, it *looks* warm, and I want to talk about weddings."

Mal put the tray of coffee down on the grass and disappeared, returning with the blanket from the sofa.

"Obviously, you won't need this," he said. "But I'll share if you ask nicely. Now talk to me about weddings."

"I don't want one," Daniel said, then held his hand up to stop Mal speaking. "I do want to be married, to you, and I do want a party to celebrate. What I don't want is what Rhiannon and Huw had: a Venue with a capital V, and a guest list, with labels for who sits where, and months spent choosing the menu and the flower arrangements, and booking a disco and deciding on the music for the first dance, and party favours for people to take home, and all the rest of it. I would like a new suit, but that's pretty much it. I could even compromise on the suit."

"Just you, me and two witnesses at the registry office?"

"Maybe Mum and Dad, and Megan, Dave and the kids. Huw and Rhiannon, Hector and Sasha and their two, Sophie and Veronica. And then a party. With everyone. A tea party, but with booze as well as cake and cucumber sandwiches. Here. Bring your own blanket."

"What if it rains?"

"We'll go to the pub."

"Can I have a new suit too?"

"Only if it isn't black. I was thinking that we'd both look good in very dark blue. You could pretend it was black."

"White shirt, rainbow tie?"

"What else? You would do the ironing, obviously."

"Obviously. When were you thinking?"

"How does the end of May sound?"

"You've already booked it haven't you?"

"I've enquired, that's all. Just to see if they had availability."

"Daniel, you know I'll agree to anything you ask. New suits, dark blue, end of May, big party here."

"*Anything* I ask?"

Daniel felt Mal nod beside him.

"Then let's go in, I'm bloody freezing."

ACKNOWLEDGMENTS

Thanks are due to many people for their help with this book.

To Bill Millward for always being there when needed.

As always, Austin Gwin provided encouragement, especially at those dark moments when I'm convinced I have written something utterly dull and boring.

JL Merrow's insightful comments and thoughtful editing have made this a much better book. Thank you so much.

To everyone who has said that they hoped for more Daniel Owen books, or has left a positive review, or has suggested online or IRL that other people might like to read the books, THANK YOU.

Cover Design by Pixel Studios.

ABOUT THE AUTHOR

My aim in writing these mysteries has been to provide you, the reader, with the kind of book I like to read - a good mystery, with characters to care about, set somewhere interesting. I hope I've succeeded. If so, please be kind enough to leave a review for other readers.

I do most of my writing in a cabin in west Wales, set under the trees. I look out of the window, and what I see are birds and squirrels, and in the evening, bats. At night, I hear the battering of rain on the tin roof, or the cry of an owl or a fox. I love the place, and it's why there are so many Welsh woodlands in my books.

I didn't start writing fiction seriously until I was *a woman of a certain age*. I should have started much earlier, but then, I wouldn't have had so many things to write about, would I?

You can find pictures of forests, a blog, and some free stories on my website ripleyhayes.com, and you can join my newsletter list at the same place. The newsletter has details of the forthcoming books and special offers.

I'm on Facebook at Ripley Hayes Author.

ALSO BY RIPLEY HAYES

All books available on Kindle Unlimited, as Kindle e-books and as paperbacks.

Daniel Owen Books

1: Undermined

2: Dark Water

3: Leavings

4: A Man

5: Too Many Fires

6: An Allotment of Time

Peter Tudor and Lorne Stewart Cosy Mysteries

1: *No Accident in Abergwyn*

I just wanted to be a caring son. So why was I relying on gin and cake to keep the boredom at bay?

Peter Tudor was an adrenaline-fuelled emergency nurse, until he decided his duty lay in caring for his disabled mother in the dull seaside village where he grew up.

Out for an early morning run, Peter stumbles over the body of a hated village resident. The police say it's an accident. Enigmatic stranger Lorne Stewart insists it's murder, after a 'message' from the dead man.

The police aren't keen to investigate, and neither is Peter. Then an attack on his home makes it personal.

There's more to Lorne than meets the eye, and his magic is reeling Peter in ...

2: No Friends in Abergwyn (April/May 2022)

Teema Crowe Books

1. Badly Served

Her job was to look for Harry. The trouble started when she found him.

It looked like a simple task: serve divorce papers on failed businessman Harry Smith, who's run off to rural north Wales leaving his wife with a baby and a mountain of debt. A welcome distraction from the implosion of her personal life.

But it turns out that Teema Crowe isn't the only one looking for Harry when she — literally — trips over his body, lying face down in a pool of oil, with a knife in his back.

The police think Teema makes an excellent suspect for the murder. Her employer and her cheating ex-girlfriend know far too much about it but they aren't telling. There's an illegal money-lender who wants Teema silenced, and doesn't mind hurting the people she loves, and a widow who just wants the insurance.

It's a race against time for Teema to find out who killed Harry, before the police or the murderer find her.

2. *Feeling Badly:* Available 31/8/22 pre-order available

The truth can set you free. Or lock you up forever.

Jamila, a young homeless woman has disappeared from the streets of Manchester. Teema gets a bizarre message asking for her help, hinting that Jamila holds the secret to Teema's birth. Teema's never known where she came from, and she told herself that she didn't care. She's slowly getting her life together after losing her girlfriend, her job, and being accused of murder. The last thing she needs right now are more secrets and lies.

Then Jamila is found -- dead -- with a letter to Teema in her pocket.

Did Jamila know the secret of Teema's identity? Can Teema find out who she really is before the truth is buried again, along with Jamila's body?

Printed in Great Britain
by Amazon

13175035R00144